I0586827

FOOL'S
paradise

A CARTWRIGHT
BROTHER ROMANCE

lilliana
ANDERSON

INTERNATIONALLY BESTSELLING AUSTRALIAN AUTHOR

FOOL'S PARADISE

CARTWRIGHT BROTHERS, BOOK 5

LILLIANA ANDERSON

Ebook & Print Edition

Copyright © 2018 by Lilliana Anderson

All rights reserved.

No part of this book may be reproduced in any form or by any electronic or mechanical means, including information storage and retrieval systems, without written permission from the author, except for the use of brief quotations in a book review.

Cover design by *Ember Designs*

Editing by *Making Manuscripts*

❀ Created with Vellum

For You. Because you're still here and that makes you one of my favourite people xx

Here we are. The end of an amazing year following five thieving brothers and the women who stole their hearts. How will we cope?

One thing I know for sure, is that I am going to miss these men something severe, massively, hugely, a hole is now in my heart. Ugh. If you can't tell, I'm sad that this is the end....

This entire experience started as a dream and turned into this epic journey. Toby's book was an absolute delight for me to write. He's been a solid character throughout the series and I feel that his story is the best way to wrap it all up.

Blair, the voice of our story, is Toby's equal in every way. I had two women in mind for him, but a woman who was his female counterpart with enough vulnerability to suck him in seemed the perfect fit.

There's a lot more action in this book, because both parties are pretty badarse. It's like one of those crazy bad-guy story lines in one of your favourite soaps with a lot of fun and sexy times thrown in along the way.

OK. That's where I'll leave it so you can turn the page and say a bittersweet goodbye to the Cartwrights.

CHAPTER ONE
BLISSFULLY ALONE

REGRET CLANGED ABOUT inside my skull as a bleating ring pierced my consciousness and roused me from an alcohol-induced slumber… coma… *whatever*.

Slapping my hand on top of my phone, I squinted with one eye then punched the accept button. "What?" I croaked, balancing the handset on the side of my face as I continued to lie on my side, head throbbing, manners nowhere to be found.

I need to quit drinking.

"Blair. You sound like shit." Big Jim, my boss and mentor. His voice sounded like gravel and most of his words joined. The only reason he'd call this early was if he had a new job for me.

Taking hold of my phone, I grunted a little as I forced myself to sit, squinting against the light of the new day. "You *are* a shit, but you don't hear me complaining."

"Always hilarious," Big Jim said with a chuckle.

"It's why you love me."

"I love the money you make me." It was true. I'd been

working for the guy since I was sixteen. Originally as a filing clerk then later as a member of his elite team. I'd made his private investigation firm a heck of a lot of money over the years. I could track down practically anyone with a bare minimum of clues then deliver them to the highest bidder. If I was a decent person, I'd work for the cops and get that 'most wanted' list of theirs cleared out in no time. But, I wasn't that kind of girl. I didn't trust the authorities and would never work for those bastards.

Instead, I took jobs from less than savoury people, finding rats on the run and anyone else they paid me to find. It wasn't the kind of living that would get me through the gates of heaven, but it provided plenty of cash for me to live a cushy life. The way I saw it, people who got mixed up in the underground had made their bed. I was just putting them back in it.

"And how much are we lookin' at this time?" I asked, just as a body shifted beside me, startling the crap out of me until I remembered the guy I'd met in the bar last night. I barely remembered bringing him up here.

I really need to quit drinking.

"Hold that thought," I said, slipping from beneath the sheets.

"Man in your bed?"

"Something like that." I grabbed my dress from the pile of discarded clothes on the floor then pulled it over my head before I stepped out on the balcony, the cool morning air a blast against my warm skin. Goosebumps covered my arms as a chill ran down my spine. I closed the door behind me. "I can talk now."

"When are you gonna quit fucking those randoms and find yourself a steady guy?" There was amusement in his voice, but I knew he was serious too. Big Jim was the closest thing I'd ever had to a father. See, my mother had never introduced me to my real one. She was a working girl who'd met an untimely end when I was only nine. I'd been unfortunate enough to be watching as she foamed at the mouth with a needle hanging out of her arm, not having a clue what to do to help. That background made me too damaged for placement with a decent foster family. By the time I'd gone to Jim and demanded a job, I was living in a girl's home with a massive chip on my shoulder and rage swimming in my blood. He'd asked why I wanted to work for a private investigator, and I'd told him I wanted to find out who my father was so I could cut off his nuts for abandoning me. He'd laughed, told me I was too young to be a PI then offered me a job anyway. I was the office shit-kicker until I turned eighteen and got my license. Then I'd worked my arse off until I was the best PI he had. I even found out who my father was with minimal clues. Much to my chagrin, I was still yet to take the man's balls. *One day....*

I rubbed my hand over my face and sighed, the idea of settling down prickling uncomfortably beneath my skin. "I don't do happily ever afters, Jim. You should know that by now."

"Never said nothin' 'bout bein' happy, kid. Just settlin' down. Sowing some roots and shit." He coughed, his chest rattling from decades of cigars balanced between his teeth.

"Like you?"

"Ah, don't use me as your example. I'm old and I fucked up my life years ago."

In his late sixties, Jim had had three wives and four children, none of whom talked to him. He'd always been married to his job above all else. Probably why he and I got along so well, even though I was half his age.

"All right, old man. Enough of the chit-chat, what have you got for me?"

"Like that, huh?" I could hear the smile in his voice as he clicked at the computer keys.

"Gotta get rid of the guy in my bed," I said with a smirk, causing him to chuckle then cough.

"OK. I got a call from some guy's mother. Mid-level crime family, oldest son has taken off, she wants him back running things."

"That's more information than I need," I told him. I never liked knowing why I was finding someone. Having that kind of knowledge made it too personal for me. I just needed a photo, a list of his habits—you know, likes and dislikes kind of shit—if they're dangerous and their last known whereabouts. The rest I could figure out on my own. "Just send me what you have and I'll get on it."

"Sending now. They haven't heard from him in nearly a year, so I'm not sure what you're gonna find."

"And they left it this long to hire me? Must be a real tight-knit family." There was sarcasm in my tone.

"Who the fuck knows. Just watch your back, and if you find any bodies, get the hell out of there."

It wouldn't be the first time I'd discovered a body. Some people weren't missing at all. Just gone.

"I'll be fine. I'll call when I have something."

"See ya, kid."

He disconnected as my phone vibrated in my hand, indicating a new file had been received. Opening it up, I swiped through the basic information and brought up the most recent photo they had of him. *Whoa.* He was dressed in a suit at what appeared to be a wedding, smiling for the camera. Everything about the man was perfect: broad shoulders, hard body with sun-kissed skin, neatly styled chocolate-brown hair, and a face chiselled from stone. He was definitely gorgeous, so gorgeous that it felt like a punch in the ovaries to look at him. But when I zoomed in, my lust leant itself to curiosity. It was those eyes. Clear blue that spoke of something beyond his well-put-together façade. They told me of pain, pressure and loneliness—all things I understood at the very core of my being.

As I pressed my fingers against the screen and zoomed in on his expression, I felt my heart tighten in my chest. It was strange to react this way over the photo of a man I'd never met and knew little about. It was just that... looking into his eyes made me feel like running away too. *So strange....*

"Hey, you." The door to the hotel suite slid open, and the man I'd spent last night with stepped out onto the terracotta tiles. "Thought you'd ditched me." He smiled. And it was a nice smile, nothing like the guy in the picture's; but any man would appear lacking next to a male of that calibre.

He doesn't remember my name.

Powering off my screen, I slid my phone into my dress pocket and smiled back. *I can't remember his name either.* "No ditching. Just had some business to take care of."

"Speaking of, I actually have to get going. I'm late for, ah, a thing." The awkward morning-after brush-off. I'd heard it many times in my thirty-four years. Excuses ranging from family events to appointments and meetings. I'd heard them all, but preferred it when they left with no excuse at all.

"See you round," I said, turning my back to him. The hotel looked out over a golf course, green as far as the eye could see. The groundskeeper was mowing the rough on the closest hole while a flock of sparrows dove for bugs in the cut grass.

"I, uh, had a good time. Maybe I can call you sometime?"

Turning my head slightly, I sighed against his discomfort. I'd lost count of how many times I'd done this. Sex was my thing, along with the drinking. Everyone had a vice; I had two. I loved to drink, and I loved to fuck. In that order. I rarely did close connections, but I enjoyed the physicality of two bodies joining. I had zero interest and zero time for anything more. And in the 21st century, you'd think a woman could play the field without the stigma. Not the case. That's why I chose not to keep many friends outside work. I didn't need anyone's judgment either.

"I doubt I'll be back in town anytime soon." I gave him a flash of a smile. "Don't let me keep you from your... thing." I turned my attention back to the view, relieved when the door slid closed again and his footsteps receded. The moment I heard the main door click open and shut, I released my breath.

Alone.

Blissfully alone.

Taking a clearing lungful of air, I pulled my phone out again and reactivated the screen. And there he was: *Toby Derek Cartwright. 41 years old. 188cm (6'2"). Last known whereabouts: Torquay, Victoria.*

Torquay. It was a holiday destination known for its endless beaches and great surf. Looked like he grew up there with his mother and four younger brothers. Must have been nice growing up near the sea.

Not everything seemed rosy though. His father was incarcerated, siblings were all married and still lived within a few kilometres of each other. His list of known associates was empty; as was his list of enemies.

Hmm.

Not that having his list empty meant much. There were a lot of people unwilling to share that kind of information with a third party, especially when there were illegal activities involved.

"Toby." I tested out his name as I looked at his photo again, flicking through to find a few more: him surfing, walking a small black and white dog... There was a picture of him working on a fishing boat, shirt off, the sun on his slick skin. A quiver went through me as I absorbed the strength of his body and the genuine smile upon his face. So different from the first photo. I zoomed in and saw a different pair of eyes. These eyes were happy, hopeful, content even. *Interesting.* When I swiped to the next page, I found a note saying he'd left with the boat, the dog, and nothing else. "What do they need me for then?" There were only so many places in Australia to moor a fishing boat. And the fact he had a dog with him made it even easier to narrow it down. *How strange.*

Dialling the office, I walked back inside the hotel suite and pressed my phone to my ear. Big Jim answered on the second ring.

"Problem?"

"No. A question. Did the family look for him themselves?"

"Thought you didn't like extra information."

"This case is a walk in the park. They could easily locate him with a few phone calls if they wanted to. It makes little sense to hire someone like me."

"You hate money all of a sudden?"

"No. But this doesn't sit right. I'd like to know what I'm walking into."

His breath heaved slightly down the line, laden with the weight of his words. "From what I hear, them Cartwrights are mixed up with the Grim Order."

"The Motorcycle club who blew up that drug convoy last year?" They were bad news. Barely a week went by when they weren't suspected to be involved in some crime or another. The cops rarely proved their cases though, meaning they continued their reign of terror on society. *Biker scum.* They were the worst kind of criminal. Well, next to smugglers. But, I had bigger reasons to hate them.

"The very one. The mother made no mention of trouble with them, but she did say they were under watch and needed someone outside the family to bring him back."

"Under watch. By the cops or the MC?"

"Didn't say. Just be careful, kid. When you locate him, don't make a big scene. None of this 'naked and tied to the bed' business."

I couldn't stop the smile that curved my lips. "That was *one* time."

His chuckle rumbled heartily in my ear. "Yeah, but I saw this guy's picture. Even I got a hard-on lookin' at him and I'm straight as they come."

"TMI, boss." I laughed and shook away the image. Imagining Big Jim with a boner was crossing the line with me. He was a giant of a man with a big belly that hung over the top of his pants and a comb-over that wasn't fooling anyone. Not naked mental image appropriate at all.

He chortled at my obvious discomfort. "Just call me when you have eyes on him, I'll get one of the guys to help you with this one. He's huge."

"Whatever you say, boss."

"I mean it, Blair."

We disconnected for the second time that morning. Then, unable to resist, I took another look at Toby Cartwright's photos. *That man is HOT.* There was seriously something about him that drew me in. The eyes. Or maybe I was incredibly shallow, and it was the body? The face? Either way, I was curious about the guy. There was a big part of me that wanted to break some rules because of that.

I knew it was a terrible idea. But my life was one massive collection of terrible ideas, so that wasn't going to stop me. And I hadn't exactly promised Jim I wouldn't try to bang the guy before I handed him over, so I didn't have to break my word—something I never did. My word was my bond.

No. There was nothing keeping me from undertaking a more lustful investigation. I could get as close as I wanted since Toby Cartwright didn't know me from a bar of soap. And a honey trap was a hell of a lot more enticing than showing up and tasing the guy to his knees. Especially when silk ties and bedposts were involved….

CHAPTER TWO
AND I'M LEAVING

A WEEK later I was in Western Australia, walking along the Port Bouvard marina while following a lead on Toby Cartwright's boat. In the year he'd been missing, it had changed hands twice before disappearing from record altogether; they cited suspicions of it sinking or being stolen as the reason. I'd followed that damn boat around the country, travelling to different marinas it had been penned at, asking questions and showing photos, all to sift out what happened next.

Where did Toby Cartwright go?

I struggled to believe a man who seemed so at peace on his boat would willingly get rid of it. And after doing a ridiculous amount of footwork, I found I'd been right. Several people recognised Toby from his photo. They even mentioned the dog.

However, they all knew him by different first names. Something one expected in my line of work. Aliases were a dime a dozen. Hell, I even used them myself. But, it was people's unwillingness to part with things close to their heart that made it easy to track them down.

Toby was smart, taking on new identities and moving from town to town. But the fact he had a tie to the sea, to his dog, and to his boat, kept his trail hot enough for me to follow with a little effort. Once again, I wondered why his family hadn't hunted him down themselves. They'd said they were under watch, but a few internet searches in the early days of his disappearance would have led them right to him. What was so important that they needed him back so suddenly almost a year later?

It was probably better if I didn't know.

With Toby's boat listed as missing on official documents, I had hopes he'd just given it a makeover and assumed another identity to cover his tracks. After searching for any new fishing boats applying for licenses or paying for pen fees, I hit the jackpot when a boat matching Toby's make and model turned up. It had been at the marina in Wannanup for the last three months, its owner setting up business and running tours three times a week for tourists wanting to throw their line in and catch a big fish or spot local sea life.

Jackpot.

Wanting to inspect the boat in person—and possibly catch a glimpse of the current owner—I armed myself with the registration and pen numbers before heading out. I also took an extendable baton in case things got ugly, you could never be too safe when it came to these criminal types.

As I stepped along the grey swollen wood of the pier, the planks shifted slightly under my weight. I wasn't the daintiest girl in existence, but I certainly wasn't overweight either. I had curves where I should and a big set of tits which I willingly used to my advantage. I was five-nine—not so tall that I was intimidating, and not so short that I gave off a helpless vibe— with an attractive face, green eyes and thick blonde hair I paid a lot at the salon for. I had a strong body that I maintained with hours spent at the gym, lifting weights and working out. My favourite activity was MMA training, which I took part in as often as I could. Self-defence and a robust attack were essential tools required in my line of work. Those attributes made me muscular and confident; everything my foster carer told me a woman should never be. *She had no clue.*

I smiled to myself as the sea breeze kissed my skin and ruffled my hair, thinking about my third foster mother who would lecture us girls—there were three of us at the time —on the qualities a woman needed to make a man marry her.

Insert eye roll here.

She listed things like, being demure, taking care of others, learning to clean, sew, and cook, looking after our appearance—shit like that. It was basically lifted out of a 1950s housewife magazine. But at thirteen, I couldn't imagine anything worse than modelling myself in the hopes of finding a 'decent man to look after me'. After seeing the way men treated my mother, the last thing I wanted was to be *anything* to a man. Instead, I decided I needed to be better than all the men I'd ever known so I could look after myself. I learned about cars, I learned to fight, I picked up odd jobs, and saved every cent I could. I refused to be reliant on anyone for *anything*. When my foster mother found out what I was doing, she labelled me as 'unteachable' and 'belligerent' before she sent me back to the home. I labelled her as 'moronic' and 'blind'. Her 'decent man' of a husband was as handsy as a guy could get. I was glad to be out of there.

"Miss?" A man doing something with a rope beside one of the boats called out, stopping me in my tracks. "You have business here? This is a private pier. Public access is restricted."

Turning to him with a bright smile, I tucked my shoulder length hair behind my ear. "I'm looking for pen number thirty-eight. Am I in the right place?" That wasn't quite the pen I was looking for, but it was directly across from it. I kept my voice light and my chest out. His eyes travelled down, taking in the low V-cut of my fitted shirt, the tight-fitting jeans, red lipstick and nails. He'd clock me as a tinder hook-up or an escort, which was precisely why I dressed the way I did when working on foot. It made life easier whenever I looked a little lost if people thought I was some guy's date. *See, I could be demure…*

"Down there a way," he said, pointing. "But I don't think anyone's on board. I've been here all morning and haven't seen anyone."

I frowned a little then pouted. "Well, I'll check and come right back if that's the case." I took a step away then paused and placed my hand against my chest, hoping he had more information for me. "There aren't any guard dogs up there I hope, this being private property and all. I'm awfully frightened of those ferocious jaws when they growl, like they wanna make a meal out of my behind."

He chuckled and smiled, his eyes dropping to appreciate my *behind*, which was easy for him since I jutted out my hip to show it off. "Definitely not at thirty-eight, but there is a little terrier at thirty-three. He barks sometimes, but he's old, so nothing to worry about. He won't bite." A terrier at thirty-three? *Perfect.*

"Well, that's a relief. Is he one of those scruffy looking things then?"

"No. A Boston terrier, I think. Short hair, black and white markings. He's a good dog, always happy and excited." People were far too free with other people's information. *Thank you, Mr. Sticky-Beak.*

Rocking my shoulders lightly from side to side, I looked at him through my lashes. "So, he's not gonna jump off the boat and chase me away?"

"I'll be here to catch you if need be." He winked, and I giggled. *This is too easy.*

"I might just hold you to that." Then I thanked him for his time and headed towards the end of the pier, even more certain that my gut had been right.

When I found myself standing in front of a freshly painted *Kong Halvorsen Island Gypsy* cruiser moored at pen thirty-three, I *knew* I was right. The boat had been built in the late eighties, but it was still impressive to look at—all forty-four feet of it. If I was Toby Cartwright, I think I'd have a hard time letting go of this beauty as well.

As I admired the vessel before me, the snuffling sounds of the Boston terrier caused me to look up. "Hey, little fella," I said quietly, clicking my tongue in a friendly manner at the panting dog my file had listed as 'Rogue'. "You got a master on board, or you all by yourself?" My gaze moved along the length of the hull, lingering on the cabin windows, looking for movement. The dog barked twice, and I stepped back, hands up. Seemed no one was home. "All right. I'm backing off."

With a quick glance down the pier, I made sure Mr

Sticky-beak wasn't watching before I climbed onto the deck of the boat at thirty-eight. Being a girl who was thorough with her research, I knew no one was onboard and picked the lock on the cabin door before heading inside. The owners of this particular vessel weren't locals, and they had adult children who sometimes used the boat to entertain their friends. Facebook was a treasure trove of information, it could arm me with a believable story just by clicking through some pubic photos.

Opening the tiny galley fridge, I gave the beer a longing look then pulled out a water—I never drank while on the clock. That was one rule I didn't break—then I took a seat at the tiny table and gulped down a long drink while staring out the window. *Why is Western Australia so damn hot all the time?* I didn't think I'd ever been on this side of the country without sweating my face off. I was born a Melbourne girl, so the cooler climate suited me.

Finding a piece of paper to fan my face, I observed the dog sunning itself on deck, its belly pointing towards the sky as its ear flicked occasionally to ward off the buzzing flies. *Oh, to be a dog.* It must have been nice for them when they had good owners. They got to laze around all day, go for walks and eat good food. I often thought dogs were people who'd had it so tough in their last life they needed a rest in this one. I wouldn't mind coming back as a lucky dog. I could do with the rest.

About half an hour into my stakeout, I heard voices floating down the pier, carried far on the warm breeze. That guy who'd stopped me was talking to someone else now. A man.

Getting up from my position at the table, I moved closer to the window and looked out, spotting a massive man holding two overflowing green bags as Mr Sticky-Beak tried to engage him in conversation. The massive guy looked disinterested. He also looked a lot like Toby Cartwright.

His hair was a lot longer and there was enough scruff on his face to make me take a second look. But men that size weren't exactly a dime a dozen, and there was no mistaking the way my heart pounded just by looking at him. It was definitely my mark.

I held up my phone, the attached 12x lens allowing me to zoom in for a clearer picture. I snapped several photos as he fought to end his conversation with the sticky beak up at number twenty-seven, even managing to catch one of him rolling his eyes when he finally turned away and headed for his boat. The little dog jumped up and rushed to the guardrail, his tail wagging excitedly as his master approached. I snapped more pictures, my heart skipping happily because this job had been a cakewalk. I'd found him. Now I just had to call Big Jim and wait for the cavalry to arrive.

Slipping the zoom lens into my bag for safekeeping, I was effectively done.

Done.

Did I want to be done?

Call it in, Blair. The Grim Order is involved with his family. You don't know this guy or what he's capable of. For once in your life, do as you're told.

That's what I would have thought if I was a sensible woman. But, I wasn't a sensible woman. I was a risk-taker, which was why I was so good at what I did. It was both a curse and a blessing.

Before I could give it much consideration, my feet

were propelling me forward, and I was heading in his direction, my eyes on my phone and a scowl on my face.

I could have been an actress if I'd wanted, I always had a character teed up, ready to present to the world. The real me was reserved for me and me alone. No one knew what really went on inside my head, not even Big Jim.

"Hey," I said to Toby, stopping him mid-stride. "You know when Devin is supposed to be here? He said four and I've been waiting thirty minutes already." I shook my head and snapped a sneaky close-up photo before slipping my phone into my back pocket.

He took a minute to assess me, those blue eyes of his so much softer and calmer than I'd seen in his photos. The fisherman life obviously agreed with him. "You know him well?"

I pressed the toe of my wedge heel into the wood under my feet. "It's new. We've spoken back and forth a bit, and I'm in town a few days, so we thought we'd catch up in person, ya know?"

"You met online?" His brow shot up.

I pulled at my bottom lip with my teeth and shrugged. "You probably think I'm stupid meeting some guy on a boat for the first time, huh?"

"Not the safest location I could think of. Most of the houses here are empty outside the summer months." He moved his gaze, doing a sweep of the surrounding houses that were smack on the water with their own private jetties.

"If it's so scary, why do you live here?" I asked, widening my eyes.

"Who says I live here?" His mouth quirked in a half grin.

"I don't know. The groceries. That dog wagging its tail at you. You're at least staying on that boat right there."

"Good observation skills."

I shrugged. "Well, they tell us girls to be wary of our surroundings." Lowering my voice, I took a step towards him, looking up into that handsome face of his. He was even better looking up close than he was at a distance and he smelled good too, soap and sea breeze. The photos didn't do him justice. "But, between you and me, I came prepared in case things went sideways." I held out the strap on my bag, showing him the extendable baton sitting safely inside. "A little insurance."

"You thought of everything."

"I am always prepared." I placed a light touch on his forearm, flirtatious as I held eye contact. His pupils dilated, and he licked his lips. "Anyway, I should get going. Hey, you know somewhere I could get a decent drink and something to eat?"

"You staying in Mandurah?"

"No. I'm in Wannanup at a little B and B."

He nodded, his eyes dropping a touch before lifting back to my eyes. "There's a place at the end of the marina. Or if you don't mind roughing it a little, there's an Irish pub a few streets over. Great food, great beer, great people. I'm partial to the Guinness pie myself." *His voice sounds like honey. I'm in lust.*

"You eat there often?" I wanted him to keep talking, imagining that soft rumble of his voice whispering erotic things in my ear while those strong hands roamed my body.

"Occasionally."

"Want to join me?"

He grinned and glanced away before meeting my eyes again. "I'd love to. But not tonight." He lifted his bags to show me his groceries. "I have plans." *Would it be rude if I invite myself for dinner?*

"Cooking for two?"

He laughed a little, the sound light and easy. Something I hadn't expected from the brooding man I'd been looking for. He seemed... happy, free....

"I am."

Now I'm jealous.

I shrugged. "Makes sense. You have that first date air about you."

"It's not a date. Just dinner. But it is the first time I'm cooking for her. So, yeah. I'm nervous."

Her.

Forcing a smile, I placed my hand on his bicep and gave it a squeeze. *So firm.* "As long as you can cook, I'm sure you'll be fine."

"Here's hoping." He lifted the bags again, and I suddenly felt shitty for making him stand here talking when those bags seemed heavy.

"I should let you go then. Thanks for the recommendation. I'll check that pub out. Enjoy your date."

"Dinner. It really is just dinner."

I moved past him, throwing a smile over my shoulder, "You don't need to convince me."

"I'll tell Devin you were looking for him."

"Don't bother, I'll tell him myself." I lifted a hand and waved over my head.

"I'm Tom," he called out.

Tom.

"And I'm leaving."

I heard Toby laugh as I passed Mr Sticky-beak's boat. He popped up his head, so I winked and blew him a kiss then quickened my step. I would need a new vantage point. Toby, I mean 'Tom' was having a woman over for dinner. If it wasn't a date, then I wanted to know exactly what and who she was. I told myself it was research, that I was doing this investigating to present our client with a thorough picture. But if I was honest, I was doing it for me. Because I was selfish. Because I liked looking at him. And because I wanted him, date or no date, I wanted him to be mine. Just once.

Maybe twice.

CHAPTER THREE
STUCK ON THINGS

AFTER DROPPING CLOSE to a grand on Airbnb, I found myself inside one of those beautiful big houses Toby Cartwright had indicated when I spoke to him on the pier. From my new position, I had a view of the entire marina. With a good set of binoculars, I could easily see what was happening on his boat. He was wining and dining some twenty-something woman with wavy dark hair and a tall slender body that a swimsuit model would sell her soul for. She moved like a ballerina, and I hated her instantly.

Snacking on a couple of meat and salad sandwiches I'd bought at the service station, I sat in the dark, camped out by the window for three hours straight. Toby and this woman—who was at least half his age—sat on a small table he'd set up on the deck, eating in the open air and talking quietly. Well, it was quiet for me, at least. From my vantage point, all I could see were moving lips and awkward smiles.

So many awkward smiles. How was this not a date? Their body language said, 'nervous but interested'. I kept waiting for one of them to make a move—a hand sliding across the table, a dance in the moonlight—but nothing came. They stood, hands smoothing clothes with relieved smiles. *They're not into each other.*

Good.

Toby needed a more mature woman, anyway.

I rolled my eyes and shook my head. *Like I'd know.* I was acting weird over this one.

When she gestured that she was going to leave, he lurched forwards, his movements jerky as he offered her a hug. It lasted maybe two seconds then they pulled apart and the girl held up her phone, saying something that caused him to shake his head. The girl's shoulders dropped as she seemed to say, "OK". But before she could put the phone away, he flicked his hands in a manner that said, "What the hell," which made the girl smile. Next, they leaned their heads together while she took a selfie then tucked her phone into her handbag, her lips curved in a small smile. After that, they said a quick goodbye, and Toby helped her down from the boat before waving her off. She got about ten steps away before he chased after her and walked her all the way down the pier and into the carpark. There, she got into a light-blue hatchback, spoke to him through the window for a few minutes then drove away.

Interesting. I jotted all of this down on paper in point form, splitting my attention between my notes and my binoculars.

I placed the pen back on my notebook while Toby stood and waited until her car was out of sight before he ran his fingers through his hair, shook his head, and smiled like he was bemused by the way the evening went. Then he slipped his hands into his jeans pockets and took a slow walk back to his boat where he cleaned the dinner dishes and disappeared into the cabin with his dog at his heels.

After noting his final movements, I continued to sit, watching the vacant window until the light switched off. 10:45pm. I wrote that down then added the words, 'end surveillance', underlining them twice before taking a moment to study the list detailing his evening: a romantic home cooked meal, a beautiful young woman, nervous actions, gentlemanly behaviour....

It wasn't a date, he'd said. But, I could feel the expectation of something more than friendship as I watched them converse. Their happiest moment was just after the hug and the photo. She was obviously something to him. The question was *what*?

As I stood and stretched my legs, I swiped through the pictures I'd caught of her on my phone, zooming into her face, trying to read her expression. *She wants to like him.*

Not a date.

Was that true, or did he lie?

A lie was certainly possible if he was a player. Lots of men downplayed their romantic connections when they wanted to keep their options open. *But was there romance here?* I tapped the screen and flicked through the pictures. *Maybe.* Especially if he was playing the long game with this one. I'd seen it before. Some guy acting the gentleman, wining and dining a woman, making her feel safe; as though she was the only woman in his world. And while he was waiting for her to be ready to give it up, he satisfied himself elsewhere. *With women like me.* It happened all the time. Men were ruled by their dicks.

Pulling the telephoto lens off my phone, I walked over

to the couch while I cropped a picture of her face and uploaded her to a facial recognition data base. It wasn't the same one the cops used. They only had access to known criminals because of all those privacy acts out there that protected the layperson from the authorities. For us, there were other databases that combed the Internet like little ants piggybacking on legitimate code, gathering data from social media and smart phones then reporting back. It made it so the people with the right kinds of connections—people like me—could figure out who anybody was. That's why, if you didn't want to be found, you disconnected entirely. No photos. No social media.

As I watched the search bar creep incrementally along the screen, I yawned and blinked through heavy eyelids. Surveillance was tiring work, but I wasn't ready for sleep yet. I was restless.

From what I could tell, there wasn't a hell of a lot of anything going on in Wannanup besides the marina. And being late at night, there wasn't a lot open besides a tavern a few streets away.

"Bloody hideaway towns," I said as I slipped my feet into my shoes. If I hadn't been so eager to get in this house and spy on Toby Cartwright, I would have searched for a bottle shop to pick up some vodka: my drink of choice. "How do people even live here when there's no nightlife?"

Thankful for the cooler night, I enjoyed the sea breeze as I walked through the dark towards the marina. The pathway running along the water was a straight shot to my destination: a tavern positioned right next to the bridge overlooking the Dawesville Channel. When I got inside and saw the massive windows showcasing the view—the lights from the bridge glittering against the water—I sucked in my breath. it was pretty fucking spectacular.

"Vodka, lime, and soda," I said as I approached the bar, a handful of other patrons dotted around the room.

"We close at twelve," the bartender said, sliding my requested drink in front of me.

"Line up three more and I'll be out of here by 11:55."

He laughed through his red middle-aged nose then got to mixing my drinks.

"Hard day?" he asked as he set the last one in front of me and took the fifty I held out to him.

"Nope. This is how I always drink." I answered him honestly, but his laugh told me he still thought I was joking. Or at least hoped I was.

"Didn't like the Irish Pub?"

Based on the way my skin prickled, I didn't even have to turn my head to know who it was. *I thought he'd gone to bed.*

"I decided to eat in." I locked eyes with Toby Cartwright, my heart kicking up a beat at the connection. "Date didn't turn out the way you wanted it to?" *What the hell is it with this guy? I'm wet just looking at him.*

"It was fine." He laughed as he paid the bartender, who placed a beer in front of him before he even ordered it.

"*Ha.* So you admit it was a date."

He took a sip of his beer and pressed his lips together, the pink of his tongue poking out to lick away the foam. "I'm just not going to argue with a person who couldn't even give me her name, but seems overly interested in my personal life."

I let my eyes do an obvious and lazy drag down his hard T-shirt clad body then back up to his eyes. "Have you seen yourself? I'm sure every woman you meet is interested in you."

He smiled, and I moved on to my next drink. "More friends who didn't show?" he asked, indicating the row of vodka limes.

"Nope. These are all mine." I drank the entire glass in two gulps and reached for the next.

"Drowning sorrows?"

"I'll let you know when I figure it out."

He lifted his dark brow and took another mouthful of his drink. "Listen, I'm not sure what you had going on with Devin. But from what I can tell, he isn't the most stand-up guy."

I smiled. *How sweet. He's playing the 'good guy' card.* "And you are a stand-up guy?"

An amused breath burst past his lips as his knee bounced on the edge of his stool. "Far from it. But, I know you don't ask a woman to meet you on a boat then not show up."

I rested my head in my hand as I leaned on the bar and angled myself towards him. "You're pretty stuck on that, huh? What if he had a really good reason?" He did, of course. The man had no idea who I was and was currently on the other side of the country in Sydney. I checked.

"There's never a good reason to give someone the runaround."

"Says the man who had a date tonight, but is drinking here with me."

"Speaking of being stuck on things." He chuckled then finished his beer, placing the empty glass on the bar with a thud before he stood up. "This place is closing. I'll walk you back to wherever you're staying. A B and B, right?"

"An Airbnb, actually. But there's no need. I'm perfectly capable." I finished my last drink then stood and grabbed my bag, slinging it over my shoulder.

"Another thing a man should never do is let a woman walk home alone in the dark when she's been drinking." He held out his hand.

Lowering my eyes to his upturned palm, I couldn't help notice how manly his hands were, well-worn with small calluses under each of his joints, a testament to the hard work they'd seen. Another thing I noticed about them was the fact they were very large. *And you know what that means...* Gulp.

"I don't know if that's a good idea," I said, meeting his eyes. "I mean, I just meet you today."

"I don't bite." He grinned in a way that made me think perhaps he did.

I shuddered. "How disappointing."

He laughed and scraped a hand over his stubbled jaw.

"Just give me a minute to use the ladies and we'll leave," I said with a slight smile.

Lowering his hand to his side, he nodded once then stepped back until he was leaning against the bar, watching me walk away. I had never met a man so... *beautiful* in my entire life. I'd seen handsome, attractive, manly. But never beautiful. Despite the scruff on his face and the too-long hair in his eyes, he took my breath away.

The fact he was so confident approaching me told me he was aware of the power he held over women. He didn't seem douchey about it, just conscious of it.

As I walked away, I threw him a smile over my shoulder, my own awareness of *my* effect on men causing me to sway my hips in that hypnotic way all lust-filled men enjoyed. It never ceased to amaze me how easy it was to lure men into my bed. I guessed the apple didn't fall far from the tree with me. The only difference between my mother and myself was that I did this for free, which meant I got to choose who I shared my bed with. And the payment never came in powder form, only orgasms. Big difference.

Once I relieved myself, I stood at the sink washing my hands and checking my appearance. Despite the long day, I still looked good. My hair was straight as a nail and shone like sunlight was trapped in it, and my makeup had held up against the warmth. I swiped a thin layer of gloss on my lips, rubbing them together as the stall behind me flushed then opened.

A woman in her mid to late thirties stepped out, straightening her skirt and running her hands down the fabric to smooth out any bumps. I smiled at her in the mirror as she stepped up to the basin and switched on the tap.

"Was that Tom I saw you talking to at the bar?" she asked, her voice slightly husky and her smile knowing.

"I think that's his name, yeah," I said, capping my gloss and sliding back into my bag.

"And you're leaving with him?" Her eyes met mine via the mirror. She was pretty with that 'mum's night out' kind of vibe.

"He's offered to walk me home. Is that a problem?"

"Not at all." She smiled and leaned in conspiratorially. "I was actually just going to wish you luck. I hear he's a devil in the sack."

"A devil?"

She nodded. "Between you and me, a girlfriend of

mine spent the night with him, and she couldn't walk properly for almost a week." She lifted her brow before holding her hands out to show his size.

My eyes widened. "Well, I did notice the big hands."

She smirked and nudged me in the arm with her elbow. "And big feet."

I pressed my knees together.

"Did your friend say whether it was worth it?" I asked as I hooked my bag on my arm.

A massive grin spread across her face as she met my eyes and nodded. "Best experience of her life."

CHAPTER FOUR
HEY SIRI

"THIS IS ME," I said, standing on the driveway of the Airbnb I rented. We'd walked along slowly, making conversation about inconsequential things. He talked about his boat and his fishing charter, plus a little about his dog, Rogue—no name change there—who was old and enjoying the sea life. I spoke about a job in marketing that didn't exist and told him I travelled a lot, having no time to consider settling down like my (imaginary) high school friends had. In between the lines of our conversation we were actually saying things like, "I'm only interested in you in this moment," and "I'm emotionally unavailable," letting us both know this would be nothing more than a one-night stand.

My favourite kind of something.

"Right near the marina. Nice." His gaze took in the expanse of the waterside property. It truly was beautiful. A six bedroom home with three living areas and outdoor entertaining. I imagined it would be a family's dream home. For me, the size was wasted. All I needed was a room with a bed.

"Tom." I'd avoided saying his name as much as possible so I didn't call him Toby accidentally.

His gaze dropped to mine and held, the blue of his eyes as clear as the surrounding ocean. My skin tingled with the expectation of his touch. "I still don't know your name," he said, his eyes crinkling at the sides as he almost laughed about it.

I smiled then lifted on my toes and pressed my mouth to his. He froze for a split second, his lips pursing to receive the kiss, but not parting right away. It seemed he needed to consider what was happening before responding. Then he was on me, his tongue pushing past my lips, and his hand in my hair. He took over, devouring me, controlling the depth along with my movement.

Fuck me, fuck me, fuck me.

A low hum rumbled in his chest as his tongue slid against mine, the beer he'd drunk earlier mixing with the tartness of my vodka lime. It tasted like a good time, and I wrapped my arms around his neck as his other hand found my arse and pulled me flush against him.

Hmm. That thing is big.

"Inside," I whispered, pulling at his shirt when he pulled back to allow us to catch our breath.

He shook his head and released my hair. "You've been drinking. I should go."

Did my ears hear right? "I'm not drunk." Not even close.

Still a little out of breath, he ran a gentle touch down the side of my face, sending waves of longing all the way through me. "Still, I like my women sober." He ran his thumb over my bottom lip, dragging it down before he dropped his hand to his side. "I also like to know their name."

I smiled as he waited, still getting nothing from me.

"OK. It's like that." He took a step back, teeth pulling at his bottom lip. "I guess I'll see you around, stranger."

"You don't have to leave. It's not like I'll ask you to call me in the morning."

His grin got bigger. "You're forward."

"Then you won't be shocked when I tell you I want you to come inside, fuck me and leave without saying goodbye."

A sound that could be described as both contemplative and erotic vibrated in his chest. "Tempting. But I'd still need your name."

If he hadn't kissed me the way he did, I'd be wondering if I'd lost my touch. This guy had some serious restraint. *Kudos.*

I grinned. This was a game now. "It's tattooed on my arse. You'll have to undress me to find out what it is."

A laugh burst out of his chest as his eyes twinkled, taking me in. "Seems we're at an impasse."

"That it does."

Sliding his hands in his jean pockets, he took a step back. "Good night, enigma."

I laughed at the name as I pulled out my keys. "Good night, Toby. Thanks for walking me back." Flicking my hair over my shoulder, I headed for the front door with a giant grin fixed upon my face. I was enjoying him even more now he'd shown restraint. It was rare to meet a man willing to walk away from a sure thing. But here was one, standing in my rented driveway with a giant hard-on after kissing the life out of me. It had to be uncomfortable.

"Last chance to get inside me," I called over my shoulder as I slid the key into the lock. With no response forthcoming, I turned on my toes and found nothing but empty space where he'd been standing. *Damn. There goes my orgasm.*

"Thank god for vibrators and a vivid imagination," I muttered as I unlocked the house and stepped inside.

AFTER REMEMBERING I had a half full bottle of vodka tucked inside the boot of my car, I inserted my earbuds and had myself a little alcohol induced dance party. I had energy that needed to be burned that multiple self-induced orgasms couldn't overcome. So, I drank straight from the bottle, jumping around and singing to my favourite songs until my mind and body went numb. *Bliss.*

I woke to a cotton wool mouth and a pinching at my wrists. When I went to move... I couldn't.

"What the fuck?"

"Stay still." I looked up to find Toby holding the Touch ID on my phone up to my zip-tied hands. *Shit.*

"Don't." I thrashed about, trying to make a fist so he couldn't get into my phone. But it was no use. He was far too strong for me, and I was bound, hands and feet tied to the bed frame.

No. No. No.

The moment he got past the lock screen, he backed away from the bed, the glow of the display illuminating his features in the dim room as he swiped with his fingers.

His jaw tightened. "You shouldn't drink on the job, Blair. Big Jim should have taught you that. It makes you sloppy." *How the hell does he know who I am? Who I work for?*

"What I do and when is none of your business," I spat, bracing my arms against my restraints.

He jabbed at my phone, his eyes busy as he continued tapping around, probably deleting all the information I'd gathered about him. I cursed myself for holding off on the upload. I should have sent it all off last night instead of letting my curiosity lead me astray. *Sloppy.*

"This life you lead isn't a nine to five, Blair. The job ends when you get paid." He stopped his assault on my phone and met my eyes. "Or does it end for you when you get *laid.*" His eyes travelled slowly down my body, a singlet and a pair of black panties my only clothes.

"Fuck you." That was a low blow, even for a criminal.

"You wish," he said, sniffing as he went back to working on my phone. "Tell Jasmine you couldn't find me. Better yet, tell her I'm dead."

"What's to say she isn't already on her way?"

He glanced at me and rolled his eyes. "You haven't called in for almost twenty-four hours and nothing has been uploaded to your server. I'm deleting your pictures, your notes are coming with me and I've canceled the facial recognition search you instigated. That girl is of no consequence to you."

"She is to you. Why?"

"That's none of your goddamn business," he growled. "If I find you *anywhere* near her, you won't just wake up tied to a bed. I'll make sure you don't wake up at all."

Scowling, I clenched my teeth and pulled at my

restraints. *Who the hell is this guy?* "I'm not promising you a fucking thing."

"Considering you're nearly two hours away from the nearest major city, I'd be promising the world if I were you."

"You don't scare me, Toby Cartwright. I've met and overcome far worse than you."

In response, he just shook his head and concentrated on my phone. Once finished, he shut off the screen and held the slim device between his large palms. "You better not become a pain in my arse, Blair."

"I wanted to be the finger in your arse, but I guess that ship has sailed," I said with a shrug. I swear I saw the corner of his mouth quirk.

"Wanna know?" he asked, his eyes pointing out my current state.

"Sure." I rolled my eyes. This wasn't the first time a mark had confronted me, and since it seemed Toby wasn't planning on ending my life today, I doubted it'd be the last. During the course of this job—this life—I'd been beaten, tortured, and then some. There wasn't a thing a person could do to me I hadn't been through already. I wasn't afraid of pain. Or death. Being tied to a bed was almost boring to be honest. "But, if I had to guess, I'd say you're paranoid and think everyone is after you."

He actually smiled at that, and despite my prone and vulnerable state, I still found that smile attractive. My stomach even flipped. *Crazy.* "I was. It took me forty years to get away from those people. But lately…" He took a deep breath and ran his teeth over his bottom lip. "You know, for the first time in a *year*, I was feeling relaxed enough to move here. Wannanup. My own slice of paradise. I set up my dream business, was even looking into getting a house closer to—" Stopping, he pressed his lips together and shook his head, closing his eyes with a sigh, like he couldn't believe he was unburdening himself. "You called me Toby."

"I did what?" My mind raced, trying to figure out when and how that happened. *I'd been so careful... how?*

"Last night. Before I left, you said goodbye, and you called me Toby."

Holy shit. What was I even supposed to say to that? Wasn't like I could deny it. He had the proof of what I'd been doing in his hand. Well, he *had* the proof before he deleted everything. *This is what I get for listening to my clit instead of my head.*

"That's why you don't drink. It's also why you don't hit on your mark. Gets messy. Believe me, I've seen it all firsthand." He threw my phone on the end of the bed between my bound feet. "You come on too strong, by the way."

"Excuse me?" *He's coaching me on how to pick up men now?*

"If seducing your mark is part of your thing, you're coming on too strong."

I couldn't stop the smirk from curling my mouth if I tried. "Hasn't been a problem before. Most men like a sure thing." Although, truthfully, most of the men I captured, I took down with a taser or a tranquilliser dart. I only slept with the *really* good looking ones. And *those* guys had liked a sure thing.

"I guess I'm not like most men. I like to be the one in control."

I lowered my lashes. "I guess that makes two of us."

He shook his head. "See? You're doing it again. You're beautiful, and from what I can tell, you're smart—when you're not on the bottle." He tapped the empty vodka bottle with his foot, and it rolled along the wooden floor, hitting the wall near the bathroom. "You don't need to walk around acting like you're just a hole to fuck. That's no way to live."

Anger flashed behind my eyes, blinding me momentarily. "Who the fuck are you to tell me how to do anything?" I snapped. "I'm a grown woman who can fuck whomever she pleases whenever she pleases. There's no shame in that." *Pig.*

"Hey, if that's all you want to be..."

My eyes widened and my cheeks flamed. "You don't know me. You don't know a damn thing." *Whoa, Blair. Why let him push your buttons? He's not worth it.* I needed to get control of myself.

He shrugged. "I don't need to know you. I can read you. Besides, I looked into your background. You have quite a reputation."

"I don't give a flying fuck about any reputation besides the one that says I'm the best damn human tracker in the country."

"And I'm the best damn problem solver you'll ever meet. Mess with me, mess with anyone I care about, and I'll make you sorry. Consider yourself warned." Then he walked out the door, leaving me strapped to the bed like a southern cross spider in the centre of their web.

"Toby!" I called after him. "You can't just leave me here."

"Someone will find you," he yelled from what sounded like the bottom of the stairs.

"Toby! Get the fuck back up here!" The silence returning told me that my screams fell on deaf ears. *That motherfucker. He actually left me here.*

Pulling as hard as I could against the zip ties, I tried to stretch them so I could slide loose. But it was no good. I was stuck.

"Great." Puffing out my breath to get my hair out of my face, I looked around the room, trying to figure something out. My options seemed limited to waiting until the owner of this place came when I didn't return the keys, or until Big Jim got worried and sent someone looking for me. Either of those options could take days.

Unless… My eyes landed on the phone sitting between my feet.

"Hey Siri," I said, sighing with relief when the screen lit up and I heard that telltale beep. "Call Big Jim."

"WELL, well, well. What do we have here?" Nick Jennings appeared in the doorway a few hours later, a shit-eating grin on his dark-tan face as he slid a cigarette between his full lips and lit up. "Lookin' good, Blair."

Of all the people who could come to my aid, Nick was the last person I wanted.

"Just untie me, fuckface."

My job didn't exactly have the Christmas parties or social gatherings more typical vocations did, but I knew most of the guys on Big Jim's roster. Mostly because I made it a point to, but also because I occasionally worked as part of a team. Not easy for a loner like me, but sometimes it was necessary.

"Is that any way to greet your saviour?" he said, casually walking to the foot of the bed and chuckling. His jet-black hair pulled back in an elastic at the base of his neck, a thin wavy strand of it falling free and hanging about his masculine yet attractive face. His mother was Chinese and his father was Greek, giving him hooded eyes, a roman nose, and a heart-shaped mouth. And he was charming to boot. Women fell for him easily. Including me once upon a time.

"Just untie me, Nick. *Please*." It hurt me to say the word, especially to him, but I was busting to pee, and I didn't want to dick around.

"Give me a minute. I'm getting myself a nice mental image so I can jack off to it later. Even after everything, you still get my blood going, Blair." A few years back we were working a job together. The sex and chemistry between us was great, so we gave a relationship a shot. But he had issues with anger, and I had issues with trust and vulnerability. Neither of us could let our guard down long enough to have anything meaningful, so we cut our losses and moved on when it all got too ugly. Now, we avoided each other as much as possible; mainly because I threatened to break his nose the last time we spoke.

"Nick. Please. You know how uncomfortable I am right now."

He reached into his pocket and pulled out a flick knife. "Yeah. I remember." His voice and gaze softened a little before he slid the blade between my ankle and the bedpost, slicing the plastic tie with a snap.

With a relief-filled groan, I bent my knee as my blood flowed and prickled beneath my skin. Nick made quick work of the next two ties, but paused before cutting the last. "How'd this happen, anyway? It's not like you to participate in any sort of kinky shit." His eyes slid down the length of my body, pointing out the fact I was wearing nothing but my underwear.

"Some guy I've been watching figured out who I was. He broke in while I was sleeping."

He cut the final tie and met my eyes. "He hurt you?"

Sitting up, I rubbed at my wrists and shook my head. "Just got rid of everything I had on him and left me here for you to find." I got up and headed straight for the ensuite bathroom, closing my eyes in sweet relief as I emptied my bladder. "He's probably long gone by now," I called out when I finished and headed for the basin to wash my hands and brush my teeth. "I'll have to start again."

Nick entered the bathroom and dropped his finished cigarette butt into the open toilet. It fizzled out with a hiss as it hit the water. "About that…"

I stopped brushing and spat my toothpaste into the sink. "No."

"Big Jim wants you to turn everything you have over to me."

"I don't *have* anything. "

"Then tell me what you know."

"No. This is *my job*. My mark. I found him."

"And like you said, he's probably long gone now. *I'll* be basically starting again, anyway."

"That is total bullshit." Big Jim could be way too protective of me. He'd never do this to one of the guys.

"I don't make the calls," he said, following me out of the bathroom as I gathered my things. "But I do think it's a good idea." When I whipped around to confront him, I found him holding the empty vodka bottle. "How much are you drinking these days, anyway?"

I snatched the bottle from his hands and threw it in my bag. "Just enough to help me sleep."

"You smell like you're drinking more than that."

Pulling a hairband from my purse, I scraped my hair

into a ponytail, huffing out my breath. "Leave it alone, Nick. I'm not hurting anyone. It isn't affecting how I do my job."

"Says the woman I just cut free from her starfish position on the bed."

"He did that while I was sleeping. Not because I let him."

"Sleeping? Or passed out?"

"Fuck you, Nick."

"He could have really hurt you, Blair." His voice softened as he stepped towards me.

I sat on the edge of the bed and shoved my feet into a pair of chucks. "I know," I snapped, tightening the laces. "I fucking know, all right. I know I got lucky. *I know*."

Releasing his breath, he sat down beside me and placed a gentle hand on my thigh. "I'm worried about you, Blair. Take this as a sign that your shit is getting out of control and get some help. Check yourself into one of those fancy clinics or something. I don't want to walk in one day and find you dead instead of just zip-tied to a bed."

"What part of 'I'm fine' aren't you getting? This is *my* job, and I'm not letting you swoop in and steal my hard earned money. I don't give a fuck what Jim says."

"Jesus fucking…" He got up and shook his head. "You never fucking change."

"Neither do you, you glory hogging arsehole!"

"Are you serious right now?" His eyes widened, lacking understanding. "Whatever, Blair. I'm not dealing with you right now." He lifted his hands and headed for the door.

"That's right, run away, Nick. Run like you always do."

Huffing out a growl, he muttered under his breath, slamming the bedroom door on his way out.

I moved over to the window and watched until his car pulled away and made it to the end of the street. Then I let out a sigh. *Alone.* Thank god. I couldn't take any more of his words. People always wanted me to change, they commented on my drinking, my sex life, my attitude... it was none of their fucking business. If I cared about any of that shit, I'd change for myself. I'd be that demure little girl my foster mother had banged on about.

No. I was just fine. They all needed to learn how to mind their own business and let me live my fucking life. I didn't need any of them.

Once I saw Nick's car leave the quays and head towards town, I collected the rest of my things and moved into the living room, ready to work out where Toby had run to this time.

I made a coffee in the little pod machine then walked over to the large window overlooking the marina. As I sipped the bittersweet brew, I sought out his boat pen, expecting to find a vacant spot of sea where Toby had moored his boat.

Instead of water, I saw a fucking boat. *He's still here? What. The. Actual. Fuck?* He knew everything about me. About Big Jim. Why I was here. Did he really think I wouldn't come back at him? Because of a few zip-ties?

That man was a whole new level of messed up if he thought that way.

With my heart thudding in my chest, I dumped my coffee in the sink, excited that I could complete this job and prove I still had what it takes. One stupid mistake shouldn't mar an exemplary career.

Rushing downstairs, I opened the boot of my car and pulled up the lining, revealing the compartment underneath that contained my takedown kit. I pulled out my taser and checked the batteries. The prongs crackled perfectly.

Wait. Toby is a big guy. He might not go down with the taser alone....

Reconsidering, I pulled out the black case containing my tranquilliser gun, loaded it with extra strength darts then tucked it into the back of my jeans.

That'll do the trick.

My phone rang.

"Jim," I said, holding it to my ear as I straightened up my car mat with the other hand.

"Glad you're OK, kid." He paused for a second then chuckled. "Gotta admit, I laughed at your expense over this one."

"Yeah well, I'm sure I'll laugh about it one day too."

"It's like he read your file." He kept laughing before his cackle turned into a cough.

"He probably *did* read my file. You might want to check your firewalls for a breach."

"Ah, fuck. I'm on it. But kid, I need you to turn this one over to Nick. Tell him everything you know then step down."

"I'm fine, Jim. I don't need protecting."

"Well, I think you do. It's my call, and I'm telling you to back off. I don't want this to turn into another Adelaide job."

I closed my eyes, shuddering at the memory. "Sure, boss," I murmured, shaking off the chill crawling across my skin as I reached up and closed the boot. I didn't want to argue after he hit me in my Achilles heel.

"Thank you."

"I'll fill Nick in right away," I lied, there was no way. "Thanks for checking in, Jim."

"Just make sure you do the same. I don't like the idea of losing my best tracker to a psycho just because she didn't call it in like I asked."

"Duly noted."

Disconnecting, I pocketed my phone then headed straight for the marina. I didn't care what Big Jim or Nick Jennings wanted. Toby Cartwright was *my* job. And I was damn well going to finish it.

CHAPTER SIX
DON'T TURN THAT KEY

WITH MY HANDS in my jacket pockets, I hunched against the morning wind, one foot stepping sure in front of the other. It was 10am and Mr Sticky-beak wasn't being his nosey self just yet. *Probably had something better to do.* The marina seemed relatively quiet; the only people I ran into were two men—one in his twenties, the other middle-aged, both too different to be related—walking in the opposite direction. They wore caps down low, their collars pulled up around their necks to shield their skin from the unusually cool bite in the air.

"Morning," the older man said, meeting my eyes and flickering a memory locked tight in my brain. It felt like the flutter of a shadow in the corner of my eye, uncomfortably familiar.

"Morning," I replied, staring at him a little more intently during the moment it took us to pass each other. *I feel like I know him.*

"Rough on the water today," he said, tapping a finger on the brim of his hat and flashing a gold-toothed smile.

I nodded in response, a creeping, crawling feeling settling beneath my skin as I continued on, my mind flashing, threatening me with a headache I didn't want. *No. Don't.*

No. I needed to find Toby.

Forcing my mind to focus, I concentrated on propelling my feet forwards until I was standing in front of his boat and looking up.

The little dog wasn't on the deck this time, and when I climbed on board, there was no other sign of life. *Maybe he left on land?*

Entering the cabin, everything seemed clean and tidy. A single cup and plate were sitting in the drain tray, the bedroom—or berth—seemed untouched. I ran my hand across the hanging shirts before opening the drawers. Still full of clothes.

Maybe he isn't running at all?

Continuing my search around the room, I pulled open the drawers at his bedside, rummaging through papers and personal belongings, trying to get a handle on who this guy was, and what was important to him. There were the typical things—random receipts, batteries, tangled headphones. I found a pair of cuff links, old looking, gold and square with a green stone set inside them.

Dropping them back in the drawer, I slid it closed and opened the next one down. A bottle of lube rolled and hit the back of the drawer, returning to me and knocking against a pack of extra-large condoms. "Guess the rumours are true," I said, peeking inside and seeing it was mostly full. I didn't know why, but it pleased me that maybe he wasn't having that much sex.

Still pissed over the 'hole to fuck' comment, I took

every condom out of the box and shoved them in my pocket. *He won't be sealing the deal any time soon, either.*

Kneeling on the floor, I opened the small cupboard and rifled through the books inside. *One Flew Over The Cuckoo's Nest*, *Norwegian Wood*, *Slaughterhouse Five* and *The Great Gatsby* to name a few. I ran my finger along the spines, well worn with creases and fine lines that cut through the colour of the covers, telling me someone had read them over and over, that they were favourites.

I pulled out his copy of *Norwegian Wood* and studied the cover while the Beatles song of the same name ran through my head. I hummed a few bars as I traced over the upside-down butterfly then flipped the book over to see what it was about. The motion caused a sharp corner to press into my palm. A photo.

Sliding the print from between the pages, I stared at the image it contained. Toby, possibly in his twenties, sitting on a porch swing, laughing while a small girl sat in his lap with her head thrown back and a massive grin on her face. She couldn't have been over five or six with long brown hair and a mouth that was achingly familiar.

Is she...

I flipped the picture, hoping for some sort of clue printed on the back, but there was nothing.

Flicking through the rest of the book, I found a folded piece of paper—a child's drawing of two people and a rainbow—a school photo of the same girl at around nine or ten, a pressed flower.

Who is this girl to Toby?

Pulling out the other books, I continued my search, finding more photos—from a baby right up until high school—when it became obvious that this girl was the same one I'd watched him have dinner with the night before. I picked up a photo of her in her graduation robe, her clear blue eyes shining happy as she smiled for the camera. *Those eyes.* I held it next to the first photo. *I've looked into those eyes before.* The resemblance was unmistakable.

"He has a daughter?" There had been no mention of any spouse or offspring on his file. But their features where too similar to deny a family connection.

Is this why he ran away?

Movement on the deck snapped me into action. I gathered the photos and shoved them back in the books, slipping them into the cupboard and closing it up before I got to my feet and moved closer to the door.

Thud. Thud. Tap, tap, tap.

With my hand on the tranquilliser gun, I listened as the movement got closer.

"Settle down, Rogue. I need to pack these supplies away first." The little dog barked, its nails tapping against the flooring as it jumped about something.

Oh shit. Maybe he's trying to tell Toby where I am.

With a slow release of my breath, I reached one hand forward and flicked the lock on the door. I needed the element of surprise and having a dog sniff me out would mess that up.

Claws scratched at the door. *Shit.*

"Hey, you can nap later. There's work to be done." He whistled with two short bursts of sound.

With a slight whine, the dog left, its nails clicking away while I sighed with relief. I could hold my own in a fight, but even I knew I'd be no match against a guy of Toby's size in close quarters.

When I heard footfalls on the deck above, I unlocked the door and peeked out. If I could get him out in the open, I could hit him with a dart without any risk to my person. The only problem I'd have would be with the dog. I figured I could deal with the pooch using every dog's weakness—food.

Opening the fridge, I found what Rogue had been excited about when Toby had entered the cabin: a bone with some meat on it.

Pulling it from the plastic, I held it by my side and crept up the stairs to the deck, finding Toby at the helm performing what looked like a system check. The dog's head whipped around and its tongue slurped at his chops.

"Hungry?" I whispered, so soft that even I could barely hear it. Rogue could, however, and ran straight for me, chasing the bone into the cabin when I dropped it down the stairs.

"One down. One to go."

The engine flared to life, vibrating the entire boat as Toby eased us away from the pier.

Quiet step after quiet step, I crept up behind him.

"I hope you know how to dock a boat this size," he said as I moved in. "Otherwise you're gonna have a bitch of a time getting me off it."

How does he know I'm here?

"Maybe I have a helicopter on the way?" I held my tranq gun in front of me, keeping my distance as he glanced over his shoulder.

"Doubtful."

"Well, I guess you'll just have to wait and see." Flicking the safety, I placed my finger on the trigger and aimed for the meaty part of his arse.

The engine stalled.

Stumbling forwards as I fired, the dart hit the back of his shoe, not the ideal place for a tranquilliser injection.

Toby grunted and leaned down, pulling the dart and throwing it so it landed in the water. "I should take you to the deep and throw you overboard for shark bait," he growled, nostrils flaring as he turned the key and the ignition clicked without catching. "Great." He tried again, and suddenly all those pictures I'd been struggling to keep buried in my mind came to the front. *The eyes. The voice. The gold tooth.*

Shit.

Adelaide.

"Stop!" I yelled, shoving the gun in the back of my jeans as I rushed forwards. "Don't turn that key!"

Too late. The engine made a chugging sound as I dove at Toby, catching him about the waist just as a rumble erupted from beneath us.

"Jump!"

The force of the blast shot us higher into the air before we tumbled down into the water, heat and debris chasing us, forcing us deeper down.

Frog swimming as far from the explosion as we could, we came up for air near a small jetty in the quays, gasping and spluttering as sirens wailed in the distance, flames and black smoke licking the air.

"My dog was on that boat!" Toby gasped, grabbing my arm and sneering into my face, his eyes wild.

"I didn't do that," I yelled back, panic settling in as I tried to keep my head above the lapping water with only one arm available. "It wasn't me!"

"*Fuck.*" He released me with a shove as he swam

towards the wreckage, nothing more than fire and drift-wood at this point.

"Toby, Stop. You can't go back there."

"I need to find Rogue." Emotion and panic coated his words.

"Your dog is gone." He stopped swimming and met my gaze. "I'm sorry, there's no way he survived that. But, if you swim out there, they'll find out *you* did."

"Fuck!" He ground the word out through his teeth and slapped the water.

"We need to get out of here. *Now*."

Emergency services responded, their lights flashing and sirens blaring in almost every direction. Edging our way through the quays, we used jetties and runaround boats as our cover, needing to stay hidden as residents emerged to watch the chaos. Eventually, we made it back to my rental and sloshed our way inside.

"I don't have any clothes that'll fit you. But there's a washer and dryer. You can wrap yourself in a blanket while your clothes clean." I gestured to the laundry beside the kitchen.

"Where's the bathroom?" His question came out in a monotone, the shock of the explosion settling in.

Pressing my lips together in commiseration, I pointed down the hall, and he disappeared without a word. *Shit.* How the hell did this happen?

Upon hearing the shower switch on, I grabbed towels and a blanket, hesitating slightly on the other side of the bathroom door when I thought I heard a sob. *Is he crying? Oh god.*

A knot formed in my throat. He'd just lost his dog, his boat and all of his belongings. The photos of his daughter, the books, the history. That boat held his identity. Of course he was upset.

Whoa. When did I learn empathy? Emotion wasn't really something I *did* well.

Staying as silent as possible, I cracked the door open and slipped the items I held inside, grabbing his wet things then slipping back out again and heading to the laundry where I stripped out of my own clothes and started the washer after removing everything from our pockets.

Our phones, his wallet, my tranq gun, and the condoms I'd stolen sat on the counter, soaked with seawater. At least I'd thought to leave my purse behind, so my personal stuff was fine. But everything Toby owned was wet, destroyed or dead. *Was this* my *fault?*

Wrapping myself in a towel, I went upstairs and took a quick shower so I didn't stink of fish. Then I dressed in a fresh pair of jeans and a T-shirt before heading back downstairs. I found Toby standing at the window overlooking the marina, watching the rescue boats attending to the scene. Moisture beaded on his bare shoulders as small drips fell from the ends of his overgrown hair. The strong defined muscles in his back rippling with tension, and I longed to reach out and place my hand against his skin. *Now is not the time to get all aquiver, Blair.*

"I'm sorry about your dog," I said as I approached, my eyes dropping to where the towel hugged his hips. He was a stunning sight to behold. All man. Even after his nasty words, he took my breath away.

"I had him since he was a pup. Almost fourteen years now. The vets always said he wouldn't last that long. But he was healthy...." He frowned then swallowed without continuing.

"If it helps, he was gnawing on that bone you bought him when it happened."

His mouth quirked slightly. "It doesn't." He met my eyes. "But thanks."

I shrugged and moved to stand by him. There were four boats crowded around the wreckage now, lights flashing as divers entered the water looking for survivors, or at least evidence there were none. I swallowed hard. *That poor dog.*

People did shitty things and survived all the time. I always hated it when innocents, like animals and kids were caught up in the mess. Rogue didn't deserve that end.

"Why does your family want you dead?" I asked after a while, thinking about the man I'd seen on the pier. He was a freelancer who specialised in munitions, went by the name Irish. I'd only seen him in the flesh once before. Right after a house blew up in Adelaide and….

No. Don't.

"What?" He looked at me like I was insane. "This wasn't my family. They'd never…"

"Hey, I was just asking." I held my hands up for a brief second before folding them across my middle. "Someone wants you dead and since *they* sent me to find you, it makes sense they also did this."

His jaw ticked as he stared at his destroyed boat and shook his head. "This wasn't them. They don't… I just know it wasn't them."

"Then who? And how did they know you were here?"

"You tell me."

I took a step back, insulted that he'd question my professionalism. "I haven't told anyone shit about you. You deleted every photo and destroyed my notes before I uploaded a thing. Either someone has been watching you all along, or…" I let my voice trail off as I gathered my thoughts.

"What?"

"Would someone be running an active search on you? Waiting for a picture of you to pop up somewhere?" The database I'd used to run the image of the girl I now suspected to be his daughter wasn't just used by private investigators.

"It's possible."

"That girl. The one you had dinner with. She took your photo."

He shook his head. "She wouldn't."

"But what if she did? What if she uploaded it to her social media? Even if she sent it in a private message, it could get picked up."

His jaw tightened before he growled out a name. "Grey."

"Grey *what*?" My blood went cold.

"The smuggler."

Holy shit. "Brendan Grey?"

He nodded. "You know him?"

My eyes went wide as my cold blood turned freezing and stopped up my heart.

I knew the man. Everyone who had access to a news outlet knew about Grey these days, but I'd had my own special reasons for hating the man. Grey and his organisation were responsible for smuggling most of the drugs, guns and people into the country, making himself wealthy off the back of the resulting misery. And that was just the start. He'd gained public notoriety a little under a year ago when he was arrested after a cache of stolen drugs were found in a warehouse he owned. Since then, his name had remained in the papers alongside the Grim Order as they waged war against each other. It was speculated the MC had planted the drugs on the smuggler's property, setting him up to remove suspicion from themselves, or weaken Grey's operation so they might take over. No one outside really knew for sure, but the turf war had been getting increasingly heated in the last few months since they released Grey. Insufficient evidence, they'd said. I was thoroughly disappointed the man was at large again and suspected his release involved foul play.

"Why's he after you?"

Toby's eyes met mine, their focus far away. "I killed a bunch of his men."

"A *bunch*?"

He nodded in slow motion. *Fuck.*

"Oh." I took an involuntary step backwards.

"Regret saving me?"

I shook my head. "No. The only good smuggler is a dead one in my opinion." In fact, seeing Grey dead would be my greatest joy. I moved closer so Toby and I were standing side by side. "What do we do now?"

His brow lifted. "We? There's no *we*."

"The man he sent saw me get on that boat. They see me walking around, they're gonna realise you probably are too."

"I don't give a fuck what they think."

"And what if they know about your daughter? Isn't it better for her if they think we're both dead?"

He spun so fast, his hand shooting out to grab my arm, that I didn't have time to counter. "What the fuck do you know about my daughter." His fingers pinched my skin.

"I figured it out. After your dinner that wasn't a date, and the photos hidden in your books."

"You were in my room?" His grip tightened, and I winced.

"Yes," I admitted. "But maybe they weren't. Maybe they found you the same way I did and have no idea about your girl. Or maybe, just maybe, they found that photo of you two and they know exactly who she is."

"They can't possibly know she's my daughter. No one knows. I've made sure of that."

"You look alike. That's how I figured it out. What's to say they didn't too?"

"Shit." Releasing my arm, he scrubbed a hand over his face. "Shit. Fuck. *Shit*." He took a step back, turned, then faced the window again, lacing both hands behind his neck. "I can't stay here. I need to make sure she's safe."

"Let me go. You don't even have any clothes." I gestured to the towel around his waist.

"Then give me my wet clothes. I don't care. I'm going."

"They're in the washing machine. They'd be full of soap."

"I'm *going*," he insisted.

"Fine. Just give me ten minutes. I think I can help."

He placed his hands on his hips then let out a growl. "You have five."

CHAPTER SEVEN
SPILL

"HUH. Those clothes are baggy as fuck on me," Nick said, when Toby emerged from the bathroom, dressed in what Nick had called his 'eating pants' and a plain black T-shirt.

Nick was a fit guy. Coming in at five-eleven, he worked out regularly and wouldn't be described as tiny by anyone. When compared to Toby, he was practically a waif.

I covered my smile with my hand as Toby ran a hand over his chest where the fabric stretched so much it became a second skin. "The shirt's a little snug, but the pants are fine."

Nick nodded knowingly. "Elastic waist," he said, pride in his dark eyes.

"Just don't flex or that shirt's gonna tear," I said from behind my hand trying not to laugh. The hem of the shirt barely touched the waistband of the khaki pants.

He pulled at the hem and rolled his eyes. "I need your car," he stated.

"No way, mate. I'll drive you," I said, hands on my hips and a 'don't even try to argue' expression on my face.

"Whoa, whoa," Nick put in, touching his fingers to my shoulder. "We seem to be forgetting that this is my case now. *I* do the driving."

Twisting my body towards him, I narrowed my eyes. "You can't possibly think I'm handing my collar over to you. I put in the time and effort. *I'm* delivering him to his family."

Nick leaned in, his face only a few inches away from mine. "Your fuck up is my success."

I shoved him in the chest to get him out of my face. "So typical. Always ready to claim the glory just for showing up."

The roar of an engine cut into our little tiff. At the same time, we turned to where Toby had been standing, only to find him gone and the front door open.

"Now look what you've done," Nick said, pulling his keys from his pocket and rushing for the door.

"You can't blame me. He's *your* collar," I shot back, following close behind.

"Oh, *now* he's mine." Nick slid into the driver's seat of his Cherokee as I jumped into the passenger side. "Where's he even going?"

"To check on a girl," I said, leaving out the fact they were related as I held out my hand. "Give me your phone."

"You seriously think he's gonna answer if you call?"

"No. But my iPad is in the car. We can track it."

"Fine." He slapped his phone in my hand and started the Jeep, heading out of the quays as I logged into my Apple account.

"Here." I brought the map up on the screen and

connected it to his hands-free. "He's just at the edge of town."

"Reckon he's hittin' her up for one last bang before he pisses off again?" Nick grinned lasciviously as he looked my way then took a corner.

I chose to ignore his comment and change the subject instead. "I'm gonna need you to stay here and play the worried partner role."

"What? Stay in Wannanup?" He glanced at me, frowning, his hands still on the wheel.

"Yeah. I need you to act like you're waiting for them to find our bodies. Act upset, ask questions. You know, sell it."

"You reckon whoever blew up his boat is still watchin'?"

"Of course. Wouldn't you?"

"Well, yeah. But why can't you be here? Who even knows you were on that boat but him and me?"

"You remember a guy called Jasper O'Keefe from your commando days?" Nick practically grew up in the armed forces and was discharged in his early thirties after failing one too many psych evaluations.

"Irish? Yeah, I remember him." Every guy coming out of the military seemed to have a nickname of some sort. Jasper O'Keefe was Aussie through and through, but since he had an Irish sounding surname, the nickname had caught and stuck. He went into demolition once his time was up with the forces, but the bad guys paid better and he soon became the go-to guy whenever you needed something exploded. Grey had hired him on more than one occasion I knew about.

"He saw me get onboard."

Nick jerked his head back so hard he almost lost control of the car.

"Nick!" I grabbed for the wheel reflexively, but he deflected me with his left arm.

"You saw Jasper O'Keefe, and you got on that boat? Are you *insane,* Blair?"

"I didn't recognise him until it was too late."

"But, you know what he does, right?"

"I know."

"Then why, in god's name would you get on the fucking boat of a guy you *know* is a criminal?" He gestured to his head, emphasising what a dumb idea it was.

"I know."

"You're losing it, Blair. Fucking losing it."

I clenched my teeth. "I'm *fine.*"

"No. You haven't been fine since Adelaide, and you know it. You drink to forget and you fuck to feel something. But all you're really doing is messing up your life. You're better than this."

Gritting my teeth so hard my jaw hurt, I focused my attention on the blip of my iPad on the map. "Save your lecture, Nick. We're almost there."

With an aggravated sigh in the tension-filled air, Nick pulled up behind my Captiva. I jumped out before he even cut the engine, thankful he stayed in the Cherokee as I walked right up to my car and got in beside Toby.

"What was your play here?" I asked as soon as I shut the door. Toby turned to me and grunted in annoyance. "Realised you can't just storm in there in case they're watching?" He grunted again. "Which place is hers, anyway?"

"Yellow brick." He stretched one long finger towards

the end of the street at a single-storey house with a rose garden and white-framed windows. "It's pretty."

Another grunt.

"Do you think anyone is watching her?"

"Not that I can tell." He kept his eyes on the house and didn't look at me. "Why are you even here? Haven't you done enough?"

"If you're talking about saving your life today, then you're welcome."

"Occam's Razor."

"What?"

"The most obvious answer is the right answer. Everything was fine before you showed up, and now it's gone to shit."

"Occam's Razor? You think this is my fault?"

"Absolutely. I've heard talk about a female bounty hunter who shows up right before people disappear for good. My guess is that's you?"

"I'm not the only one. And there are also male versions of me. And we aren't bounty hunters, we're private investigators."

"Same shit, different smell."

Whatever.

"For the record, I had no idea Grey's men were watching. Grey is probably the one person in this world I'd rather die than do a job for." And that was putting it lightly.

"You two got beef?"

"Beef?" I laughed a hollow laugh. "If I can ever get close enough, I'll cut the balls from his body and stuff them down his throat until he chokes to death."

He nodded slowly, eyebrows up, impressed. "That's some beef. What'd he do to you?"

"What didn't he do?" I shuddered as the memories rattled against the vault door of my mind, mingling with a distant scream. *No. Don't.*

God, I could do with a drink right now.

"I suppose that would be a shorter list with a man like that," he agreed.

"What would you do if you could get to him?"

"Could?" He met my eyes. "There's no 'could' because I *will* get to him. Once I make sure they haven't found out about Lucy, I'm going to do what I should have done in the first place: track him down and put a bullet in his head. No one I care about is safe until he's out of the picture."

"That's a big ask. The Grim Order have been at war with him for the last year, and they still haven't taken all his men out. Although, I honestly don't know which is worse, the bikers or the smugglers."

"Neither is ideal, but I prefer the bikers. At least they have a code."

"And you know them, don't you? Your file said your family was affiliated."

"We're kind of… related by marriage."

"So from your point of view, the Grim Order is much safer than Grey and his evil band of mercenaries."

"Evil band of mercenaries." A shadow of a smile crossed his lips. "Sounds like something out of a movie."

"Except worse, because he doesn't have a fatal flaw. That man doesn't give a fuck about a single person in this world except himself, he'd kill his own kin if it benefited him some-how. I'm honestly shocked he has such a loyal following."

"How much have you had to do with him?"

I shook my head and looked down at my hands. "Too much. He was responsible for a job going horribly wrong a few years back. I barely made it out."

His gaze softened a little as he observed me intently. It made my stomach flip and my chest ache, so I shook my head and changed the subject as fast as I could. "Have you always known about her?" I pointed to the house at the end of the street. "About Lucy?"

Sweet relief came as those intense eyes quit searching my face and returned to watching his daughter's house. "I have."

"And you hid her all this time?"

He nodded.

"That must have been hard."

With a slow release of his breath, he furrowed his brow. "We do whatever is necessary to keep the people we love safe."

I didn't think anyone had ever loved me with such ferocity. The thought caused a lump to develop inside my throat. "Well, she's lucky to have you."

"Is she?"

Our eyes met again, and I could see the doubt in the depths of his. But I felt sure of it. He was risking being found to make sure she was safe. He'd spent years trying to escape his life so she'd have a father. She was lucky he cared that much. My own father couldn't even care if I was alive or dead; actually he'd almost killed me twice now.

"Yes," I said with certainty. "Very lucky."

His gaze landed back on his daughter's house as a quiet settled over us like soft gauze. "Listen, you don't need to be here for this. I'll wait till sundown, then if all is clear, I'll say goodbye and meet you back at the house."

I settled into my seat, folding my arms a little tighter to get comfy. "No offence, but we haven't exactly established trust here. I'll stick around if it's all the same to you."

Releasing an amused burst of air from his nose, he shook his head. "Where am I gonna go? I'm checking on my daughter then I have to go back home and finish cleaning up my brother's stupid mistake. This doesn't end until I do that. So, I'm a sure thing, lady. You've got your bounty."

"I'm not a bounty hunter."

"Yeah? Well, it fucking feels like it."

I shrugged. "I'm staying."

"Whatever."

Pulling my iPad from the glove compartment, I messaged Nick and told him he could go back to the house, warning him to be careful of Grey's men since I had no idea what they knew or how they found their way here. I had assumed it was the photo, but Toby was right, it could have been my investigation that tipped them off. I was always careful not to broadcast my location or ruffle any feathers during my search. But, if the Cartwrights hired me and they were being watched, perhaps I was being watched too. We had to be cautious.

Tension radiated from Toby's body and filled the car with a thick and stifled air. I cracked the window and watched the street. A neighbour arrived and unloaded groceries while their kid screamed about not getting a Kinder Surprise. Then a man jogged by with a grey cattle dog on a blue lead. Thirty minutes ticked away in what felt more like an hour.

"So, what's your background?" I asked after a while, needing something to cut the air a little.

"We don't need to play this game."

"What game?"

"Getting to know you."

I shrugged. "What's it hurt? We almost died together today, and I already know your biggest secret." I gestured to his daughter's house. "Come on. It'll help pass the time."

A long pause drew between us, making me think the travel from Wannanup to Torquay would be an absolute nightmare of uncomfortable silence.

"Burglary," he said finally, glancing my way.

Thank fuck. He's speaking.

"How'd you get into that?"

"Jesus. Are you going to ask me if I *enjoy* it, next? You're almost making it sound *normal*."

"Isn't it though? To you and to me, the darker side of life *is* normal."

He rubbed a hand over his face and leaned back in his seat. "I guess. How'd you get into your job, then?"

"Big Jim took pity on me. I was practically homeless, living in one of those girls' homes for the kids no one wants. He gave me a job, trained me up and took care of me. I've always had to fight. At least this way I'm more in control over who that fight is with. Unless I'm being strapped to a bed, of course." I smiled at the last part, watching him for a reaction. He barely gave a flicker. "Your turn." I nudged him with my elbow.

Placing his fingers on the steering wheel, he traced the silver lion badge with his thumb. "It's the family business;

tradition. My father taught my mother, and she taught us kids."

"There's five of you all up?"

He nodded.

"And how did you go from burglary to killing off a bunch of Grey's men?"

Scraping his teeth over his lip, he stared off into the distance before answering. "My brother got mixed up in some shit he shouldn't have. It got us all in over our heads until it became kill or be killed. I needed to eliminate some threats, make people pay."

"Just you?" I asked, picking up on the 'I' over 'we'.

He nodded. "As the oldest, it always fell at my feet to keep them safe."

"Because your dad wasn't around." I nodded, understanding it was natural for the oldest son to take on the role of the protector when the father was out of the picture.

"Thank god. Bastard used to burn me on the thigh with his cigarettes and was an all-round bastard to everyone else. I haven't missed him for a second. But Jasmine did. Lord knows why; he beat into her every chance he got." He shook his head.

"Maybe she felt like she deserved it," I mused, my voice quiet. The human mind was a tricky thing, our inner voices the harshest of every voice available to us.

"Who would ever believe they deserved a beating?" he asked, his brow pinched as he stared at me in disbelief.

"So you kept your daughter away to protect her from a messed up family life?" I looked out the window, avoiding the question.

"Pretty much. I was twenty when we had her. Broken condom with a girl I barely knew. I was determined to be a good dad though." Looking over to the house, he worked his jaw from side to side. "We were still doing low level stuff at the time, but I always knew the life wasn't for me. I was planning on getting out even before Lucy. But I tried even harder once she was born, thinking I could make a go of it with her mother. Every time I was close to leaving, something happened with the family that made me stay. It was like they couldn't plan anything without my help, and whenever they did, there was a fuck up I had to fix. So, as my responsibility grew, it became more difficult to see myself living any life but the one I had."

"You gave up?"

He knitted his brow. "On myself, yeah. But never on Lucy. We had this friend—my brother's and I—this girl we grew up with. Her grandfather was our safecracker and had kept her shielded from all the shit we were involved with. He gave her a pretty normal life. I thought, 'hey, I can do that with Lucy. I can keep her safe and hidden while I bide my time, waiting for the right moment to leave and come be with her'." He paused and stared out the window as someone crossed the street in the distance. "I had this plan to set up a fishing charter and live a simple life out here. That was the dream." Dragging his teeth over his bottom lip again, he looked at Lucy's house and released a heavy sigh. "Now she's twenty-one. Engaged to be married, and I've only ever met her a handful of times. I sent money. I kept in contact. But I wasn't a good father. Not like I wanted to be. There was always something else. Something only Toby could do. Until I had so much blood on my hands I couldn't see my own skin anymore." He lifted his hands and looked at his palms before placing them against his thighs. "Finally, I said enough. I left, and I felt happy for the first time in… god knows how long." He swallowed and sighed again, his voice getting coarse and gritty as he swung his gaze my way. "Then you show up and I'm dragged straight back in. All my dreams. Gone." He clicked for effect.

"I'm just doing my job," I said, folding my arms back across my chest because his predicament wasn't my fault. I *was* just doing my job as I always did. But seeing this side of him, knowing his family seemed semi-functional, made me wonder again *why* they came after him now. He'd sacrificed a lot for them. Waiting for him to settle into a new life before they sent someone like me seemed overly cruel. *What's the play here?* Something felt off.

"I get that this is your job." His eyes held mine, unwavering. "But don't you get sick of it? Tracking people down so someone else can kill them?"

"That isn't always how it works. Sometimes I send people back home, find someone being held against their will. I've even found teenage runaways and reunited them with their families." My virtues were few and far between. But I had some.

"And most of the time you find people who have flipped and gone to the cops or left because they're trying to go straight like me."

"No one really gets out of the life, Toby. Changing your mind doesn't change what you are, or what you were."

Lifting a hand, he raked it back and forth through his hair, agitated. "You know they call you Black Widow, right?"

I looked out the window to the other side of the road. "Other people's opinions don't matter to me. I'm damn good at my job. That's what counts. I don't ask why I need to find someone. I just find them. The *why* and the *what* comes after aren't any of my fucking business. I do a job. I get paid and move on. End of."

"Turning a blind eye doesn't change what you do." His eyes flashed, his words clipped.

"And running away doesn't change the fact you've got all that blood on your hands. We're all the bad guy here, Toby. Don't act like you're above it when you're as ruthless as the rest of us."

Silence. It descended rapidly, heavy with unspoken words and accusations. I understood that he was in a shitty situation and blamed me for it. I got that he wanted me out of his way so he could do what needed to be done. I *understood*. But that didn't change my role. I needed to return him to get paid and figure out what the hell was going on. He couldn't scare me away with threats or forceful words. I wasn't afraid of him.

"Listen," I said after a while. "I know you don't like me much, but the way I see it, we've got common goals. Most notable being we both wanna see Grey rot in hell. I reckon I can help you get to him."

"I can get to him fine on my own."

"You can't, actually. He's always surrounded by security. You'll need an 'in' to get close."

"And you have this magical 'in'?" He seemed doubtful as he swept me with those intrusive eyes of his.

"I do." *I can't believe I'm about to admit this out loud.*

"So, spill. Explain how you can get to Grey and I can't."

Hating the words, I closed my eyes while I said them. "Because Grey is… he's my father."

CHAPTER EIGHT
DON'T CALL ME DADDY

I'D ONLY HEARD of O'Keefe AKA Irish by name until a few years ago when we crossed paths during the dreaded Adelaide job. I'd been searching for the daughter of some stockbroker—one of my more noble jobs. The cops had been incapable of getting her back, despite saying they did everything they could.

Cue hiring me.

I tracked her down to a particular kind of whorehouse in Adelaide. It was one of those den of pleasures where any kink was for sale. They'd find pretty girls and get them hooked on narcotics, promising them the world then luring them away from their families, one hit at a time. The job got a little too personal for me because I'd grown up in a place like that. I decided to save more than just the one girl.

After I tipped off the cops, I stepped back so they could raid the place and get them all out. I'd continued my surveillance until the raid team showed up, which was when it all went horribly wrong. The moment they approached the entrance, the whole place went up in flames, girls and all. I'd stood with a crowd of people attracted by the blaze and watched in horror as it burned to the ground and no one came out alive.

The screams. Ear piercing agony.

The smell. I could only describe it as death.

"The boss doesn't like people meddling in his affairs," a man had said from beside me. When I'd looked his way, I saw a flash of a golden tooth as he blew out a lungful of cigarette smoke.

"You did this?" I'd asked in a horrified whisper. He winked then told me his boss—who turned out to be Grey—wanted a word. It wasn't a choice. I was forced into the back of a car and taken to meet my father for the first time. What happened next was the stuff of nightmares. I couldn't even think about it without needing a drink.

That was kind of when the whole drinking thing started.

When Grey released me, I lived at the bottom of a bottle for weeks, trying to forget. Big Jim and Nick had needed to hunt me down and force me to sober up, get my shit back together, and return to work. But, nothing could stop the screams of those girls in the night. I still felt those awful blows and rough hands on my skin.

That job was my open wound. One that wouldn't close until I learned of Grey's death.

"His fucking *daughter*?" Toby stared at me with his mouth open, body tense like he wanted to throttle me.

"I'm not supposed to tell anyone, but yeah. My mother was one of his hookers. She OD'd when I was a kid, and I guess he didn't know about me back then. I only worked out who he was after I started working for Big Jim."

"Grey knows about you now?"

"He does."

His eyes went wide. "And you're *surprised* his men followed you? Is this some kind of joke, Blair? A fucking *trap*?" His body shifted back as though I were made of venom, his chest inflated, ready to pounce.

I held up my hands in surrender. "I give you my word, I have nothing to do with the man. We basically agreed to deny all knowledge of each other. It's been years since I've even seen him. Except in the papers, of course."

"And you seriously don't think he's been keeping tabs on you?"

"I didn't. But, now… I don't know. But, I need to tell you, that guy I saw on the pier before your boat blew up. I know he knew who I was, and he didn't stop me getting on board. I think it's safe to say Grey is cool with his daughter biting it."

"Then how do you think you'll get close to him?"

"Because he asked me to join him once. If I show up there, alive, maybe I can get in?"

"Or maybe he'll kill you on sight. No. This is a suicide mission as it is. I'm not using you as bait. Think of another plan."

"That is the plan."

"Listen, if a man is willing to let his daughter explode into chunks for fish food, he's not gonna be waiting with open arms when it turns out she's still kicking. No. If you really want to do this we'll come up with another way. Maybe one we walk away from."

"We?" I smiled. "We're in this together now?" I nudged him with my elbow. He wasn't immune to my charms.

Pressing his lips together he rolled his eyes. "Yeah, well, I don't see myself getting rid of you anytime soon. And you're good at finding people, so…"

I grinned, happy because not only was I going to get more time with the delicious Toby, but I would also get the chance to kill Grey. It sounded horrible, a daughter wanting to commit patricide, but I had dreamt of ridding the world of the scourge of a man who fathered me for years.

FaceTime popped up on my iPad with its bopping-popping tune, Nick's name listed as the identifying number.

"Hey," I said as I held it in front of me, brightening my smile for the camera. "What's up?"

Nick's face appeared on screen, slightly glitchy before clearing. "I'm thinkin' it's not a good idea for you two to come back here," he said.

"Are they watching?" I asked.

"Not the house. But they're watchin' the marina. Here"—he switched the camera to rear facing—"see that grey sedan with the dark windows? That's them. I spotted Irish gettin' some food at the café down there a while back. I've no idea if they're lookin' this way, but I reckon you two stay out of sight and get out of town ASAP. You might wanna ditch your car, too."

"OK. But I'll need my stuff," I said to him. "Can you get it to me?"

"Don't you have a grab bag in your car?"

"Of course I do. But my computer…"

"Then use what you have. I'll get your stuff back to you when it's safer. I'll stick around and keep an eye on things, keep you appraised on the situation. Just, I don't know, stay dead I guess. I reckon it'd be safer for you both until we know what's what."

"You're probably right. Thanks, Nick."

"No probs, toots."

He disconnected, and I turned to Toby. "Looks like we're ghosts for a while."

"Obviously. Does Nick know Grey's your—"

"My father? No. You are literally the only person I've ever told. I'm trusting you to keep it between us."

"I thought we hadn't built any trust yet."

I shrugged. "Well, I know your longest kept secret. It's only fair you know mine."

"So that makes us even then?"

"We'll be even when you save my life."

He frowned. "Um… I'm pretty sure you're the reason my life was in danger."

"Uh. No. I accept that Grey's men might have followed me here, but you got in his crosshairs all on your own, buddy."

He rolled his eyes. "There's no such thing as a coincidence. If you aren't in on this, your boss is."

"Big Jim would never. And I swear on my life I'm not in on any of this. I almost got blown up as well. If I was in on it, I'd have sat in that house and watched you explode."

He grunted.

"Don't sulk just because I'm right, it ruins the whole hot tough guy thing you have going on."

He glared at me, unimpressed.

I rolled my eyes. "Why don't we go see your daughter while we know for sure they're at the marina?"

"You are *not* coming in."

I scrunched up my face a little. "Yeah, actually, I am.

This talk, and the sharing and shit, has been great and all, but we're gonna be joined at the hip until this thing is sorted out. Get used to seeing this face." I used my index finger to draw a circle in the air around mine.

He shook his head, rolled his eyes then got out of the car with me following hot on his heels. "Let me do the talking."

Lifting my hand to my forehead, I saluted him and smiled. "Sure thing, daddy."

"Don't call me daddy." He frowned, and I giggled.

"OK, daddy."

With an unimpressed growl, he shot me an unamused look. "Shut the fuck up."

"Daddy," I whispered, deciding that riling him up was my new favourite thing to do.

"HE'S ACTUALLY HILARIOUS," I said, swallowing the last mouthful of tea in my mug while reaching for a fourth biscuit. "You wouldn't think it with that scowl he always has on his face, but he really is. Aren't you, sweetheart?" I smiled and turned to Toby, placing my hand on his knee. He sat on the couch beside me with his arms crossed and a grimace on his face. This guy didn't understand how to have fun with a good cover story. He was way too serious.

"I don't think I'm funny at all," he grunted. *My point exactly.*

Lucy giggled and covered her mouth with one hand to make sure the shortbread she'd just bitten into didn't spit out. "I have to agree with Nikki, dad. You can be pretty funny when you let your guard down a bit."

I'd told her my name was Nikki since Toby had called me the Black Widow. It had made me think of *La Femme Nikita,* making it seem like the perfect nome de plume for this particular personality.

"See," I said, gesturing towards Lucy. "She agrees with

me. We obviously know you better than you know your-self, Tom." At least I remembered to give him the right name this time. I was still kicking myself for fucking that up.

"Seems that way," he said with a doubtful press of his lips as he took my empty mug and placed it on the coffee table.

Lucy's eyes shone happily as she looked between us. "I really like you two together," she said. I beamed happily while Toby suppressed an eye roll.

All her life, she'd been told that her father's name was Tom Clancy (ridiculous, I know). Although, instead of being the famous writer, he was an officer in the navy, off to sea for long stretches at a time. It gave credence to his extended absences and gave Lucy a cool story about a father who was fighting for our freedom, instead of one who was stealing shit for his own family's gain while killing off a few smugglers on the side.

I was pretty into his cover story and couldn't help insert myself into it, giving myself the character of the girlfriend who was currently on leave, wanting to take him on a romantic getaway to Melbourne. I told her we planned to set sail that evening. Lucy thought it was a fabulous idea.

I wasn't sure what Toby thought, but he'd thank me later. The stuff coming out of my mouth was pure gold.

"I like us together too," I said, nudging Toby. "I also think you're pretty great. Every bit as beautiful as your pictures."

"Oh, thank you. That's so kind," she said, smiling as she touched a hand to her chest. Her eyes and smile were so similar to her father's it was uncanny. Sitting this close to her, I couldn't believe I didn't pick them as relatives when I watched them dine the night before.

"You kept her a secret for so long." She directed that at Toby. "I've been sitting here feeling bad for you living all alone on that boat." When she shook her head and laughed, it was musical, happy, innocent and free. I was jealous of her when I thought her a woman Toby was interested in. But now I was jealous because she was the embodiment of the perfect life. Such a thing didn't really exist, but growing up in a beautiful seaside town with a mother and father who protected you from the evil of the world sounded pretty close to me.

"Well, I, uh—" Toby started, stuttering a little over his words.

"He's never been one to kiss and tell," I finished for him as I threaded my fingers through his, holding onto his hand while I smiled and met his eyes. His seemed to say, 'I'm going to kill you for this.' So I winked at him. This story was so much better than his 'I've got to go away for a while to take care of some stuff' version.

"How long are you planning to spend in Melbourne?" Lucy asked. "Oh, do you want me to look after Rogue for you? I can keep him in the backyard."

Oh dear. Poor Rogue.

With a frown, Toby looked down then cleared this throat. "Rogue, ah, he passed, Luc. He was old, had a great life, and uh, it was quick."

"Oh no. It wasn't the fright from that explosion at the marina was it? It's all over the news. I was going to call you just before you showed up, actually. I was worried about you."

"No." He cleared his throat again. "It was in his sleep."

I gave Toby's hand a reassuring squeeze. The one thing I felt horrible about during this whole ordeal was the loss of his beloved dog. It didn't seem fair he had to lose his life for being nothing more than a loyal companion.

"I'm sorry, dad. That's... that's horrible news. He seemed so happy last night. Puppy like, even."

Toby just nodded, and I reached over and placed my other hand on top of our already joined ones. He squeezed mine back. "It's partially why we decided to get away for a while, give Tom the chance to get his mind off things."

"Of course," Lucy said, pressing her lips together and twisting them downward as she leaned forward and placed a hand on her father's shoulder. "Make sure you do something Rogue would have liked to honour him."

With his eyes shining, I watched Toby's Adam's apple bob before he nodded. "I will. But, uh, we should get going. Right, um, babe?" It seemed to hurt him calling me that. I smiled wider.

"Yes. That ship isn't going to sail itself." I released his hand and stood up, holding my arms out to Lucy. "I'll make sure he calls you while we're down there. It was lovely to finally meet you."

"Oh, same to you." She stepped into my arms and gave me a brief hug. "I'm so excited that you even exist. I really hope we'll see more of each other."

"Maybe when my next tour is up," I told her, another easy lie falling from my tongue. "Your father's been hinting at me to leave the navy and settle down with him, but, I don't know. These legs are made to live on the sea." I sighed and shrugged.

"Well, if you can get the time off, I'd love it if you were dad's date for my wedding. It's in November next year, so there's plenty of time to decide."

"I'll do my best," I said with a smile, stepping back so Toby could say a proper goodbye. I moved into the background as he held her for a little too long, knowing this could well be the last time he saw her. The reality of this mission we were now on was that it may be the last thing either of us did in this world. And I was OK with that. Toby, on the other hand, had more to live for than I did. Despite his insistence we 'find another way', I wasn't kidding myself by thinking we'd walk out of this alive.

"Talk soon, kiddo," he said when they parted, his voice a little thicker than it was before.

Lucy didn't seem to notice. "Have a wonderful time, you two," she said as she walked us to the door. "Take lots of pictures. I can't wait to hear all about it."

With a wave and a fake smile, we both got back into my car and drove away, not saying a word until we hit the next town over.

CHAPTER TEN
ALWAYS IN CHARGE

"MY GIRLFRIEND NIKKI?" Toby asked with a shake of his head when he stopped at a set of lights.

"Your *commitment phobic* girlfriend Nikki. There's an important distinction. Without that, we would have had a bunch of questions about why she doesn't know more about me."

"I told you to let me do the talking."

"Stuttering isn't talking, sweetheart," I teased.

He clenched his teeth together. "I'm not your *sweetheart*. And I don't like her thinking you and I were together all this time."

"Get fucked, Toby. I gave you a believable story. Live with it." I wanted to punch him in the nose. "I'll have you know I'm a fucking catch and extremely hard to pin down. You should be honoured I'd even consider having a fake relationship with you."

"She'll think you and I were a thing before her mother passed away," he said in a quiet tone.

"Oh." I closed my eyes. I kept messing up with this

guy. "I'm sorry. I didn't know. I also didn't realise she thought you two were together all those years."

"She didn't. But… I don't know. I never wanted her to have the impression there was anyone else."

"Did she think you had no one?"

"No. Maybe. I don't know. I always stayed with them when I was in town and we... her mother and I *enjoyed* each other during those times."

"And she never married?"

He shook his head as he indicated to pull off the main road. "Maybe there were other guys during the time in between, but I don't know. She liked to sell the happy family story to Luc."

Reaching across the console, I placed my hand on his forearm. "It was a good story, Toby. You did the right thing protecting her."

He almost flinched away from my touch. "She'll think I abandoned her if we don't come back."

Pressing my palms together in my lap, I tried to ignore the burn that tingled beneath my skin from our connection. "Then we organise a safeguard that will tell her we died at sea. Surely you had something like that in place before."

"I did."

"Then what's the problem?"

Shaking his head, he blew out his breath. "I'm… I'm just… I'm tired."

Tired.

We were all tired.

All tired and faking it.

We drove for another thirty minutes in silence before he slowed in front of a rundown looking house, manoeuvring the car down the driveway until he tucked it next to a shed.

"What's this?" I asked, unclipping my seatbelt when he cut the engine.

"Safe house," he stated, his hand still on the wheel, gripping tight.

"Are we going in?"

With his brow pinched, he focused on nothing as he spoke. "This thing we're doing. Are you dead serious?"

"Absolutely," I said without hesitation.

"The man is your father. You're willing to kill, or least help to end his life? He's part of you."

"Yes. But he's the very worst part of me. His death..." I snuck my tongue out and licked my lips. "Have you ever watched the *Princess Bride*?"

"I have."

"Well, you know that character, Inigo? He always talks about the six-fingered man and how he won't rest until that man is dead."

"I remember."

"Well, Grey is my six-fingered man."

"He killed your mother?"

"He played a big part in her ending her life, and he played an even bigger part in robbing me of mine. When he's dead, maybe I'll find my peace too."

"What if he kills you first?"

"Then at least I tried."

Turning to meet my eyes, Toby studied my expression, my sincerity. I had nothing in my life except work and a hope that one day I'd get the chance exact my vengeance. This mission with Toby, it was the first time I'd felt true purpose in years. I needed this.

"OK," he said, nodding slowly.

Gathering my things, I opened my car door then went to the boot, taking out my grab bag as well as the handful of weapons I had inside hidden compartments. "We need to ditch this car somewhere," I said. "If we're staying here overnight, I don't think we should leave it out in the open."

"How do you feel about torching it?" Toby said, holding his hand out to help carry my things.

"Uh, won't that draw attention? I was more so thinking about parking it inside the shed instead of next to it so no one could see it." I pointed over my shoulder as we walked towards the rear door of the house.

"There's already a car in there. I figure we get that started then drive out to this gully about an hour away from here, dump your car then rest here for the night. We've got a fair way to travel back to Torquay, so we'll need sleep, and I don't want to worry about someone tracking your car to us while we do that."

"Torquay? You think it's wise to go directly back to your family? They're under watch."

He slid a key in the door and jiggled it before it turned, tossing a frown over his shoulder as he said, "By who? Cops or Grey?"

"The file didn't say, but maybe I can get Nick to find out?"

"Do that. And get rid of your iPad. I have an old Blackberry here that's untraceable, you can call him on that." Pushing the door open, it scraped against the linoleum floor and kicked up dust.

I waved my hand in front of my face and coughed as I

stepped inside. "I take it you haven't been keeping tabs on whatever is going on back home?"

"I wasn't planning on ever going back there," he said, pulling dusty sheets off the lounge room furniture and rolling them up into a ball. "I didn't see the point since it would only make things harder."

"Harder on you, or on them?"

He stood motionless for a moment. "If I knew they were struggling, I would have gone back."

"Strong sense of duty. I dig it," I said, helping remove the sheet from a side table and testing if the lamp worked. "Hey, there's electricity."

"I'd hope so," he said, throwing the sheets on the floor in the corner of the room. "I pay enough every month to keep all the utilities on." Clearing his throat from the dirty air, he pulled open a desk drawer and dug around until he came out with a set of keys.

"Reckon I can risk opening a window or the front door to clear this funky air out?" I asked.

"Yeah. For a bit so we can at least breathe. I haven't been out here in forever to air it out."

Pulling the front curtains open, late afternoon sunlight spilled into the house like a tractor beam in a sci-fi movie, the floating dust defining it perfectly.

Waving my hand in front of my face again, I pushed past the horizontal blinds and found the lever for the windows, spinning it rapidly until they were open as far as they would go. Then I opened the front door and made sure the screen door was locked, taking a moment to look out at the street before I headed out back after Toby.

"Seems quiet out front," I said when I found him in the shed leaning over a yellow Datsun with the bonnet open.

"There's no reason to think anyone would be watching. No one followed us or even knows we're alive." He was confident in that assumption. I was overly cautious though, knowing how easily I'd tracked him down the first time. If it was all the same to him, I would keep making sure we were alone.

"Can you even fit inside that thing?" I asked, moving closer to look at the tiny 1980s car. "Does it go?"

"Yes," he said, using a little contraption to check if the battery had any charge. "And once I jump this battery, it should go just fine." Moving to a storage cabinet at the back of the shed, he grabbed a portable jump box and handed me the extension cord. "Can you plug this in at the house for me?"

"Sure," I said, grabbing the yellow cord and walking it across the patchy lawn. It was neatly trimmed—Toby undoubtedly had someone mowing it for him—but in a fairly decent looking suburb, this place was quite the eyesore.

"Flip the switch on the charger for me?" he asked from where his head was still under the bonnet when I returned from the house.

I did as he asked, waiting until the lights changed to show the battery was now charging. "Now what?" I turned to face him.

"Now we wait."

"How long do you think?"

He shrugged. "We'll give it an hour? It needs enough charge to get us started, the alternator will do the rest on the drive."

"And what do we do with my car in the meantime?"

"There's a canvas tarp in the cabinet. We can cover it up so it's out of sight. We'll get rid of it when it's dark."

I stood on the other side of my car as we unrolled the tarp over the car. "Just because I keep doing the things you ask doesn't mean you're in charge," I said, securing the fabric by tucking it behind the numberplate.

He walked back over to the Datsun and grinned. "You wanna be in charge?" he asked, checking the oil and coolant levels.

"I'm always in charge."

With a shake of his head, he pointed to the small toolbox he had out. "Chuck me that rag?"

"Are you asking me or telling me?"

His eyes dropped a little, and a smirk kicked up half of his mouth. "Which do you prefer?"

With a smile, I slapped the rag into his upturned hand. "Hmm, depends on what we're doing."

He continued smiling as he used the rag to clean the grease from his hands. "I can see I'll have to watch you."

"You can watch me do whatever you like." I grinned as he shook his head, amused. "You got anything to drink in there?"

"Should be something in the fridge. Beer and water."

"Anything stronger?"

"Cabinet under the sink." He dropped the rag on the edge of the car then ran his hands through his hair, pushing the long strands out of his eyes. "Pour two. I fucking need it after today."

"WELL, there goes forty thousand down the drain," I said, taking a seat on the creaky green vinyl chair in the kitchen with a sigh. It wasn't easy watching my car go up in flames. All I could think about was the hard-earned money that had gone into paying for it.

"More like fifteen with depreciation." Toby opened the fridge and pulled out two beers, placing one in front of me.

"This isn't gonna cut it," I said, touching the slim neck.

Within seconds, he whisked the beer away, a tumbler taking its place with amber liquid poured inside to match the width of the four fingers I held up.

"Thank you." Taking a gulp of the scotch, I blew out a raspberry as I placed the glass back on the Formica table. "Who needs a nice car, anyway?"

Opening a bag of nuts, Toby poured some in a bowl and sat it in the table's centre. "I'll make food, but it might be an idea to eat before you get all maudlin."

"I don't get maudlin when I drink. I get hyper then I get exhausted."

"Can't wait," he said as he rummaged through the cupboards and came out with two tins of chicken soup. "This is about as exciting as it gets."

"Soup is good." I popped a few cashews in my mouth, watching him rinse a small saucepan then dump the contents of both cans inside before turning on the stove. I liked the way he moved, such grace for a man of his size. My favourite part was when he bent over to find a wooden spoon inside one of the drawers.

Toby had a great arse.

"This place is well appointed for a safe house. If I didn't know any better, I'd think this was your grandma's," I said to his back as he stirred. "There's even a spoon collection on the wall."

He glanced over his shoulder to where the wooden fixture was, decorated with a layer of dust and a few cobwebs, filled with hanging spoons. "You'd be right in thinking that way. She wasn't my grandmother, but she was someone's. I bought this in an estate sale."

"Wooden spoons and all, huh?"

He nodded. "The entire contents of the house and shed."

"So that Datsun was hers?"

"Sure was."

"Low kilometres because she only took it shopping?"

"Thirty thousand on the clock. It's perfect." He grinned my way as he lifted the saucepan and divided it between two off-white ceramic bowls.

"And what name did you buy this place under? Dan Brown?"

He chuckled as he set the bowls on the table and found spoons. "Todd Smith."

"Do you always use T names?"

"Makes it easier in case someone from my past runs into someone from my present. If the name sounds similar, I can explain it away."

"Smart," I said.

"And for the record, Tom Clancy wasn't my choice. Lucy's mother came up with it off the cuff one day. Luc was asking about me and she lifted the name right off the spine of a book. She wasn't super imaginative when she was put on the spot."

Stirring my spoon through the milky-looking soup, I blew amused air out of my nose. "What was she like?"

"She was kind, understanding, patient."

She sounded like a saint. "What did she look like?"

"Lucy."

"Lucy looks like you."

"You think?"

"Very much. How did she die?"

"Bowel cancer. Around eighteen months ago."

"That must have been hard for you. To mourn someone you weren't supposed to know."

"To be honest with you, I didn't really *know* her. Not completely, anyway. I mean, we were in touch for nearly twenty years, spent the odd month together here and there, but we were on our best behaviour, you know? There was never any time to discover our flaws. I think that's the part that hit me the hardest. She died, and suddenly there was no more time for anything."

"Did you love her?"

He shook his head and wiped a hand across his stubble. "No. I was in love with what I imagined my life could be with her though."

"Did she know about your real life?"

"A little."

"She sounds like she was a good woman."

With a nod, he smiled with half his mouth then stirred his spoon inside his soup. "I need to apologise to you for some things I've said during the last twenty-four hours," he started, surprising me with the sudden change of subject.

"Don't worry about it," I said as I lifted my spoon to my mouth. "It's nothing I haven't heard before."

"Still, I was angry, and I attacked you on a personal level when I had no right."

Swallowing the salty liquid, I lowered my utensil and lifted my glass. "Listen, I pride myself on being unflappable, and I'll admit you were very successful at hitting my buttons with little effort. So, I take my hat off to you, sir, for that. Still, I'm not holding it against you, I said plenty of shitty stuff in return."

"I called you a hole to fuck, Blair. That's pretty fucking low, and you didn't deserve it."

I took a sip of my scotch then inhaled slowly as I placed it back on the table with little sound. "Maybe I did. I get that I can come on a little too strong for some people."

"You really didn't," he replied before I held my hand up.

"Let me finish, because I know I do. And luring men into bed has never been a part of my job, so I took offence to that. I sleep with whom I want, when I want to. It's my choice. I think the best thing that god gave us humans was the ability to orgasm. It trumps free choice in my opinion. And I've had more than a few men try to damage my ability to find sex an enjoyable activity with their words or their abuse. But I *refuse* to allow anyone to take the most basal human enjoyment away from me. I love sex. I have fought hard to continue loving sex, and no one—man or woman—will ever make me feel ashamed of that." I downed the rest of my scotch and pushed away my soup as I stood from the table.

"I have a huge amount of respect for you, Blair. It wouldn't have been easy finding me, I made it hard on purpose. It's why I was shocked when you called me by my real name. It's no excuse, and I can't apologise enough for my behaviour or my words, but I do need you to know I regret them. I don't really think of you that way."

The sincerity in his eyes tugged gently at my heart-strings. It took a big man to admit his failings, and Toby was the embodiment of that both in size and action. I was coming to respect him myself, which was a big thing for me. Especially since I'd only known him for twenty-four hours.

"I need to take a shower," I said, clearing my throat. "I smell like soot." I stepped away, our conversation feeling heavy and unfinished. "Thanks for the food, and... I accept your apology." The last part came out in a rush before I turned towards the bathroom and practically scur-ried away. He was softer than I'd expected him to be. Far more open and possibly... *good*. I rarely felt bad for tracking people down and sending them back to their lives, but with Toby, I wished he'd been left alone. Seemed to me he'd spent his life trying to do the right thing by others while no one had ever done right by him, including me. I was using him for my own gain from the get-go. First as a payday, then as a conquest, and now I was using him as a tool for my revenge. I was a really shitty human being.

When I came out of the bathroom, I found him tucking clean sheets into the couch cushions to make a bed. "There's only one room. You take the bed and I'll sleep out here," he said.

I smiled. *He's a gentleman too.* I hadn't met many of them in my time on this earth. Such rare creatures. "That couch is barely big enough for you to sit on, Toby. I'm smaller, you take the bed. I insist." After everything that had happened, everything he'd lost, I needed to do the decent thing.

"I really don't mind," he said. "Doubt I'll sleep much, anyway."

"Well, that makes two of us, but I'll rest better if I know you aren't all scrunched up and uncomfortable."

Pausing with a pillow in his hands, he turned to face me, his eyes travelling slowly down the silk negligee I'd put on after my shower. One thing I didn't own was boring sleepwear. He gulped and forced his focus back to the pillow, fluffing it before dropping it on the couch. "Feel free to switch with me if you get uncomfortable."

"I'm sure I'll be fine," I said, moving past him before I slipped beneath the sheets he'd set out. "Thanks, Toby."

Picking up a blanket, he placed it on the end near my feet. "In case you get cold."

I smiled at him as he looked at me with confusion or perhaps longing in his eyes. *Come and get me,* I told him with mine. He swallowed again then stepped back.

"Well, good night then," he said.

"Goodnight, Toby," I replied, watching him walk away

before I rested back on the pillow and stared up at the ceiling.

In the last twenty-four hours, I'd been tied to a bed, come face to face with one of my attackers, stirred up my most repressed memories and almost exploded into nothingness. Oh, and I'd helped torch my car. Now, I was on the run with the man who was supposed to be my mark, both of us aiming to kill the one man responsible for our current situation—my father.

Yeah, I wouldn't sleep at all tonight. I hadn't had enough booze to achieve that. I probably wouldn't even close my eyes.

CHAPTER TWELVE
HE'S A DEVIL

HEAT PRESSED against my skin as I ran towards the screams. *No. Don't.* Hands pawed at my skin, dragging me back, their smiles glinting and leering. *I'll teach her a lesson she won't forget.*

"No." I sat bolt upright, gasping, drenched in sweat from forcing myself out of the jumbled nightmare. "Don't."

Shoving the sheets from my body, the cool air collided with my hot skin, causing me to shiver at the sudden change. I stood and stumbled, heading for the kitchen where I splashed water on my face, heaving great gulps of air while I grabbed a glass from the strainer. With a shaky hand, I twisted the cap off the scotch, filling the glass halfway and gulping it down like it was cordial, forcing the memories back into their box where they belonged. "No," I gasped through gritted teeth. "Get out of my fucking head."

Taking the glass and the bottle back into the lounge room, I set them on the coffee table and refilled my glass, flicking on the television but finding nothing but snow on all channels.

"Great," I said, throwing the remote on the couch while leaving the TV on, the static of dots soothing to my aching head.

With my eyes closed, I focused on the white noise and drank slowly, each swallow burning at my throat but adding to the quieting of my mind. *This is why I drink.*

Comfortably numb, I rested my head against the back of the couch and cradled the glass in my lap. *No.*

I hated the nights. It was always a shit fight as to whether the nightmares would surface. Drinking helped. Fucking even more so. Both together were the magic drug that led to a dreamless sleep. I wanted to be strong. I wanted to be unaffected by everything that had gone on in my life. During the day I could put on a brave face and attitude to convince myself that I was unchanged. But at night, the monsters came. I hated the nights.

The scrape of a cupboard door startled my eyes open, drawing my attention towards the kitchen where I spotted Toby on one knee, crouched over and digging through the shelf beneath the sink.

"I have it here," I called out, causing him to jolt and bang his head on the bench above.

"Shit," he hissed, rubbing his head as he stood and closed the cupboard, picking up a glass before he headed towards me wearing nothing but a pair of boxer shorts. *Gulp.* As he moved, I could see every one of his muscles rippling beneath his taut skin, begging for a hand or two— or a tongue—to slide all over him.

A man this well built should be considered porno-graphic, one look, and I was squirming in my seat, staring at those arm cannons and wondering if I could even wrap both hands around them while I licked the vein that ran along his bicep.

My nipples hardened as his eyes held mine hostage, warmth flooding the best parts of me. It'd been a long time since a man had elicited this kind of reaction. Most men I slept with these days were a means to an end. I took from them what I needed and barely registered their faces. But with Toby, I wanted to explore every inch of him. I wanted *him* to use *me*.

"Here," I said, reaching my hand out for his glass as I unscrewed the lid from the scotch.

Our fingers brushed as he handed it over and held on for a moment too long. "Did I wake you?" Releasing the glass, he sat in the single-seater diagonal from me.

I shook my head, blinking off his closeness and breaking eye contact. "Nightmares," I stated, pouring him his drink before pushing it towards him.

He leaned forwards to collect his glass. "You too, huh?"

Tilting one side of my mouth, I bounced the opposite shoulder. "You can run from everything else but never yourself, right?" I held up my glass, and he tapped his against it before we both drank.

He sat back, draining the liquid with a small groan at the end. He held the cool glass against his temple with one hand and ran the other hand through his damp hair, the muscles in his arm bulging with his movement. *My god, he is so incredibly beautiful.*

Part of me wanted to ask him what his mind tormented him with, but the other part of me didn't want to know at all. Asking him meant sharing my torment, and I wasn't there. All I wanted was to make the noise stop, to be beautifully broken together.

Standing up, I moved until I was in front of him, taking the glass from between his fingers and filling it a third of the way. "More is better," I said, handing it back to him. His eyes lifted to mine as he wrapped his fingers around the side of the glass, sliding in next to mine and sending a heat up my arm that was far more powerful than the curling fingers of the alcohol in my blood.

"Sometimes it's required," he said, lifting the glass to his lips, still watching me as I remained standing in the space between his feet.

"To quiet the screaming," I added knowingly, watching the soft light from the static TV flicker across his bronzed skin.

He nodded slowly, his eyes never leaving mine as he drank. Then he held out his glass, and I refilled it, lifting the bottle to my lips and drinking with him.

"Do you know what else helps?" I asked, taking the glass from between his fingers when he finished.

He shook his head, his elbows resting on the arms of the chair, fingers of one hand pressed to his jaw. He watched me carefully as I set the glass and bottle back on the coffee table then turned back to face him.

"Orgasms," I whispered, placing one hand on his bare shoulder as I rested my knee on the sofa beside him. He made no move to object, said nothing in protest. So I slid my other knee into position, running my hands over the smooth skin of his chest as I straddled him. "One good fuck"—I rocked my hips lightly, delighting in the soft sound that escaped his chest as his manhood responded, hardening against my centre—"and the mind goes quiet as a mouse." Reaching down to the hem of my negligee, I pulled it over my head, exposing my breasts to the night air, my nipples pebbling as the cool brushed across them.

"You've been drinking," came the soft rumble of his voice as his interested eyes perused my bare flesh.

"So have you. Makes us even."

One large hand wrapped around the ribs on my right side, his thumb moving to caress the underside of my breast as we locked eyes, his expression calm, searching. "You are painfully beautiful, Blair."

Painfully beautiful.

"You don't need to compliment me, Toby. I'm not that kind of girl."

A flicker of something passed through his gaze before he swallowed hard then lifted his other hand and slid his fingers into my hair, pulling me closer. "Achingly beautiful," he whispered, his voice rough as he pressed his mouth to mine, the kiss deep and strong. Lips sucking, tongue exploring.

I sank against him, my hands remaining on his chest where I could feel the thumping of his heart against my palms. *Thump, thump. Thump, thump.* Solid, sure, yet nervous. I was making him nervous.

Done with my mouth, he pulled back on my hair, angling my head so he had access to my neck. His teeth slid along my jaw, down until he ran his tongue along my pulse point, nipping me lightly as I moaned and rocked my hips, pressing against his hard girth. The pressure was sublime between my legs as his mouth and fingers explored my chest, kneading, pinching and sucking. One hand slid in an arc across my back, fingers finding my spine and trailing featherlight touches down to the top of my arse.

Sliding his hand beneath the elastic waist of my panties, he ran his tongue back up my neck, his mouth pausing at my chin. "I want you naked and in my bed." Then he scraped his teeth over my chin before sucking my bottom lip into his mouth.

He could have me anywhere.

Wrapping his arms around my body, he stood with zero effort, making me feel light and dainty for the first time in my life, before he strode towards the bedroom, the tip of his erection tapping against my arse as he moved. I was so wet and aroused that all I wanted to do was ride him to kingdom cum—and I meant that in the dirty way.

Leaning forwards to lay me on the bed, Toby bit my lower lip before immediately sucking the pain away, causing me to moan and whimper for more.

Giving me just that, he slid his hand between us, shoving my panties to the side as he thrust two fingers inside me. He moaned as my juices coated him, and I rocked up to meet the depth of his movement. "Is this what you wanted?" he asked as he curled his fingers inside me, massaging my G-spot. "Last night when I walked you home, did you want me to do this?" He thrust his fingers deeper, adding a third.

An involuntary moan left my mouth as I nodded. "And more," I gasped out.

He grinned and pulled his fingers from inside me, running my juices over my bottom lip before leaning in and sucking it into his mouth, tasting me before he slid his tongue against mine and shared my flavour. "Oh, there's more," he said, pressing his massive cock against my thigh.

"Give it to me."

"How's this?" He slipped all four fingers inside me, filling me further so that my eyes rolled back in my head.

"Yes," I groaned, arching against him as his mouth returned to mine and his fingers pushed gloriously into my depths. Unable to take the beautiful torture of his touch, my body let go, coming around his hand as I howled into his mouth.

He slowed his movement as he brought me back down and ran the tip of his nose across the soft skin of my cheek. "Good girl," he whispered, kissing my swollen lips as I melted into the mattress. "I hope you still want more?"

Numb, I nodded. "Everything you can give me."

"Mmm, good, because you taste almost as amazing as you look." His mouth collided with mine, kissing me fiercely before he slid down my body, paying particular attention to my nipples before hooking his fingers into the sides of my panties and pulling them past my feet.

"I want you inside me," I gasped, reaching for his hair and sliding my fingers through the soft tousled waves.

"Not yet," he murmured, kissing the inside of my thigh. "I need you good and ready first." I loved the way he panted, his arousal thick in his voice.

"I'm ready now. Please."

"Soon." He slid his tongue out, sweeping it through my core, flicking at my clit.

I lifted my hips off the bed. "Holy fuck!" Most men who engaged in meaningless sex didn't tend to go down on a woman unless it was something they enjoyed themselves. Even then, they weren't always that great at it, and

I had to instruct them more often than not on what to do. But Toby—holy hell—he *knew* what he was doing, and from the soft hum that left his mouth as he fucked me with his tongue, he enjoyed giving oral too. *Oh yes.* I would not be disappointed.

When he centred his focus on my clit, tongue swirling and sucking at the tiny bundle of nerves, I had an intense desire to clamp my thighs around his head and refuse to let him go. I hadn't been handled this well in, well, ever. The conversation I'd had with that woman in the bathroom slammed into me moments before my second climax hit and I cried out his name. *He's a devil in the sack.*

I'd barely caught my breath by the time he'd shed his boxers and donned a condom, that massive cock held in his hand as he paused at my opening. "Relax and breathe," he instructed, ice-blue eyes locked with my green ones as he pushed his tip inside me, stretching me to the point where I cried out cross-eyed.

"Oh god."

"Relax. You're clenching," he winced. "I won't last long if you clench."

"You're big," I gasped, relaxing my core around him, breathing slowly as he inched his way inside, filling me more than I'd ever felt possible. "Oh, wow."

"Think you can handle me?"

I nodded before he moved. And oh god, I could barely control my moans.

"Toby."

"Blair. You feel… fuck me. You feel amazing."

In and out. In and out. He fucked with agonising precision, a slow torture of the senses dancing along that fine line between pleasure and pain.

So. Full.

Almost ready to explode for the third time, I tipped my head back and let the sounds escape my throat. I would happily walk with a limp for the next week if this was the kind of lover he was. No wonder Lucy's mother had waited on him all those years. *Oh God. Fuck that feels sensational.* No other man could compare to this... his size and skill. *Amazing.*

Starting at my toes then zapping its way to my scalp, my third climax hit with a blinding light. "Hold it," Toby heaved, picking up the pace as he laced our fingers together and held me against the bed, something I'd normally fight against, but with a pleasure this intense, I lost myself in the feeling, writhing up to meet him, thrust for thrust.

"Fuck," he hissed through clenched teeth as he spilled himself inside me. "Blair. *Fuck.*"

"Toby. My god. That was—"

My voice got lost in his mouth as he kissed me with a fierce passion, pushing against our connection, touching me so deep I thought I might die.

"More," he gasped, his damp hair brushing over my forehead as our sweat slick bodies buzzed in tangled togetherness.

"There's more?" I could barely speak, my hands still tangled with his.

"There's definitely more." He grinned and grated his teeth along the side of my jaw.

"Show me," I said, wanting to drown in his body and die from his skill.

Pulling from inside me, he crouched back on his knees

then grabbed my hips, rolling me onto my stomach then shifting me back on my knees.

"Your skin feels like satin," he said, running his hand up my spine then back down until he cupped my arse cheek and nudged my knees apart. "And inside"—he smoothed two fingers along my slit before pushing inside —"silk." Pressing against my arse cheek, he opened me wide then leaned in, fingers still inside me as his tongue touched my opening then ran back until it was circling my back-door entry, running enough pressure along the nerve-filled edge to make me howl and squirm.

"Holy fuck," I moaned, my back arching, doing involuntary yoga poses as he poked and prodded, licked and kissed. I erupted. Again.

No man has ever gotten me off this many times in a row.

Toby Cartwright was a god, and I was his humble servant.

With every nerve in my body humming in pleasure, I held myself on shaky arms, listening as he tore through another foil packet and slid a fresh condom over his length. Then I took a breath and floated up the steps to heaven when he pushed inside, the angle and stroke the perfect combination to bring tears to my eyes as ecstasy took over. All I was was sex and raw nerves.

"I don't want to stop fucking you," Toby forced out as he fought against his ejaculation and lost, his hand squeezing my arse as he panted out his breath, slowly coming down. I could barely speak, barely breathe. "You feel too good." He leaned down and pressed his teeth gently into my flesh. "Too good." His hot breath washed over my skin before he bit a little harder this time, kissing and sucking to cancel out any pain.

For a woman who loved to fuck as I did, a man like Toby was dangerous. Heroin in the vein of a borderline nympho.

I was in trouble.

"We need a shower," he said, still inside me, sweat dripping from our bodies as he slid his fingers over my skin.

Nodding, I pushed my hair from my face. "And water," I gasped.

"Kitchen first then."

Following me to the fridge, he waited until I opened the door to place his hand on my back, his fingers digging possessively into my skin as I leaned into the cold. Closing my eyes, I pressed back into his touch then turned with a bottle of water in my hands. "Still want more?" I asked, my eyes dropping to where that massive cocked stood stiff and proud, wondering how the man didn't pass out from a lack of blood to his brain while maintaining an erection this long. He was in his forties and going at it like a twenty-year-old. I wasn't complaining.

With a telltale grin, he removed the bottle cap for me and watched with hungry eyes as I drank. "If you can take it." He lifted the bottle from between my fingers.

"I can take it." I wasn't sure if my body *could* take more, but I'd already come this far, and I wasn't a quitter. I'd happily risk a trip to the ER if it meant getting blessed by his huge man rod again.

His eyes locked with mine as he drained the rest of the water and threw the empty bottle over his shoulder, bouncing it against the floor. With a smile that turned my insides to mush, he bowed his head and kissed me softly, cold tongue to cool tongue. "Hold on to something," he said with a wink, before dropping to his knees in front of me.

"Oh god." My legs almost gave way as his tongue lashed out and stroked through my slit. I grabbed hold of the open fridge door for support and yelled, "*Toby*," while the shelving pressed against my back. Hooking his forearm behind my knee, he shifted one of my legs and draped it over his shoulder, giving him better access to my overused core as he licked and sucked, dipped and fucked me into yet another screaming quivering mess.

I'm dying. Fucked into oblivion by the man I should have captured but saved instead.

Wait. *Did I die on that boat?*

Is this heaven?

I didn't think they'd let someone like me into heaven. But endless orgasms couldn't possibly be hell.

I've lost count of how many times I've come.

After eating me out at the open fridge, he took me to the bathroom and pressed me against the tiles in the warm shower, fucking me from behind as his teeth dug into my shoulder and I pulled at his hair. This was pure and carnal and I loved every second, thriving on our bodies connecting in the most biblical of ways. When I came again, my cries echoed around the small room. I practi-cally slithered down the wall and into a smiling puddle on the floor.

"You OK?" Toby asked as he steadied my failing legs by catching me about the waist.

"I'm fan-fucking-tastic," I replied, grinning as I turned in his arms.

With a chuckle, he shut off the water then scooped me up in his arms, drying me off before placing me in the bed, my body a boneless weight that sunk down into the mattress. He fucked me good.

Did I say I wouldn't walk for a week? Make that a month. At least.

"Think you'll be able to sleep now?" he asked in a whisper as he curled behind me, the double bed too small for us both. I nestled beneath the weight of his arm.

"Hmm," came my faraway reply. Toby's breathing had already evened out.

CHAPTER THIRTEEN
FILTHY

"SWEET BABY JESUS," I moaned, placing my hand against the wall. "I think you fucked my uterus into my rib cage last night." Waking up to bright sunshine and a hunky man wrapped around me had been pure bliss. Until I moved.

Every muscle ached, especially the ones in my thighs and my pelvis. When I'd rolled out of the bed and hobbled towards the bathroom, I'd run myself a salt-filled bath just to soak my swollen muff. Somehow, I'd fallen asleep in there. And by the time I got out of the tub, Toby was up and making breakfast in the kitchen.

"Can you walk OK?" He moved to help me, but I held my other hand up to stop him.

"I can manage," I said, shuffling over to the table before I eased myself down. "That cock of yours is huge. I feel like I've been punched in the vagina."

"Maybe we should have called it quits after round two," he said, setting a plate of scrambled eggs in front of me. "They're powdered, but they do the trick."

"I'm no quitter." I blew out some air from my lungs then shifted on the seat so my thighs were further apart. *Ow.*

Setting his lips in a straight line, he moved to the freezer where he pulled out one of those long gel-filled ice packs, wrapped it in a tea towel then handed it to me. "For your, uh, lady parts."

"My lady parts?" Trying not to laugh, I looked from him to the ice pack.

"Just use it OK?"

I took it from his grip and placed it between my legs, the cool bringing me sweet relief. "Sweet Jesus." I closed my eyes and breathed in deep. "You know, I don't know what's funnier. That fact you call a vagina 'lady parts' or that you keep vagina ice packs in your freezer."

He shot me a long suffering look. "They're regular icepacks. And I can call it whatever I want."

"*It?*" I teased. "Call 'it' a 'cunt' then." I smiled as he rolled his eyes.

"That's not going to happen."

"Aw, come on. Just once."

"I don't like to speak about women that way."

I took a moment to let my eyes absorb this fine specimen of a man before me. He wore a navy T-shirt that gently hugged his torso, and a pair of dark grey trackpants that hung low on his narrow hips. His hair fell forward as he bowed his head over the stove. He'd cooked me breakfast, he'd gotten me an ice pack and he wouldn't use crass words to describe my swollen parts, and he was *amazing* in bed, spending far more time taking care of me than he did himself. *Who is this guy?* Men like Toby Cartwright didn't exist. Not in my world, anyway. Women like me didn't attract men like him. And if they did, they certainly didn't get to keep him.

"Freaky between the sheets and a gentleman in the streets," I said, nodding as I stared at his arse. "I dig it."

With a soft burst of laughter, he shook his head and slid his eggs on another plate before joining me.

"How sore is it, really?" he asked, his eyes dropping to where the ice pack rested against my crotch as he slid a fork against his plate.

"Swollen. But I'll live to fuck another day, I assure you."

He scooped some eggs into his mouth and grimaced a little. "I think I have anti-inflammatories in the first aid kit if you need them. You were pretty voracious last night. I tried not to go too hard, but..." The corner of his mouth kicked up and his eyes shone bright, telling me he enjoyed my sexual appetite just as much as I enjoyed his. *Too good.*

"*I* was voracious?" I said, trying the eggs. They weren't horrible, but I didn't particularly like them either. "Says the man who quite literally ate every part of me. I have teeth marks on my arse and on my shoulder, thank you very much." I scooped more eggs into my mouth before deciding I was done.

"I didn't hear any complaining," he said, finishing his plate then eyeing mine. I pushed it over to him since he was far bigger than me and had given us an equal serving.

"I'm not complaining at all. Just... interested, I guess."

"Interested?"

I bounced a shoulder. "Yeah, well, it's rare I meet a man who can go me round for round like that."

He paused his eating and lifted his brow. "It's rare I

meet a woman who can *take* me round for round like that. Most give up after one, maybe two. Never four."

"Well, I'm honoured to be a unicorn pussy for you."

He rolled his eyes but laughed. "I'll get you those pills," he said, clearing away our plates before heading into the laundry. When he returned, he was holding a bright red bag with a white cross on it. "OK, I have Nurofen or Voltaren."

"Voltaren," I said, pointing to the bottle. "That's quite an extensive medkit you have there." Taking a peek inside, there were enough supplies to perform any number of minor surgeries.

Handing me a bottle of water with the tablets, he repacked and zipped up the bag. "I like to make sure I'm over prepared."

"Over prepared, huh? I hope you've got a big supply of condoms in there."

He laughed. "I do, actually. Got plans for another round?"

"Or six. A little swelling isn't gonna stop me. The way I see this, we've got a week, maybe two, together at most. Might as well make the most of the time we have left." I stretched back in my seat, wincing a little when my inner thighs protested. "And I don't know about you, but I slept like a baby last night."

A grin crept across his face, and I couldn't help admire how stunning he was when he smiled. "I did too."

"Well, Mr Cartwright. I think we both just found a solution to our sleeping problems."

Responding with a slow nod and a hungry perusal of my cleavage, he picked up the first aid bag. "Coffee?"

I adjusted the ice pack against my vag. "Love some."

PACKING up the Datsun with our things, we locked up the safe house then hit the road mid-morning, heading to Perth where Toby said he needed to make a stop. The only answer he'd give me was 'for supplies' when asked. It didn't matter how much I pushed.

After dropping me off at a motel where he paid cash for our room, he left me to my own devices and told me he'd be back in an hour.

Not one for idleness, I used the Blackberry to contact Nick and find out who was watching the Cartwrights and why.

"Seems they've got trouble all round," Nick said when I reached him.

"What kind of trouble?" I leaned back on the bed, my body feeling less achy as the day wore on.

"Cops are keepin' tabs on them, the Grim Order has a man in their house—think the mother is his woman—and your smuggler problem is also the entire family's smuggler problem. Brendan Grey has men watchin' there too. Seems there's some kind of stalemate goin' on between them all. Not sure if they're watchin' for your guy to turn up or if there's more to it. Either way, it's a mess back there. Be careful when you get close. You don't wanna get exploded again."

"Speaking of, is our bombing duo still there?" My eyes lifted to the wall-mounted TV, flickering silently as I pressed the phone to my ear. There was some fishing show on, and I caught myself wondering if Toby liked watching this kind of stuff. *Since when did I care about what a guy liked to watch on TV?* Shutting it off, I rolled my eyes. He was in my head and it'd barely been a day. That wasn't normal. But then, our circumstances weren't normal either.

"Yep. Still watchin' the marina. Don't know what they reckon they're gonna find now that the search is called off. I'll fill you in if there are any changes though."

"Thanks, Nick. Don't let them out of your sight, OK?"

"Sure, Blair. I'm on it like a rash on sweaty balls."

"That is so gross," I said with a laugh.

"Ah, I live to serve. How are you doin' anyway? That Toby guy OK around you?"

"Yeah. He's not giving me any trouble."

"Still escortin' him home? He cooperatin'?"

"Everything's fine, Nick. We're heading back, but you've heard what Grey's like. He doesn't like loose ends, us showing up alive will really piss him off."

"Then at least stay hidden until you get to Torquay. Maybe I can try to meet you there."

"So you can collect half my finder's fee?" I asked with a smile.

"No, Blair—but I deserve some compensation for all this work—it's so you have backup. This Cartwright guy has a big family, and it seems the family has the backin' of the bikers. I'll tail Grey's guys wherever they go, but he doesn't command a two-man army. There might be more out there. Just keep your head down. You've got a lot of ground to cover, and I don't want you disappearin' somewhere out on those desert roads. I'll never find you out there."

"Worried about l'il ole me, Jennings?"

He grunted in response. "Crazy, I know. Just keep in touch."

"I will. Goodbye, Nick and thanks."

"See ya, toots."

Disconnecting, I smiled, resting the phone on my chest as I looked up at the ceiling. Despite the fact we didn't work out as lovers, Nick was a great colleague, and possibly the closest thing I had to a friend. We gave each other shit a lot of the time, but when the going got tough, he kept showing up to help me out. But I had no idea what help he could truly be against Grey in the long run. Grey was the biggest name in crime Australia had seen since the Moran family. Getting to him wouldn't be easy, even *with* my parentage.

I'll teach you a lesson you'll never forget.

A cold shudder jittered down my spine, giving me a reason to shift my focus.

No. Stop.

Sliding off the bed, I hefted my bag from the floor and opened it wide, sifting through until I found my envelop of cash and a fake ID. Peeling off a couple of fifties, I shoved it all in the back pocket of my jeans and set off in search of sustenance.

Returning thirty minutes later with some sandwiches, bottled water and a bottle of vodka—that I hid inside my bag because old habits died hard—I set up a small picnic on the bed then settled back against the pillows, flipping through TV channels while I waited on Toby. *Tick, tick, tick.* He was taking forever.

Startled by the opening door, my hand immediately flew to my face where I could feel a trickle of drool sliding out my open mouth. "Wha? Huh?"

"Aw, honey. You cooked," Toby said as he closed and locked the door, placing a large black duffel on the floor inside.

Pushing up on my elbows, I looked around, disorientated. "I fell asleep?" With a frown, I moved to sitting and rubbed my eyes. "What time is it?"

"Almost five."

"You were only supposed to be gone an hour."

Pulling his shoes off, he kicked them to the side before he sat on the end of the bed.

"Miss me?" he asked, picking up the sandwich packets and looking inside.

"I might have if I hadn't fallen asleep. I never nap."

"Can't imagine what got you so tired." He grinned, a knowing glint in his eye as he held out the mayo, chicken, and salad sandwich for me. "Keep your energy up."

"Is that a command or a request?"

"A suggestion. But, take it as you will."

Rolling my eyes, I took the food then tore into it ravenously, my empty stomach cheering at its reward. "I love sandwiches. They are the *best* invention ever."

"I'm partial to burgers, myself. An entire meal stuffed into an easy to consume bun. Makes life on the road easy."

My cheek stuffed with food, I gave a thoughtful nod. "Burgers are basically just hot sandwiches."

He chuckled, taking a healthy bite out of his corned beef and coleslaw on white bread. "I suppose you're right."

We ate quietly for a moment, strangely content in each other's company for two people who shouldn't get along. The hunter and the hunted, coming together over a common foe. It was movie worthy stuff.

"I spoke to Nick," I ventured, speaking around my full mouth.

"And?" Toby did the same, holding his hand up to cover his lips. Much more polite than me.

"He said everyone is watching your family. Cops. Grey. Grim Order."

"The MC is of no consequence . They're allies."

"OK. But Grey and the cops are watching. That's a cause for concern, right?"

He rubbed his fingers against his forehead, closing his eyes before he nodded. "Yeah. We must be careful as we get close. I'll need to reach out before we see them."

When I slid the last corner of my bread into my mouth, Toby picked up a water and handed it to me with an unscrewed lid.

"Thanks." I had to admit that I liked this. Him taking care of me. It would be easy to get used to, possibly frightening if we'd met in any normal kind of way. But since we were committed to travelling back to Torquay together, it was... nice, comfortable. I liked being around him.

"What's in the bag?" I asked, needing to shift my mind back to the task ahead of us before it got carried away feeling things then twisting them into something I didn't want.

He glanced at the black duffle. "Supplies," he stated, like he wasn't planning on elaborating beyond that.

I narrowed my eyes. "What kind of supplies?"

"Things we'll need over the coming days."

"Days. So, that's the plan? Drive straight through to Melbourne?" He took a drink of water and nodded. "I hate to break it to you, buddy. But that's almost two days on the road if we drive non-stop. That old Datsun won't make it under those kinds of conditions—the desert heat, the shitty roads. Hell, a new car would struggle with that run time.

And since we're supposed to be dead, getting stranded in the desert in need of rescuing isn't going to keep us off the radar."

"You have a better suggestion?" He opened the extra sandwich—egg salad—and offered me half.

Waving it off for him to eat, I got up to get my iPad from my bag. "Actually, I do."

"I thought I told you to get rid of that thing."

"Relax, I turned off the location and took out the SIM. It's using the motel's free Wi-Fi." Sliding back onto the bed next to him, I brought up the browser. "I've driven to almost anywhere you can think of in the country over the years, and the best and safest route from Perth to Melbourne is along the coast. Lots of tourists sightseeing across the Nullarbor and Great Ocean Road. It'll take us at least a week with stops, but there are plenty of places along the way to rest. I see families and couples doing it all the time. They take their four-wheel drives or camper vans and hit the road, we'll blend right in."

"In the Datsun?"

"No. A four-wheel drive or a camper van; keep up. I can rent one with this ID." I pulled my fake one from my back pocket. "Hell, I'll buy one if that's what you want."

"And this way takes a whole week?"

I nodded. "At least. Driving straight there is insanity. This is about limiting our risk of breaking down, getting run off the road at night by a truck, or smashing into a kangaroo we can't see coming in the low light. We travel during the day with the tourists and rest amongst them at night. Look at this, there's even a tourist website dedicated to this route." I showed him the website I'd pulled up.

"This says two weeks," he pointed out, scrolling through the webpage.

"Yes, but we aren't really going to stop and sightsee at all these places. I figure we stop at every second location to cut the time in half."

He kept scrolling through the page, stopping to read the little blurb under each photograph. "You know, I've barely seen half this stuff." He paused on a stunning image of a bubblegum pink lake. "This actually exists?"

Leaning in to peer closer to the screen, I nodded. "It's literally called Pink Lake. I've seen the signs for it before when I've driven through Esperance. Wild, huh?"

Taking a breath that was deep enough to lift his broad shoulders, he studied the screen. "Yeah. Wild." Distracted, he flicked his finger, scrolling through dozens of images featuring our country's natural wonders. "I haven't seen any of this." He paused on the picture of the twelve Apostles. "How is it I can live in a country my entire life and never take the time to *see* it?" He stopped on the picture of a man holding a board under his arm while looking out over Bells Beach and just stared.

"You grew up there, right?" I said, watching the way he seemed to disappear from my vision and slide into a memory so vivid that even I heard the roaring waves.

Shutting off the iPad screen, he nodded, handing the device back. "Been surfing Bells since I was a kid. Dad taught me and Nate. Nate and I taught the rest. Probably the only time we got along with the man was when we were on the water." The shift in his demeanour was swift as he stood and collected our rubbish, throwing it in the bin. Suddenly he was business again, checking his watch with a straight back and tight jaw, that light happiness I'd found in his eyes that first day in Wannanup already fading. *What will he be once I get him all the way back to Torquay?* "It's nearing six. I say we call it a day and search for a new vehicle in the morning. I'm in no rush to get out of here."

Uncurling myself from the bed, I stood with my iPad in hand, slipping it back into my bag as I smiled to myself. "Ready for bed this early?" I teased.

He ran a hand through his hair back and forth then placed his hands on his hips, cracking a smile again, his shoulders relaxing. "Maybe. If your uterus has gone back to where it belongs."

I grinned. "From what my lady parts tell me, everything is fine."

With a soft burst of amusement, he moved in front of me, one large hand sliding around my waist and pulling me close. "Thank god for unicorn pussies."

I wanted to laugh at his words, but when his hungry eyes met mine, I couldn't. The heat simmering inside them gave me such a jolt of excitement that I pressed into his body, my hand resting on his massive chest. I liked seeing him like this. I liked being the reason those broad shoulders relaxed. It wasn't a normal feeling. Normally, I couldn't wait to get away from the men I'd been intimate with. Before the Adelaide job, I'd had a handful of flings that lasted longer than a night. But ever since, I'd limited my connections to strangers in bars, no names needed.

Until now.

Maybe that's because this too has an expiry date.

The thought hurt my heart.

It was too soon to feel this way.

Running his fingers across my cheekbone, he brushed

my hair behind my ear then cupped the back of my head, bringing our lips closer, closer.

Emotions I didn't have names for flitted about in my chest, tightening my airways and twisting my stomach. I wanted him to kiss me, to feel his hands on my naked skin while he ravaged my body. I wanted that more than anything. But I couldn't do it like this. I was too raw.

No. Don't.

Turning my head just before our mouths collided, I pushed back on his chest and forced myself to inhale a calm lungful of air. "Not yet," I said, smiling, forcing my face into an expression that told him everything was fine.

"Are you OK?"

Most men said, 'what's your problem?', 'I thought you wanted this', or 'why'd we stop?'.

Toby asked if I was OK. Toby looked genuinely concerned. *Who is this man?*

"I'm fine," I whispered, pressing my fingers into his chest, wishing I could latch on there, absorb his calm. "I need to freshen up first. Use the bathroom. Brush my teeth."

"I don't give a fuck about brushed teeth, Blair."

"Well, I do. Give me a few minutes, OK. I feel gross from travelling."

Untangling his fingers from my hair, he lowered his hand to rest on my shoulder and kept those inquisitive eyes of his on mine. "We don't have to do anything."

My fist tightened, pulling at the fabric of his shirt. "No. I want to. Just… give me a minute, OK?"

He dropped a kiss on my forehead. "Sure."

He dropped a kiss on my forehead… My heart jumped into my throat. *I'm convenient, just a fuck, a cure for sleepless nights. Why is he being so nice, no, sweet towards me?*

The man confused me.

I killed a bunch of his men. Until I had so much blood on my hands, I couldn't see my own skin anymore.

I should be terrified. Toby Cartwright could ruthlessly kill an enemy that got in his way.

I should be wary.

I wasn't.

I think... I think I understand him—his pain. Does he understand me too?

The thought felt tight in my throat. *No one understands me.* What a foolish thought.

Flashing him a smile that was a confident mask to my noisy mind, I picked up my bag and went into the small bathroom attached to the room, locking the door behind me. With shaking hands, I placed my bag on the vanity, tearing open the zip and diving my hand in, sweet relief flooding my mind as my hand connected with glass. *Blissfully numb.*

Grasping the aluminium lid, I cracked the seal, gulping vodka down until my lungs forced me to breathe, the burn in my throat causing me to hiss through my teeth. "You're OK," I whispered, grabbing my toothbrush and coating it with a thick layer of minty paste. "You're OK... stressed because of Grey and the explosion and..." I shook my head, brushing vigorously at my teeth as I spoke to myself with mumbled words. "You're OK." Spitting the paste out into the basin, I rinsed my mouth then washed my face, meeting my eyes in the mirror. "These aren't feelings."

Feeling the effects of the alcohol creep through my body, I changed out of my jeans and fitted singlet, slipping into a silk and lace negligee before fluffing my hair. "No one steals your enjoyment," I said to my reflection, relaxing as the gentle haze settled itself into my brain. "You are in control."

I opened the door with a dramatic sweep of my arm, spotting Toby over at the tea area wiping a hand towel across his face, a small toiletry bag sitting open with his toothbrush and toothpaste out. A smile crept across my features. He brushed. *He's different to other men.*

"Wow," he said, mouth dropping open as his eyes swept over my body.

I rested my hand on the door frame and posed against it. "You like?" I asked, running the tip of my finger along my neckline.

Placing the towel on the side of the basin, he moved towards me. "I have never…" He shook his head a little, a bewildered expression taking over his features as he held a hand out. "You look beautiful. Good enough to eat. I feel like I should wine and dine you first."

I took his hand then he lifted it high above my head, so I spun, landing pressed to his chest. "Just spank me and tell me I'm dirty. Keep all that mushy stuff for the regular girls."

He chuckled as his hand slid down to my arse then landed with a clap. I jolted against him and grinned, almost purring while he rubbed at the sting with a tender touch.

"Filthy," he murmured, just before his mouth connected with mine.

CHAPTER FOURTEEN
LET'S PRETEND

"GOD HELP anyone who takes a black light to this room after that," I gasped, brushing my hair from my face as I rolled onto my back, trying to catch my breath from the sexual gymnastics Toby just put me through.

With a chuckle, he got off the bed and filled up two glasses of water, handing me one before drinking his while watching me over the rim of his glass. I smiled and did the same, never one to shy away from direct eye contact. Especially when the eyes I was watching always seemed so hungry. They did wonderful things to my insides without needing a lot of words spoken.

Once I drained my glass, he took it back then returned it to the sink where he rinsed it and placed it on the sideboard to dry. I stared at his naked arse the entire time, watched his panther-like body move across the room, his cock a pendulum swaying in time with his steps. It'd been a long time since I'd met a man so mesmerising. I couldn't take my eyes off him. Lucky for me, I could keep him for an entire week.

One week. It didn't feel like enough.

"I want to take the full fourteen days to get back to Torquay," he burst out with.

"Are you serious?" I asked, tracking him as he walked around the bed and got in beside me, so at ease in his own skin he didn't even attempt to cover up.

"Yeah. We can do the trip how that website suggests, see Pink Lake, stand in two states at once, experience the Twelve Apostles before they're eroded away. What do you think?" *Two weeks.* Two weeks in this man's bed and I may never walk straight again. Still, the time felt too fleeting. How much would be enough?

"I think," I started, taking in the excited glint that lit up his eyes. I found myself smiling, getting caught up in his energy. If I was a sensible woman, I would have added, "we should travel as fast as possible. One week is already pushing it." But we'd already established that I was *not* a sensible woman, so my response went more like this: "That sounds perfect, Toby."

He grinned. "Really?" he asked, like I had to give him permission. As far as I was concerned, the journey between Perth and Torquay would be the last days of our lives. If he wanted to slow that time down, spend it fucking and sightseeing, then I was all in, baby.

"Really," I said with a laugh as he rolled onto his back and sighed.

"I feel like seeing all that beauty will fill my soul so I can get through this job. The job to end all jobs." He sucked the air through his nose and looked at me, his eyes so clear and sincere that I couldn't breathe for a moment. "Then we'll never have to fight again." He held his hand out, palm up, and I placed mine inside it, fingers tangled as we wrapped them together.

"Because it will be over."

"One way or another." He squeezed my hand. Death was so final.

"Let's pretend we're different people," I said in a whisper, sliding a little closer because I knew this would sound silly to most people, but to a man like Toby, who'd been living a double life for years, it might

just be what he needed to lose himself a little. "Invent a whole backstory of how we met and where we're headed. Maybe we're insurance brokers, tired of the rat race and taking a year off work to travel around Australia."

He quirked a brow. "We're not Nikki and Tom holidaying while you're on leave from the Navy anymore?"

I shook my head. "No way. You're never in the armed forces around strangers. You can't know who's served and what questions they might ask. You've got to choose boring occupations that no one wants to talk about—accountants, insurance brokers, maths teachers. Stuff like that."

"OK. I'll be a maths teacher."

I giggled. "You?"

"You literally just suggested it."

"Yeah but, have you seen yourself? If I'd had you for maths in high school, I never would have dropped out."

"You dropped out?"

I nodded. "Year ten."

"How about"—a grin crept across his face as he shifted his weight, bracing himself over me, looking down—"we say I *was* your maths teacher."

"Yes." I grinned back, wriggling beneath him as I slid

my hands over his corded arms. "And I was so bad in class that you always kept me in. Then one thing led to another, and—"

His mouth landed on mine, tongue pushing in and causing me to whimper from longing. I was sober. Far too sober for such intensity, but I was equally drunk on him and the way he was making me feel, like a woman who wasn't me, a woman who had hope in her heart, a life to be proud of and people who cared for her. *Let's pretend....*

"It was a bit of a scandal at the time," I said as Toby slipped his arm around my shoulders. "Even though we waited until after I finished year twelve, there were still a lot of questions. Poor Tony was raked over the coals by the school system. My parents acted as though he'd stolen my innocence. It was awful. I was eighteen, he was twenty-five, and I suppose I didn't have the maturity back then to fight. We broke up within the year and didn't reconnect until a couple of years ago when he sought me out on Facebook." I looked up into his amused face and smiled, sliding my hand over his thigh. "That spark was still there and we've been together ever since."

Toby smiled as he sipped at his wine then kissed me on the forehead for added impact. He was getting good at this.

"That's just beautiful," said the woman we'd been telling our story to. She had that soft look in her eyes that told me she'd eaten up every word. "All those years apart and you still loved each other." She clasped her hands in front of her chest as she glanced at her husband. "Isn't that just beautiful, Burt?"

"Lovely," Burt said, red-nosed and possibly onto his second bottle of wine. We were meant to swish and spit along the Margaret River wine tour, but there were some of us who couldn't bring ourselves to waste good alcohol —me included. But, I could hold my liquor better than Burt could.

Now, we were in the restaurant, sitting on a long table with several other couples, filling our bellies with stone-fired pizzas, antipasto and a selection of cheese. I was really enjoying myself.

"Well, who could forget a girl like Clair." Toby grinned. "She's one in a million."

Seemed Toby was enjoying our make-believe life too. I smiled up at him and happily welcomed the soft kiss he pressed to my lips, squirming in my seat when his lips moved to my ear and he added, "I hope Clair enjoys fucking as much as Blair does. That dress is really doing it for me." His eyes dropped to my exposed cleavage, returning to mine with an added devilish grin.

Looking at him through my lashes, I kept my voice low as I spoke. "She does. But, she's not very experienced. You might have to teach her a few things to bring out her inner goddess."

Sitting back against his chair, he chuckled. "Inner goddess," he repeated, reaching for his glass and taking a sip before engaging in conversation with another man on the table. While he was busy, I took a moment to study his profile and enjoy the relaxed smile on his face. The contrast between this man and the man in his photos really struck me. Here, he seemed happy and carefree. I didn't think it was because he was with me, pretending to be two people with completely different lives and backgrounds.

I'd seen this in him on the day I'd met him. He was happy in his own life, happy away from his family, happy just living. I had ruined all of that by tracking him down and bringing a wave of destruction that was ultimately forcing him to the place he'd run from. It was the first time in my entire career I'd felt bad for tracking somebody down. *He's too good for this life.*

Throwing his head back in laughter, he turned my way and asked if I'd heard what the other guy had said before filling me in on the story.

I smiled and laughed at the right places, all the while listening to the voice inside my head telling me I was this gentle giant's ruin. *I'm the devil in this story.*

With the tour over, we were deposited back to our holiday park where our new friend's invited us back to their caravan to partake in more wine and laughter. Toby shook his head and held out his hand in friendship. "I think we'll have to take a rain check, Burt. I need to spend some alone time with my girl here. You understand, right?"

Burt nodded with a sly grin and shook Toby's hand. His wife went bright red and giggled.

"Oh, of course! You two have fun now," she sing-songed.

"Oh, I plan to," Toby said with a wink before hooking an arm around my shoulders and ushering me towards our camper.

The moment he opened the door, I practically fell inside, laughing from the look on that woman's face. "Oh, I plan to," I mimicked as Toby placed our purchased wine on the small kitchen counter then came up on me, his intentions obvious as he pinned me against the cabin wall.

"Tony and Claire have a lot of lost time they need to

make up for," he said, lifting the hem of my dress until his hands gripped onto the flesh at my waist then pushed up over my ribs, fingers firm until he released me and lifted the dress over my head, leaving me in nothing but my panties and a strapless bra. I was heaving from desire.

"I don't deserve you," I whispered, catching his face in my hands and running my fingertips through his stubble.

"Because you didn't stand by me when the school was investigating our affair?" he asked, a teasing grin at the side of his mouth.

"Something like that," I murmured as he brought his lips to mine and kissed me with such passion, I felt lifted from the floor. I wanted to tell him I didn't deserve him at all, that I wasn't a good person, and that if I only had two weeks until I entered a war I was unlikely to walk away from, I wouldn't be spending them with me, the person who brought this shit back into his life, the person who hunts people with no remorse for what awaits them when they're found.

We'd known each other for three days, and already, he'd treated me better than every man I'd ever met, collectively.

I didn't deserve him.

As he pulled the bra from my body and gathered my breasts in his hands, he squeezed and sucked, swirling his tongue around my nipples until I was a gasping mess, taking the time to tell me how gorgeous he thought I was, how he loved the way I reacted to his touch, and that he couldn't stop wanting me.

I don't deserve him.

My eyes burned as he worshiped every inch of my skin with his fingers, his mouth and his words.

I am not this kind of woman.

Forcing myself to calm the fuck down, I gave myself an internal pep talk, reminding myself who I was: Blair-fucking-Page, private investigator, tracker extraordinaire. My hourly rate was enough to make a neurosurgeon balk. I commanded every situation I stepped into, and I was *never* a victim. Always in control. Happy on my own. *I need to harden the fuck up.*

"Wait," I said, pushing against his shoulders as he hooked his thumbs in the waist of my panties. He looked up, curiosity and a touch of concern in his gaze, relaxing the moment he saw my smile. I slid my fingers in his hair and pulled from the roots. "It's my turn to do you."

With a sly grin, he rested back on his haunches, nodding slightly before rising to his feet. "Clair likes to be in control, huh?"

I placed a hand in the centre of his chest and shoved. The man was built and steady as a rock, still; he shifted backwards until he was leaning against the counter, watching me with interest.

"She loves it," I said, licking my lips as I forced my hands steady while I worked at his belt buckle and tore open his pants. "Know what else she loves?" I touched the tip of my tongue to my front teeth.

He quirked a brow in question, seeming to be thoroughly enjoying what he considered as roleplay, but what I considered getting a hold of my stupid emotions.

Dropping to my knees, I tugged his pants down, wrapping my hand around his giant cock when it sprung free. "Swallowing giant cocks," I said, before running my tongue over the bulging tip. "She can't get enough."

He moaned as I opened my mouth around his girth,

testing to see if I could fit it in. It was a stretch, but I managed, and I wasn't willing to stop there. I wanted to take him all the way, a trick I'd learned at a young age and turned into my advantage. Men loved deep throat.

"Holy fuck, Blair."

Toby was no exception.

He hissed through his teeth as my eyes watered and my throat expanded, taking him further than was comfortable, because this was what I did. I did things other girls wouldn't or couldn't do; I did things that brought men to their knees, begging me for more. And I did them because it gave me a sense of power. And feeling powerful meant I didn't feel scared. I hated feeling scared.

In fact, I hated feeling all together.

"Fuck, Blair, I'm gonna come."

Then come.

Digging my fingers into his arse cheeks, I clamped down, letting him know I wouldn't quit until he'd let go. And he did. Seconds later, he groaned, and his cock pulsed in my mouth, prompting me to release him and run my hand up and down his shaft as his hot cum spread all over my chest and ran between my breasts, down to my stomach.

Breathless, panting, I felt the power surging through my veins as he stood above me, breathing heavy through parted lips.

I looked up, a triumphant grin on my face as I readied myself for words of praise, the ones that told me I was the best they'd ever had.

But they didn't come.

Instead, he said nothing. He took a few calming breaths as he looked down, taking in the state of me, a question in his eyes as he assessed me. "What the fuck just happened?" his seemed to say, making me feel as though I'd done something wrong. I had this instant flare up in my gut, a little voice crying, "Please don't be mad." *Again,* I was feeling things I didn't want to feel.

Damn him.

How is he even doing this?

"Blair," he breathed, grabbing a cloth then sliding down until he was kneeling in front of me. I looked at him with wide, rapid blinking eyes as he pressed his lips together then brought the cloth to my chest, wiping the semen away with gentle swipes. "I love head as much as the next guy. But I don't need this." He cleaned me like I was a child who'd made a mess while eating, everything about him soft and kind while I stayed frozen to the spot, too shocked to move, too surprised to speak. "I don't need you to act like a porn star so I can get off. Porn isn't even real, and the guys who get off on that shit aren't paying attention to their women." When he finished cleaning me up, he hooked a finger under my chin and tilted my head until I met his eyes. His captivating, windows to his emotions, eyes.

I am not going to cry here.

"I happen to love paying attention to my woman," he murmured, brushing his fingers through my hair and tucking it behind my ear before trailing his fingertips along my jaw. *His woman.* "I love tasting every part of you, drawing out your gasps and moans. I love the sound of my name when your voice is thick and you're about to explode. And I *love* the moment after you come when you can hardly speak and your breasts are heaving, cheeks and lips bright pink, your eyelids heavy. I fucking love it, love that it was me who made you lose yourself, because you're always in control, Blair. Always. Except for when I'm inside you."

"Huh." It wasn't a question or a protest, just a simple sound akin to 'oh god', or 'I can't fight when you talk like that', but in a much more basic, caveman-like language, because this man was undoing me, caring about me, *noticing* me. I didn't know what to say.

So, I didn't say anything at all. Instead, I collided with him, wrapping my arms around his neck as he caught me about my waist, our mouths connecting, tongues diving as we held on so tight that there was absolutely no space between my chest and his. It was a struggle to breathe, impossible to think, which was just as well, because I didn't want to think anymore. I wanted to be his plaything and ignore everything outside his embrace. No matter what role he was playing—Toby, Tom, Tony—it was the one place I felt entirely safe. In his arms.

CHAPTER FIFTEEN
BROKEN TOGETHER

"MAYBE PRETENDING IS A BAD IDEA," Toby said into the dark of the camper van, lying next to me, smelling like soap and warmth. I rolled into him and placed my hand on his chest, my head swimming from all the wine and sex. Touching him helped me feel grounded.

"We can't exactly tell people the truth," I whispered.

"I mean between us. I want to hope for the best here, but I don't like our odds against Grey's men. I want to be... me, unapologetically."

"Unapologetically? That's an interesting word choice."

"I've just..." His chest lifted my hand before he sighed. "I've always hidden part of who I am. I hid my real life from my daughter, and my daughter from my family. I played the part of the dutiful son, played the patriarch when my brothers needed it. And even when I left, and I told myself I was finally doing something for me, I was still hiding what I used to be, still living the lies I'd been telling all my life." The bed linen shuffled as he turned his face to mine. "If there are only two weeks left in this life for us, if you and I are the last people we ever get to be with or know, don't you want to let go of all the bullshit pretence and just be you?"

"Unapologetically."

"Yeah," he said, like I'd been the one to coin the term instead of just repeating his word back to him. "Tonight. The wine tour. It was fun. But I enjoy you most when you're not pretending to be someone else."

"Maybe I'm always pretending."

"A person can't pretend twenty-four hours a day without falter, Blair. I've seen you drop your guard. I like that part of you."

"You make me feel vulnerable," I whispered, closing my eyes when I felt his big arm slide around my waist and pull me nearer. "Don't. I don't need comfort."

"I do. Everybody needs comfort, Blair. Touch is a basic human need."

"That's the problem, though. I don't want to need anybody."

"That's a very lonely existence."

"I like being alone…" I let the words trail off. I'd said them so many times, but this time even I didn't believe them.

Moving his hand so that his fingers trailed up and down my spine—exactly the way I liked it—he waited a moment for my words to dissipate in the air. "When we were watching Lucy's house the other day, you told me you'd always had to fight. You delivered it so flippantly, then added that at least in your job you got to choose the reason you were fighting."

"I remember." *He sees. He notices. He remembers my words.*

"Wouldn't you like to stop fighting, Blair? Just for this next two weeks with me. Be you. Be raw. Be angry if you want. But don't be someone else when this may be all we have."

"I'm a mess inside, Toby. You don't want me raw."

"But I do. That first night when I walked you home from the tavern, I'd been out with Rogue so he could do his business before he settled in for the night. I saw you walk past, right down a deserted walkway in the dark. And I thought, 'Wow, that girl either has giant balls or a death wish.'"

"So you followed me?" I couldn't help but smile. If I hadn't known who he was, finding a man as huge as Toby following me in the dark would have been a little concerning.

"Kind of. I figured there was only one place you'd be going that time of night, so I put Rogue back in the cabin and headed to the tavern to make sure you got there OK, and of course, to walk you home."

"Why would you do that?"

"Because I wouldn't have been able to rest if I didn't make sure you were OK."

"Do you do that for all the girls?"

"No," he whispered, those soothing fingers of his still moving against my back. "Just the ones who get under my skin."

Closing my eyes for a moment, I swallowed down the emotions he was dragging out of me. He was so lovely, so honest, so amazingly perfect. I couldn't help wonder what my life would have been like if I'd met him, or someone like him, when I was younger and more capable of being saved. *Before Adelaide…*

I inhaled a shaky breath. "Do you blame me for your dog and your boat?"

"No. I blame Grey and his men."

"I'm sorry. I feel responsible. If I hadn't come looking for you…"

"Like you said, you were just doing your job. My mother will have to answer for it when we get to her. She should have known better than to send someone. I left for a reason. I didn't exactly hide what I'd done beforehand."

"What did you do? I mean, I know you killed some of Grey's men. But what happened? Why did you kill them?"

He went quiet for a moment, his fingers paused their movement on my back, and I worried he was about to clam up again—another strange moment for me.

"Unapologetically," I reminded him.

"You know that drug transport Grey was accused of attacking?"

"Yes."

"It wasn't him, well, not at first. My brothers and I hit it as a favour we owed to the Grim Order. It was the job that would set us all free—we'd hoped. My brother, Nate, he's the next one down from me, he was growing poppies for our not-so-friendly resident drug lords. When he met his wife, he decided he wanted out of the drug business and burnt the field down. The people he worked for didn't appreciate losing their crop and came to collect, and the only way we could pay them was by pulling massive, risky jobs on a regular schedule."

"Holy shit. That would have put you on the cop's radar."

"They'd been looking for us for years, but they'd never *found* us. They hauled Jasmine in for questioning a couple of times after my father got busted, but that was all unrelated stuff they were looking for a scapegoat on. We'd been so careful over the years it was thought that we were legitimate small business owners, slowly building our wealth through real estate holdings and clever investments."

"Except you've been stealing and laundering profits this entire time?" I put in, knowing how the criminal world worked. Even though I worked for a legitimate business and got paid through Big Jim's accountant, I knew Big Jim's books weren't exactly copasetic. We worked for a lot of criminals who paid a premium for our services. Most of those jobs couldn't go on the books and needed to be separated into smaller, more believable and *legal* jobs before the cash was legit.

"Exactly. But pulling these big jobs meant they'd created a task force whose entire reason for going to work every day was to figure out who we were and bring us to justice."

"Fuck me. So, what did you do? Go to the Grim Order for help?" The idea seemed insane, but I'd never been a thief with a task force after my arse.

"Kind of. It's complicated: my youngest brother, Kris met a girl who's like a daughter to one of the MC's top ranking guys. That guy—he goes by Breaker—became involved with my mother. She told him about the task force—which I wanted to throttle her for because only she and I knew about it—then he took it upon himself to get the club involved. They struck a deal with the cartel involving distribution and drug running that meant we were free of our debt."

"Oh, no." Bikers didn't do anything out of the kindness

of their own hearts. I held my breath waiting for the next part, knowing in my gut exactly what tied this together and set us on this specific path.

"Yeah," he said. "There was a catch. In return for getting the cartel off our backs, we owed the Grim Order a favour. One they would choose and call for whenever it pleased them. We weren't allowed to refuse."

"And that favour was the drug transport," I stated, my stomach aching as his story got worse.

He nodded. "One last huge job and we wouldn't owe a thing to anybody. We would be free."

"How did Grey get involved?"

"That's the big twist in this story," he said, rolling onto his back and raking his fingers through his hair with a sigh. "My sister-in-law, the one with the ties to the Grim Order, also had past ties with Grey. Well, not Grey, some guy who'd gone to work for him. She'd floated the idea of hitting the transport to this guy, thinking Grey might solve our drug problem for us."

"This was before the bikers got involved?"

"Yeah. Once Breaker stepped in, we called the whole thing off with Grey's man, paid him to keep his mouth shut, and that was supposed to be that. Ronnie—my sister-in-law—had a soft spot for this guy and his wife, swore they were trustworthy—"

"But they weren't." I couldn't seem to stop myself from jumping into his story. "They told Grey, then his men figured out your rendezvous point and hit you there. Oh, my god."

"That's exactly what happened. The actual hit went off without a hitch, but once we started unloading the truck, Grey's men turned up and all hell broke loose. It was an absolute blood bath, Blair. Men going down left right and centre. I thought we were all done for. But when they hit my brother"—his voice faltered—"something inside me clicked and, I don't know how, I killed them all, one after another, methodically. I killed them because they would've killed us if I didn't. I *had* to. And I was so pissed about it, *incensed* we'd been betrayed. The moment we were safe and the bikers had the drugs, I went back and took out that bastard and his wife in retaliation." He barely forced out that last word as he wiped a hand across this face and released a shaky breath. "That was my lowest point. I have nightmares where I click and shoot up shopping centres, schools." Blowing out his breath, he knitted his brow before he turned his head and focused on me. "You know, I never really wanted to be a thief, but I especially didn't want to be a killer."

"Oh, Toby," I whispered, running my hand back and forth over his chest. He caught my hand in his and held it against his thumping heart. *Thump, thump. Thump, thump.*

"That's what I did, why Grey wants me dead, and also why I left. I wasn't running away, I just needed it to stop. I'd become exactly what I never wanted to be. A person who snapped necks and put people down, the Cartwright garbage disposal unit. Each time I had to do it, it felt like I was killing off a piece of my soul, and I didn't *want that.* You know?" He blew out his air, lips tight as he forced his expression to stay steady. "Once I knew my brother would survive, I left with what shred of a soul I had left. Now I'm going to throw that away on Grey. But at least everyone else will be safe." He shrugged, trying to act like it was no big deal. But it was a huge deal. The more I learned about him, the more I learned what a selfless man he was. *He deserves freedom.*

I leaned over and kissed him before I cried. Lacking the word power, and possibly the emotional maturity, to tell him exactly how his words had stirred me. I showed him instead, climbing on top of him and using my body to convey what I hoped he understood as empathy, under-standing, sorrow and so many other things that it felt like a flood coming out of me. I wasn't frantic in my movement, not like I'd been earlier that night, I was more... loving; I suppose was the word. I was coming to care for Toby, far more than I'd ever cared for another human besides myself.

"Blair?" he whispered, as I sat back and took him inside me, his hands sliding up my sides before palming my breasts.

Moving over him, I moaned at the sensation, my entire body buzzed, live wires beneath my skin. I didn't think I could ever grow tired of feeling him inside me. "Yes?"

"I want my soul back."

There was such utter desolation in his expression that it took every morsel of strength within me not to cry. *This man bleeds goodness. Alongside his misery.* But a woman a shattered soul was incapable of locating his. I couldn't restore something I didn't remember ever having. *He deserves more than me.*

I leaned over his face and touched my lips to his fore-head, wishing it was enough, knowing I never would be. "I would give you my soul, but all I have are broken pieces." I pulled back and looked into his tortured eyes. "I'm sorry."

"Kiss me," he instructed, curling his palm around the

back of my head. "I want your moans in my mouth when you come. We can be broken together."

Broken together. I remembered thinking something similar when we started.

Doing as he asked, I placed my elbows on his pillow, either side of his head, my fingers spearing into his hair as my mouth connected with his; tiny nips, long stroking licks, biting sucks and anguished sounds. It felt a lot like need which hurt as it pressed against my chest from the inside. It was exactly what I didn't want in this world, not need, not comfort, not companionship, not… love.

Love.

I wasn't there yet. And I didn't think I ever would be— not in the short time we had. But it was the first time in my life I thought such a thing was a possibility. And it hurt what was left of my soul to know I'd probably never find out.

As I rocked above him, grinding at his base, moaning in his mouth, I knew it wouldn't be long before my orgasm wracked my body and my mind cleared, leaving me to feel foolish. And I wasn't ready to feel foolish, I wanted to feel complete, feel hope, just a moment longer.

I held off as long as I could.

"Toby," I gasped, muffled against his mouth. He groaned and gripped my hips tight as he clamped us together, grinding his cock inside me as deep as was possible, pulsing into my depths with a shudder, his kiss softening against my lips.

Moving his hands to hold either side of my head, he continued to kiss me, stealing my breath and cracking my heart. When he finally released me, he held me still, panting as our foreheads touched. "We skipped the condom."

Shit.

"What does it matter, Toby? We'll be dead soon anyway," I said, sliding off him and heading straight for the camper van's bathroom.

I locked the door and flipped on the water before covering my face with my hands and letting go of the flood. *What the hell is happening to me?*

"IS IT WHAT YOU EXPECTED?" I asked Toby as we stood on the bank of Pink Lake. Salt crunched under our feet and fragranced the air as the bubblegum pink water lapped gently, kissing our toes.

Reaching out to lace his fingers with mine, he sucked in a deep breath as he nodded. "It's better," he said, flashing those pearly whites of his as he smiled wide. Something he'd been doing a lot of lately.

We'd spent the last few days travelling along the coast, visiting tourist attractions and enjoying each other's company. We saw a stunning cave filled with helecites that glittered like gemstones. We floated in salt-heavy water while a pod of dolphins swam around us. We went paddle boarding on glass-like water then relaxed the afternoon away on soft sand, allowing ourselves to believe this was our life. Happy, calm, carefree.

In between our tourist adventures, we ate, drank and even danced a little. I hadn't been on a holiday in forever, sight-seeing occasionally if a job allowed it. I'd been a self-confessed workaholic until now, never having reason to stop and smell the roses. But now, well, things were different, and I was forgetting to act like a badass all the time and shock, horror: I was smiling too. Toby was rubbing off on me.

I probably didn't need to mention it, but the sex was great too. Mind blowing, in fact. Somehow, the intensity in our connection grew with time instead of waning. He was becoming a need, and I wasn't sure how I felt about that.

Even though I'd had somewhat of a breakdown that first night we were on the road, I had regained the vast majority of my composure, putting it down to the fact we were literally travelling towards our doom. It was intensifying my emotions. Even the toughest person in existence would have a small panic-filled moment when faced with similar odds. It was normal. I'd washed my face, glugged a little vodka and brushed my teeth so everything was better. I could face the world again.

"You know…" He stared back out at the water and sighed. "I've never used this word for anything, but this is fucking marvellous. Naturally occurring pink water. I didn't think it'd be this vivid."

"I kind of expected to see flamingos hanging out around here," I said, noticing there weren't any sea birds hanging around the water at all. "But maybe the water is too salty for anything except micro-organisms."

"That emu over there seems to think this is a good place to hang out," Toby said, pointing to the surrounding scrub to where an emu was standing perfectly still, its bluish face and beady eyes staring right at us.

"Or maybe he's going to run over here and headbutt us. Aren't those things dangerous?"

Toby chuckled. "That's a cassowary."

"No. That's an emu."

He laughed even harder, the lines beside his eyes crinkling in mirth. "I know *that's* an emu. I'm saying that the ones you're thinking about are cassowaries. They have that hard horn on their head and they're pretty aggressive. They're the ones you need to worry about."

I moved a little closer to him, never having seen an emu this close in the wild before. Normally they were always in the distance or in an enclosure so I couldn't see their fierce little eyes. "Either way, he looks like he wants to peck me in the face."

When his arm wrapped around my waist, I realised I was pulling at his shirt. "So this is your weakness, huh? Giant land birds."

Flattening my hand, I slapped against his chest. "Har-fucking-har."

"Come on, sunshine. Let's get you away from the big bad bird." He said, glancing out at the pink water one last time before guiding me towards the walking track.

"Sunshine?" I baulked a little at being given a pet name. I didn't let many people get close enough for such things. Big Jim being the exception.

"Yep."

"Care to explain?"

He glanced my way, that full mouth of his pulling up at the corners. "I think you can figure it out."

I'm his sunshine.

Suddenly, all I could think about was how much I wanted to kiss him. I wasn't one to do public displays of affection—especially in front of the wildlife—but I couldn't help myself. Turning in his grip, I wrapped my arms around his neck, stopping him in his tracks just before I lifted on my toes and planted my mouth against his, kissing him as insects chirped in the background, serenading us.

"I like you too," he said, hands on my hips before winding his fingers with mine and heading back to the parked camper. I liked that I didn't have to explain things to him. He had this uncanny ability to read my actions and know what they meant. It made it so much easier for me when the last thing I felt capable of was giving voice to the confusing tension that tightened my chest and swirled in my brain. Like he'd said the other night, I was trying to be unapologetically me. There was no point in wasting energy on keeping my walls reinforced when our time was so short. Besides, almost blowing up on a boat seemed to alter one's outlook on life. We were both trying to experience as much as possible in this strange limbo we were existing in together. It was like the eye of a massive storm, calm and quiet and almost hopeful in its peace. But once the eye passed, we'd be hit full force by the storm raging on the other side. Would we make it through?

Did I care?

"How long do you reckon it'll take to drive from here to Madura?" I asked as we climbed back into the camper van. We'd already stocked up on fuel and food because the roads from here were quite remote. We were about to cross the longest stretch of highway in the entire country, taking us across the Nullarbor with few signs of civilisation in between. So far, Toby had done the driving, but since I'd driven this stretch on my own before, I knew how monotonous it was. It had taken me six hours in a car, but with wind resistance considered, the camper van would take longer.

"About eight hours. Give or take."

"How about I drive first and we swap a few times?"

His response was clipping the seatbelt across his waist and starting the engine.

"Why can't I drive?" I argued.

Setting his jaw, I pulled out of our parking spot then headed for the road. "Because I don't know how sober you are."

"Excuse me?" *Fuck.*

"You heard me. Every time you visit that bathroom you drink from a bottle of vodka you have stashed in there, then you cover the fact you've been drinking with mouth-wash." He glanced at me. "No one uses mouthwash that often, Blair."

"They do if they have halitosis."

"Which you don't. I've smelled your morning breath and besides stale grog, it's just fine. You do, however, have a drinking problem." *What. The. Actual. Fuck?* I was struggling to keep my cool.

"You don't know what you're talking about." I set my jaw.

"Yeah, I do," he said with a gentle voice as he shifted gears. "And I'm not holding it against you. I'm not even going to ask you to stop. The only thing I am doing is asking that you don't drive."

Sitting back in my seat, I folded my arms across my middle, my lips pressed together as a sour feeling swarmed at the base of my throat. I wanted to rage at him and tell him he was mistaken, that there was no problem at all and I was fine. But those would all be lies. He'd seen my truth. He'd shown it to me and accepted what it was. Just like that. I wanted to be angry. But I couldn't because he'd been *understanding*. How was I supposed to react to that?

Looking out the window, I worried at my lip, the silence between us deafening. I wasn't stupid. I knew my behaviour was reckless. The drinking. The men. Even Nick had noticed the change in me. And that was saying something because Nick only really cared about Nick. I didn't know if I could talk about it yet, but I knew I'd been self-medicating, hoping it would get better. 'It' being the broken pieces leading up to the moment I told Grey he was my father.

No. Don't. I'm your daughter!

I couldn't have a quiet moment without my mind throwing up an image or a feeling. If I heard the click of a lighter or the weight of an object hitting a table, I felt physically ill. I hated that, hated feeling so out of control. Drinking created a soft fuzz that acted as a weighted blanket wrapped around that feeling of terror.

Lies. I'll teach you a lesson you never forget.

"On top of being their protector," Toby said, startling me from my thoughts. "My job in the family was also the planner. I thoroughly investigated every single move we made. We didn't work with anyone I hadn't run an in-depth background check on. We didn't take on a job I hadn't run a thousand simulations on. I was also the finder. Like you, I could take a couple of clues and hunt a person down then bring them back to the family, to my mother, the matriarch of our little organisation, to face whatever was awaiting them. I was really fucking good at my job too. And I'm not even being modest. I got shit done, shit that no one else could, and because of that, I was rarely blindsided."

As he spoke, I moved my head to face forwards, watching the road ahead while I focused on his movement in my periphery. He had a loose grip on the steering wheel with one hand, the other arm resting on the ledge of the open window, the wind pushing his overgrown hair to the side. Mostly, he kept his gaze on the road, but occasionally, he snuck a look my way.

"The first time I was truly blindsided was by my brother, Nate. I've spoken to you about him before. He's the one who got us mixed up with the cartel. You'd think I would have felt blindsided over that, but I suspected early, and it didn't shock me when it came out. Nate had always wanted… *more* than the rest of us." He paused and shook his head a little. "Anyway, the time he blindsided me was during a job. We'd been running a con where we targeted well-off single women. Nate would hit on them at a bar, get them to take him home then slip something in their drink before anything could happen. They'd sleep like the dead while we cleaned them out of anything of value. It was a good scam, we only hit women with good insurance policies and besides being embarrassed, no one got hurt. We could have kept it going but…"

By now I was looking right at him, my interest piqued as he outlined the ruse. *They drugged them?* That was ballsy. You never knew what medication a person was on that could cause contradictions. I was always careful who I used a tranquilliser on because of that fact, generally knowing my mark's medical background before I acted. There were times when I had to take the risk, but that was more out of self preservation than ease. I had to assume that Toby had done these kinds of checks too. A dead woman after a burglary would lead to a manhunt. He was too smart to risk that.

"The woman Nate married was the best friend of one of our marks. I'd spotted her during my surveillance and well, let's just say there was something about her that interested me. I told my brothers that under no circumstances were they to involve her."

"Did you want her for yourself?" I asked, too involved in his story now to stop my question.

He glanced at me, a small but sad smile pulling at the left side of his mouth. "Yes. I guess I liked what I saw. She was full of life, always smiling, always sure of herself. It didn't matter what anyone around her was saying or doing, she was just in the centre of it all, living her best life, the star of her own show. She was something else."

"Sounds like maybe you watched her more than your mark."

He laughed a little. "Almost."

"So, how did your brother end up with her?"

"We've always had the same type. Blonde, busty women with great arses and a spunky attitude." He glanced my way, and I actually grinned. *No wonder he'd walked me home.* "We had a rule that if we both liked the same girl neither of us would go after her. The night of the job, Holland got up on stage and belted out this karaoke tune. He saw her, and I guess it was love or lust at first sight, because all of a sudden, his word meant nothing. He cut his comms and took the girl."

"And you guys were out there ready for a job while he was cutting your grass?"

He lifted a shoulder. "I was pretty fucking livid, but we

still did the job. We cleaned the poor girl out twice, actually."

"And she still married him?"

"Not by choice."

My eyes went wide at that little bomb drop. "What the hell?"

"That was the second time I was blindsided. Holland and her friend figured out who we were and tracked us back to our place. Snuck up on us and everything. If it wasn't for Rogue sniffing them out, they might have called the cops on us."

I pressed my lips together at the mention of his dog. He was being so strong over his loss.

"Jasmine wanted them dead. She ordered me to kill them both, but I said no fucking way. She said she'd do it herself, but Nate came up with the crazy plan to marry them so they couldn't testify in court. Holland married Nate. Sam married Alesha—who was the original mark— and I stayed behind to mind the fort, drinking myself stupid and growing increasingly bitter."

Ah, now I see the point of this story. I placed my hands flat against my thighs and waited for him to tell me that the solutions to my problems weren't at the bottom of a bottle, some stupid cliché like that.

"I stayed angry for months, even made a pass at Holland. I was so pissed at my brother. I didn't think he deserved her, and I'd convinced myself she should have been mine. So I confronted her, made a total fool of myself then got the shit beaten out of me by the one person I'd always been closest to. I felt fucking betrayed, left out in the cold." *Holy shit.* His brother was an arsehole. I wanted to beat the shit out of *him* in Toby's defence.

"After the beatdown, I withdrew from the family as much as I could while still working with them. We ran some jobs without him because he wouldn't even speak to me after I'd touched his plaything. As if I was the bad guy in this story." He paused for a moment, shifting his hands on the wheel. "It was fucking bullshit, really. He was being a selfish bastard, and I was the guy who'd done wrong. The entire family was running around, figuring out how to coax *him* back." He let out his breath, shaking his head a little like he was trying to gather his thoughts or decide whether to continue or stop.

With the road stretching out in front of us, the arid plains to our left and right, there was nothing much else to do but to talk and listen, so I kept my mouth shut and waited for him to continue. There was more to this than I'd anticipated, he wasn't giving me a lesson in quitting drinking; he was sharing his own experience. Perhaps a little of his pain. Maybe he was doing it because he hoped I'd share some of mine, too. Maybe he needed it off his chest. Either way, my ears were all his. He was on a roll, I was his confessional. He either trusted me, or he was so sure we would die that he saw no harm in clearing it all out.

I'm listening.

"I've never told a soul this part before," he said, eyes swinging to meet mine for a little longer than was safe inside a moving vehicle. "But I made sure Holland found out about the poppies. I wanted to hurt him. And the best way to do that was by showing his wife exactly the kind of man he was."

"Did it work?" I asked, almost in a whisper.

"For a moment. Then I got the guilts and found her, told her he was all bent up without her. They loved each other. And as much as I wished I was the guy who got the girl for a change, I couldn't deny reality."

"Did she go back?"

"Not right away. Nate was losing his mind. He was desperate for her, not eating, drinking too much, and being generally belligerent and awful. He came up with this idea of staging a fire and faking his death so Holland would run away with him." He pulled at his bottom lip with his teeth and shook his head. "And since I'm the guy who gives the world and doesn't ask for a fucking thing in return, I helped him make that plan a reality." He rolled his eyes. "Off he rode, into the sunset with the girl I'd convinced myself I was in love with. Lucky Nate. Everybody loves him." *Not from where I'm sitting.*

"So you drank," I stated, finding that my emotions were rearing their ugly heads again, drying out my throat.

"Yeah. I drank. I drank, and I cursed, and I hated. It was eating me alive, because not only did he have the girl I wanted, but he had the freedom I'd always craved too. And I fucking *helped* him. He'd gotten himself into a fucked up mess over these poppies, beat the shit out of *me* because I kissed his wife in a drunken moment, and I helped. I tapped my beer bottle against his and said, 'Sure brother, let me make your dreams come true'."

I was suddenly glad I didn't have siblings. It sounded like one hell of a problem, and not at all what sitcoms led you to believe.

"The day of his funeral was the third time I was blind-sided. The cartel came to collect. Told us that the fire took their crop and since Nate was gone, *we* had to compensate their loss. No one knew he was still alive but me and Holland. Everyone else was mourning, my mother especially. Her response to their demands was to stab the guy in the fucking throat with a penknife. He bled out in the driveway and we couldn't leave the security guy alive." He took a breath, seeming to struggle with his next words. "He had to be put down too." He paused for a long while, staring at the unending stretch of road with tension etched upon his face, lips tight. "He was the first person I'd ever killed. I grabbed his head, took a breath and…" *Oh god. Toby.*

He didn't need to finish. I knew.

"I was a fucking mess after that. But it was also when I realised what I was capable of. I didn't want to be blind-sided ever again. Especially by my own brother. So, we hauled him back and made him deal with the cartel himself." He shook his head before glancing at me. "Fat lot of good that did us."

"Are you still angry?" I imagined myself in his shoes, fighting a fight that wasn't really mine all because of a sense of familial duty. It didn't seem fair. But what in life *was* fair? I certainly hadn't seen a lot of fairness.

"I wasn't. I'd made peace with Nate, moved on from my feelings for Holland, left to find a life of my own. But now, driving through the fucking desert to go back there and finish the problem *he* started? Yeah. I'm fucking mad. Why couldn't they do this without me? Why am I always the one sacrificing, always rescuing? Why can't I just *fucking live*?"

Something flared inside me at the strain in his voice, the desperation of his words. I wanted to protect him, whisk him away from all this, somehow make it better. With little to truly offer, I reached across and placed my hand on his. "Pull over, Toby."

He flicked his eyes towards me, red-rimmed, confused.

"Pull over."

"Why?"

"Because I can't change where we're going, but I can definitely take your mind off things." I touched my hand on his thigh. "Pull over. Lose yourself in me."

Reacting almost immediately, he steered into the dusty part of the road and slowed the camper to a stop. But he left the engine running. "You don't need to fuck away my problems, Blair," he said, turning to face me while reaching out to take my hand in his. I had a moment where I wanted to pull it away, to fall into my habit of deflecting with anger then drinking it away. But he'd just called me out on that behaviour. I didn't want to prove him right.

"I thought that's what we did," I said instead, giving him a slight smile.

"Yeah," he said. "That's what we've been doing. But right now I just want to talk. Is that's all right by you? This is shit I could *never* talk about with *anybody*. The fact I can say it all out loud around you without having to pretend I'm something I'm not..." He shook his head at the wonderment. "It feels really fucking good to get this crap off my chest and know the person I'm talking to gets it." I didn't feel worthy of his secrets.

"Why are you so sure I get it? I have no family. No brothers to fight with. No mother to rally against. There's just me, Toby. Me and no one who gives a damn."

Pressing his lips together, he brought my hand to his lips and placed a kiss against my knuckles. "I give a damn, Blair."

My heart swelled in my chest and my eyelids fluttered. "You barely know me."

He shrugged. "And yet, I give a damn. Just because you don't have a family, doesn't mean you can't understand what it's like to feel blindsided in a situation where you thought you were in control."

No. Don't.

I'm your daughter.

Lies.

Letting my eyes rest on our joined hands, I nodded slowly, pushing my intruding memories away. "Yeah. I know a little about that."

CHAPTER SEVENTEEN
A LUMBERING BALLET

"WHERE ARE YOU NOW?" Nick asked, the reception a little spotty as I leaned up against the outside of the camper van. Toby had gone inside to pay for petrol and grab a few supplies before we hit the road again, heading to a little town called Ceduna that was almost two thousand kilometres away, or twelve hundred miles for those measuring old school. It was surprising how many international travellers we were meeting along our journey. We'd spent the night before chatting to an American couple during dinner at the local restaurant. They told us of their adventures since arriving in Sydney then travelling anti-clockwise around the country. It had taken almost twelve months to get three quarters of the way. They couldn't believe how huge Australia was.

"We're crossing the border into South Australia today. Stopping to look at the cliffs at the Great Australia Bight on our way to Ceduna. Stuff like that."

He paused for longer than was normal. "You're sight-seein'?"

"You got a problem with that, Jennings?"

"Are you actually kiddin' me? Some mobster is after your head and you're out there *sight-seein'*?"

"What do you expect us to do? It's a long fucking drive towards our doom, Nick. I think we have every right to stop and smell the roses before we blow everything up at the other side."

"What about you blowin' up? You're supposed to be takin' him back to his family. The longer you spend fuckin' around in the desert the easier it's gonna be for our Irish friend to find you. They left yesterday, by the way. I was tryin' to get a hold of you."

I rubbed my hand over my forehead, gritty from the red dust in the air. A small lizard ran straight past me. "There isn't any reception while we're on the road and we only checked the phone this morning."

"We? You two besties now? Or you just fuckin' him?"

"Nick," I said, warning in my tone. I wasn't going to get into any of this with him. I didn't owe him any explanations, just a thank you for keeping an eye on Irish while Toby and I were on the road. "Thank you, OK? I mean it. But I've got it from here. You spoken to Big Jim?"

"He thinks you've gone off the rails since you haven't called in. There's been no reports of you gettin' on that boat so the only people who know are me, the Cartwright and Irish. I'm leavin' on another assignment now, so I guess you're right, you're on your own from here. I can't help you anymore."

"That's not what I meant, but sure. I get it. I really do appreciate you sticking around, Nick. You went out of your way to cover for me and it means a lot."

"Jesus, Blair. What happened? Did you fall in the desert and catch feelin's or somethin'?"

I laughed. He knew me well, and I didn't say thank you often. "No. I'm just a little reflective. I guess almost blowing up for the second time in my life, then travelling long distances on a mission to kill the guy who ordered it can do that to a person."

"That's a mouthful. Just... take care of yourself, toots. This world won't be as fun without your wise-arse in it."

"I'll do my best." I toed the ground with the tip of my shoe.

"All right. I'm out of here. Call me in a couple of days. You know, proof of life and stuff."

I laughed, feeling a little lighter for a moment as I realised that maybe a handful of people did care about me in this world. "OK. And maybe tell Big Jim I'm OK. Tell him I'm taking a holiday or something. I don't know, just keep him from looking and worrying, I guess."

"Will do. Try not to get too attached to your collar."

Before I could answer with a lie, telling him I wasn't attached to Toby at all, he disconnected, leaving me with silence on my end. "See ya," I said to myself as I sighed and lowered the phone.

"Everything OK?" Toby asked, his arms laden with bags of cold drinks and food as he approached.

I slipped the phone in my back pocket and reached out to help him. "Nick says Grey's men left yesterday. If they drive straight through, I reckon we've got a day or two before they catch up."

"Well, let's hope that they *d*rive straight through. They'll go right past us that way and never know it."

Smiling, I placed the groceries on the counter and started unpacking. "You know, I like the way you think."

He grinned in return and slapped me on the arse as I leaned over to restock the fridge. At first I giggled, then I stopped when I noticed a bottle of vodka in the bag I was unpacking.

"Is this for me?" I asked, running my thumb over the label.

"Vodka's your favourite, right?" he asked, his back to me as he topped up the pantry cupboards.

"Yeah." I swallowed down a ball of something that was forming in my throat. I didn't know if I was touched or confronted. I just knew I didn't feel OK.

"Well, put it in the freezer instead of the bathroom. It's better ice cold." He closed the cupboard and turned back to face me. "No sense in hiding it, right?"

"I suppose not," I said, sliding it into the freezer with a sense of unease. I wanted it, but I didn't know if I could bring myself to drink it. Not now that the cat was out of the bag. Not now I knew he was watching me, knowing how weak I really was. It kind of changed our dynamic a little. Suddenly, I wasn't the tough in-your-face girl I forced people to think I was, I was the angry damaged woman who drank too much to cope.

Be you. Be raw.

You don't want me raw.

But I do.

Toby saw me. Me. The person I tried to hide from view. In only a few days he'd seen peeks of the darkness inside me and he hadn't recoiled in disgust. He'd reached out, and he'd supported me. *I don't deserve him.*

He didn't deserve a mess like me. He was too good. Despite all he'd done. He was *good*.

I don't deserve him.

"THIS NEVER CEASES TO AMAZE ME," I said as the highway landscape shifted from red sand and tiny shrubs to towering trees and ocean. We were driving past the great Australian Bight, the part of the country down the bottom where it looked like a literal bite had been taken out of it. The change from nothingness to lush seaside wasn't sudden. It was this gradual alteration that crept up on you then seemed like it was there all at once. It felt like driving along the edge of the world.

"You like the sea?" Toby asked, glancing to the side and taking a deep breath of the cool ocean air.

"Who doesn't? I swear just looking at it calms me. Like, it's so vast it makes me feel inconsequential, which makes my problems less important."

"I get that. It's part of why I like to surf and sail. Everything is so much simpler out there. Mother Nature is in control and you're just taking your chances with everything else."

"Humans make life very complicated," I mused.

"That they do," he agreed, spotting the signs for the Head of the Bight Lookout. Our American friends from the last rest stop had told us the whales were putting on a show there. I'd never seen a whale off a TV screen before and hoped they'd be rolling around today too.

After trekking our way along the ridiculously long walkway, we made it to the viewing platform where a few other tourists gathered, phones in hands as they filmed the water below.

"The whales," I breathed as I placed my hands on the guardrail, watching the sleek black bodies roll about in the surf far below. They splashed, and they spun, performing a lumbering ballet that had me enthralled for hours, until the last one dove back into the depths, disappearing from sight, their ballet over.

I continued staring at the surf, long after the whales had moved on, outstaying the tourists, feeling too overwhelmed to move. They were so enormous, yet so... graceful. Free. Not burdened by life and its absolute fuckery. I wanted that. *God, I hate feeling like this, so...lost.* Toby remained by my side, steady, silent. A presence I couldn't ignore but took great strength from.

"Do you ever want to jump the guardrail and tumble down the cliff?" I asked after a while of us being alone.

"Metaphorically or literally?"

I closed my eyes, and a tear slid down my cheek, drying almost instantly in the warm air and the wind. "Both."

"Yes," he admitted, his voice soft yet harsh and painful.

Opening my eyes, I turned my gaze to his, seeing the accompanying torment that came with such an admission. "Me too," I whispered.

He moved closer, wrapping his arms around my shoulders as he pulled me to him, placing a kiss in my hair. "Do you want to jump right now?" he asked, his voice so thick I almost didn't hear the question.

I shook my head against his chest. "I want to stay like this." It was a terrifying truth, the need to have his arms around my body, the scent of his skin in my nose as the heat of his body mingled with mine, calming me, *completing* me. *I need him.*

"Me too," he whispered, tightening his grip as I buried my face in the fabric of his shirt, breathing him in, filling my lungs with everything that was him—strong, powerful, compassionate, warm. It felt good to be held, good to let out a drop of pain and have it completely understood.

Toby was quickly becoming my everything. I didn't want to let go.

I couldn't.

CHAPTER EIGHTEEN
THE MONSTERS IN MY MIND

TIRED OF THE heat and cramped accommodations of the camper van, we found ourselves a hotel room in Ceduna. I almost cried from joy over the air conditioning. We were seven days into our cross country drive, halfway to our destination. I'd started out on this journey with Toby, hell bent on getting back to Melbourne to get rid of my biological devil. But the distance we needed to travel had forced us to slow down, put the weight of our combined worlds on the back burner while we experienced an Australia most residents never saw. It was beautiful. It was life changing. It was soul affirming.

I felt so naked out here. Not just physically, but down to the bone, exposed nerve endings and sharp pieces of my heart protruding from my flesh. Toby was my grounding rod, keeping me from exploding and setting fire to everything around me.

He's a good man.

Probably the only good man I've ever known.

I don't want to let him go.

The more time I spent with him, the more I wanted to alter our course, stop Grey without Toby losing that last piece of his soul. I needed to protect that, needed to keep this kind and gentle man from losing himself to the monster he became in his nightmares.

"You cry in your sleep," Toby stated, his voice breaking into the quiet of our darkened room.

"I do?" Blinking rapidly, I realised I was crying then too. My tears pooling on his chest where I'd been resting, listening to the strong beating of his heart, the soothing in and out of his breath.

"Yes. But if I do this"—he ran the tips of his fingers up and down my spine and I curled into him blissfully—"you calm and sleep peacefully."

"You're too good to me," I whispered, feeling another tear slide from my eye and splash onto his skin.

"I'm rough with you. I pull your hair, I bite your skin and leave bruises behind when I grab you too tight. I'm not good."

"You are. None of those things are done with malice. You mark me with your passion and take care of me like I'm a child who can't do it for themselves."

"Does that bother you?"

"No. I like it. I've never had that before. Even when I was small I had to care for myself. It feels good to be vulnerable with you. I always thought I'd hate it, but I'm coming to need it. To need you."

"Is that why you cry?"

"No. I cry because I'm broken."

"Because of something Grey did to you?"

I nodded, my head moving against his chest. His fingers kept moving, doing their soothing up and down, drawing out a feeling that sat deep in my belly then crawled up into my chest before pushing against the backs of my eyes. I didn't want to face any of the things that had happened, but they kept rising up, tapping against my skull, trying to escape. Toby didn't press for me to go on, and it took a few goes at opening my mouth before the words came out. But once I started, I couldn't seem to stop. I needed him to know me. All of me.

"The first and only time I ever met Grey was a few years ago in Adelaide," I said, my voice not much more than a whisper. "I was there on a job, searching for a teenage runaway who'd found herself hooked on drugs and paying with her body." I paused and ran the tip of my finger in a circle around a small freckle on his stomach, swallowing the ball that had lodged itself in my throat. "My mother was a prostitute. Died of a drug overdose right in front of me." I pressed my finger lightly against that freckle. "I was nine." The image returned to my mind just as clear as if I were seeing it for the first time, her eyes rolled back as she shook on the floor. "She was foaming at the mouth and I had no idea what to do to help her." I flattened my hand against his skin, forcing a shaky breath as I used our connection to ground me in reality. "I suppose that's why I took the job so personally. I wanted to save that girl so badly. I wanted to save all the girls…"

Moisture tickled the side of my face before I realised an entire river of tears was streaming from my eyes, running straight down and settling at the point where my skin met Toby's. I blinked, but I couldn't stop them if I tried. I'd held them in so long that I couldn't put them back, couldn't rebuild that dam. So they fell, saturating us both while I kept my face turned away.

Toby's fingers continued up and down my spine, keeping me soothed. I didn't think I could keep talking without his touch.

"I only have a few memories from when I was small. Something about the mind blocking trauma, I'm told. But what I do remember came flooding back the moment I found that girl. She was in this brothel. The kind that wasn't registered or legal. The kind where any kink you were into could be purchased. I freaked out, and instead of just doing the job I was hired for, I decided I'd get the place shut down, be the saviour those girls and kids so desperately needed." A surge of sorrow crashed into me like a wave against a rock. I closed my eyes against the violence, furrowing my brow and focusing on getting the words out. Words I'd never spoken aloud. Events only I had the details to.

"I called the cops and anonymously reported what I knew. Waited for them to come and do their jobs, but..." My head ached as I forced myself into a sitting position, wiping my hand over my face and Toby's stomach, futilely trying to get rid of any evidence of crying. There was little point.

"The cops arrived. I was keeping watch, needing to see the raid go down. Then just as the first cop gave the order to break the door, the entire building ex—" I shook off the ill feeling that climbed into my throat and surged forward, eyes closed because I couldn't watch Toby's expression as I relayed this.

"It exploded," I tried again, glad to get the words out this time. "They were all inside. Women. Children. The only bonus was that the sick fucks touching them were in their too. But the screams." I let out a jagged breath as my voice turned hoarse. "The *screams*. I hear them still. Every time I close my eyes. It's like a kaleidoscope of that moment and everything that came after."

"That's why you drink." Toby's voice almost startled me, forcing my eyes to open and focus on the present, the dimly lit room and the only good thing in my life: him.

"Partly," I said, watching his soft expression swim away as tears filled my vision. "After the explosion, I should have just gotten out of there. But I was stupid and stood around when a small crowd of onlookers gathered, watching in horror as the place burned down. Then a man approached me—the one who blew up your boat— and told me that his boss didn't like meddlers. Next thing I knew, I was thrown into the back of a car, tied up with a bag over my head gangster-style." Pulling my knees up to my chest, I raked my fingers through my hair and cradled my aching head in my hands as I curled into myself. "The next few days, maybe weeks, are a blur. They called it, 'breaking in the new girl', told me I had to pay them back for what I'd taken from them. They beat me. They drugged me. I was... I was... r... raped." The last word came out as a gasp. I'd often alluded to an awful past, but I'd never said the actual word before. "Repeatedly." I ran my hand over my face, wiping at my nose, sniffling as I looked up to the ceiling. "Grey's men weren't gentle, and I fought. God, I fought so hard against them. And when I finally stopped, finally gave in and accepted that I couldn't escape, they sent Grey in to test me." My stomach flipped and twisted, and I placed both hands on my face, covering my eyes as I fought forward when all I wanted to do was to shut up, keep it inside, behind the vault doors. But I'd opened them up and now everything was coming out. I couldn't stop even if I tried.

"I'd never met my father in person. I knew who he was and what he did. But I'd never seen him up close. When I realised it was his whorehouse and his men who'd been defiling me, I don't know why, but I laughed. He smiled back and said, 'I heard you were being a good little filly. Seems you need a stallion to properly tame you.'" I lowered my hands and shook my head at the ridiculousness of those words, laughing a hollow laugh. "That's when I told him he didn't want to fuck me. He asked why. I told him I was his daughter. Then he struck me so hard that he cracked my cheekbone. I guess I'd lost my mind at that point because all I could do was laugh as he beat into me and called me a filthy liar and any other name he could think of. He raped me anyway, spit in my face then kicked me to the ground." I clicked the nail of my thumb against my bottom tooth as my tears dried up, replaced with a red-hot-belly rage that I needed to sate with my own father's blood. I hated the man. *Hated* him with the intensity of all the fires in hell. Only his death would fix this. It was the one thing I was sure of.

Toby had gone still as he listened, shocked, disturbed, horrified? Probably all of the above. I was opening the window on my torture and letting him climb right on in. *Welcome to my nightmares. Grab a chair, they're unending.*

"You know," I continued, needing to keep going with this hideous word vomit. "I thought he would kill me then and there, and I was honestly OK with that. But I woke up again, cleaned up, bandaged up, with him sitting in the chair beside my bed, demanding to know exactly why I thought I was his child. I explained who my mother was. Then I watched his face pale. Even the devil could feel regret. He had to live with the fact he'd fucked his own daughter." Shaking my head, I laughed a little through my nose. "Vile cunt." I released a heavy sigh. "After that, he was different towards me. He fed me, visited me, no one touched me. But they still confined me to a single room. He did a DNA test, and when the results came back a match, he offered me a seat ruling by his side." I scoffed as I relaxed my posture a little, the worst of my story over. "Rule by his side?" I met Toby's eyes, his jaw clenched as his eyes swam with fury and so much sorrow that a fresh wave of tears flowed from my eyes. "Don't, Toby. Don't feel sorry for me."

He took my hand. "I'm enraged," he ground out, barely able to contain his own anger. "He *raped* and *beat* his own daughter. Right now, all I want to do is kill him slowly, bring him back to life and do it all over again. I want to watch him *bleed.*"

Leaning in, I pressed my forehead to his. "I want that too," I whispered. "I've wanted little else since my escape. Hated myself for being too weak to kill him at the time. I just walked away like a coward licking my wounds."

"You are not a coward for getting out of there alive."

"I didn't escape. He let me go."

His eyes popped. "Grey let you go?"

I nodded. "I didn't trust it either. When I told him I'd rather die than join him, I thought death was exactly what I'd get. Instead, he unlocked the door, said it was his one and only favour to me. But if I ever did anything to cross him again, if I ever told another soul he was my father, he'd hunt me down and wouldn't be so lenient the next time."

Toby's grip tightened around my hand. "Jesus, Blair," he said, his words so strained it felt like the same debilitating desolation I felt. It felt like fury. It felt like a much-needed shield against my despair. It felt like…*everything I needed.*

"*That's* why I drink. Because I'm a fucking mess. I always have been, but after Adelaide I was chaos personified, and I had to fight so hard with my demons to become somewhat functional again." I met his eyes and gave him a self-deprecating smile. "If you can call it that."

"I think," he said, getting up and pulling out the vodka we'd stashed in our room's freezer before returning to the bed with that and two small glasses. "That you, Blair Page, are the strongest fucking human being I've ever had the good fortune to meet." He filled up both glasses half-way then handed me one. We both downed the contents in one gulp.

"Good fortune?" I wrapped my fingers around the empty glass, my hands shaking slightly as a shiver passed through my body. "Because of me you lost your boat and your dog."

"No, Blair. Grey did those things. And we'll make that scum-sucking-bucket-of-puss pay for everything he did to you, I promise you that. But you. *You* have done nothing but give me reason to live."

"Toby," I whispered, my eyes swimming. "Don't compliment me."

He took my glass and placed it with his on the bedside table before he sat on the bed next to me. "Why not? There's a hell of a lot to compliment."

"Because I can't handle people being nice to me. It's not normal. Men like you, *good* men, don't exist in my world."

"Men like me." He pressed his lips together and slid his knuckles along my cheekbone, so soft that I leaned into him like a purring cat. "I'm afraid your standards might not be very high, sunshine. I'm really not a good man."

"You are to me," I whispered, placing my hands on either side of his gorgeous face and urging him towards me. I wanted his mouth on mine, I wanted his body in me. I wanted him to take away the pain of my past and make my final days even more perfect than he already had. *If only we could be like this forever. Not just seven more days.*

He leaned in, his hot breath washing over my face before he paused at my lips. "Are you sure you want this, Blair?"

"I'm positive, Toby. Chase away the monsters in my mind. I need you."

CHAPTER NINETEEN
SUCH A BABY

WITH A SMIRK, I broke a tiny piece of toast off and threw it across the table. "What are you looking at?"

Toby watched the crouton-sized crumb bounce off his light blue T-shirt and land on the table, his eyes sparkled with mirth.

"Just you," he said, taking a mouthful of coffee. We were in the dining room of our hotel in Ceduna, fuelling up before hitting the road yet again. Most of the hotel was still sleeping except another couple sitting in the far corner, a family with two little kids, and the hotel staff.

"I'm not that interesting," I replied, dropping my eyes to my plate to hide my blush. I wasn't really the kind of girl to blush at anything, but Toby brought that out in me. I could feel myself blossoming around him—if that was even a real thing.

"To me you are. I've never met anyone quite like you."
There he goes again. My cheeks are on fire.

In response, I smiled and popped a bit of toast in my mouth, focusing on chewing so I didn't succumb to this gooey feeling that was developing inside me. Being with Toby had been an intense boot camp in feelings and vulnerability. I hadn't wanted to acknowledge or share any of the pain I carried inside, but a clock was ticking on our time together, forcing me to take risks I wouldn't normally take. *Unapologetically.* I wasn't a sharer, but with Toby, I wanted him to know everything about me—the good and the bad. Just like I wanted to know everything about him. To be honest, it felt a little crazy. Smiling this much wasn't natural. But happiness felt good on me, like a bold shade of lipstick I'd never had the courage to wear. I knew I'd only have it for the rest of our trip and in a way, I was OK with that. I didn't know if I was the full-blown relationship kind of girl, but this I could do. A shedding of old and uncomfortable skins. The gentle feeding of a shattered soul. My time with Toby would be one good memory I'd hold on to if by some twist of fate I survived my father.

My father.

Ugh.

I hated it when I thought of him that way. I tried to keep him catalogued under 'sperm donor'. It was easier, but recent events had forced that other F-word into my thoughts and vocabulary.

"Tell me it would be crazy to stay here indefinitely," I said, releasing a longing breath as I looked out the window, watching whitecaps dance away from the horizon. It would be a beautiful place to quit the rat race in. In another life, I could imagine myself staying in the beautiful coastal town, watching the sunsets and enjoying the idyllic scenery, Toby by my side.

Reaching across the table, he took my hand in his, his thumb moving over my knuckles. "I want to be selfish,

Blair. I want to disappear and leave them to figure this shit out for themselves. You and I…" He grated his teeth over his bottom lip as he gave his head a slow tension-filled shake. "We could be great together. I mean, look at us, travelling across the country, stifling heat, highway dirt and a lumpy bed. Those are shit conditions, but we're happy. We're smiling. Because it feels good to let go." He released my hand and sat back in his seat, grating his hand across this chin. "And I want to let go. It just…" He paused and met my eyes for a long moment. I knew a 'but' was coming, because I'd probably say the same thing in his shoes. "It isn't in my blood. I have to finish this. For you, for me, for my family, and every other human being that man has or will hurt. I don't feel like there's even a choice anymore."

Leaning on the table, I rested my head on my hand and pressed my lips together. "I understand. I also agree. But, a girl can dream, right?"

Sitting forwards, he took my hand again. "It's a good dream, sunshine. I wish I was the man who could give it to you."

I'm not a good man.

To me you are.

———

"TELL me the most embarrassing thing you ever did in front of a girl," I said as we walked from the hotel back to the camper van. Being early morning, the sun hadn't started cooking the bitumen yet. When we'd arrived the day before, it was sticking to the bottom of our runners and making funny tacky sounds as we walked.

"Besides getting drunk and kissing my brother's wife?" Toby shifted our duffle bags into one hand then slung them over his shoulder. All I was carrying was a handbag slung across my shoulders. Not that I wasn't willing to carry my own, he just grabbed it first. Another thing to add to the list of things Toby did for me. How this man wasn't happily married was beyond me. He was so damn charming that he could pluck any girl off the street and convince her to have his babies—criminal history or not. Women would *pay* to get a guy like Toby in their bed.

"Yeah, that's pretty fucking embarrassing. And recent too. Maybe go for something that doesn't have a sting attached to it. Something you can laugh at now."

"OK. Let me think on this for a second."

"You have to think? Ohhh, this is either going to be really good or you've always been so suave you don't have any embarrassing moments."

He chuckled. "I have plenty, believe me. I'm not suave in the slightest."

"And yet you have me. I'll have you know that I'm not easily caught, Mr Cartwright."

"I have you, huh? That's good to know." He bumped his arm against mine then caught my hand.

"See, that was a suave move."

With a laugh, he lifted our joined hands and nibbled lightly on the knuckle of my index finger.

"They call this deflecting, you know."

He nibbled a little more. "Actually, I'm pretty sure they call this thinking."

"Oh, come on." I pulled my hand from his and skipped ahead a little, turning to walk backwards so I could face him. "How can you not have anything? I can probably give you a list of thirty embarrassing moments right off the top of my head."

"Give me five," he said.

I held up a hand and counted off my fingers. "My tit fell out of my dress at a high school disco. My first actual boyfriend and I head-butted when we tried to kiss and I gave him a blood nose. I sneezed giving a blowjob once and bit the guy's dick—"

"OK, OK." He held his hand up to stop me talking, laughing while shaking his head. "I don't need to hear about you and other guys' dicks in your mouth."

I grinned. "Jealous?"

"Absolutely."

Reaching forwards with his free hand, he tried to catch me about the waist. But I dodged him and ran the last few metres to the camper van, laughing as he gave chase.

"Stop!" he yelled, the moment my hand reached for the door. The alarm in his voice caused me to freeze.

"Why?"

"Step away, Blair. Real slow."

Expecting there to be a brown snake or some equally dangerous reptile at my feet, I did as he instructed, my heart beating up a storm in my chest until I got close enough for him to grab me and pull me with him.

"What happened?" I gasped. "Why are we running?"

He led me until we were behind another camper, his back pressed against it like we were under enemy fire.

"Toby?"

"Someone's been in our van," he said, surveying the area with eagle eyes. He placed his arm across my middle to keep me well hidden while he poked his head out to see if anyone was watching. He was *protecting me*. Me. The woman who'd hunted him down and brought this rain of hell fire on him. The woman who could stand up and fight as well as any man. He was protecting *me*. I might have gone a little mushy inside.

"How can you tell?"

"The lock is bent and there's a piece of broken wire lying on the ground near the engine."

I tried to peek around him to see. "You've got a good eye." I could barely make out the wire let alone the bend in the lock. "Do you think Irish caught up to us already?" We should have had at least twenty-four hours before they made it here from Perth based on Nick's intel.

"Maybe. Or maybe it's nothing. Maybe the wire is from someone doing repairs and maybe some druggie was trying to break into all the camper vans last night looking to score."

"What do you want to do?"

He ran a hand through his hair, pushing it out of eyes. "Do you have a compact mirror in there?"

I dug into my bag and pulled one out, handing it to him.

"Thanks." He took it and jogged a few metres away, keeping a lookout as he went.

"What are you doing?" I hissed.

Bending down, he grabbed a stick and came back to me. "Give me your hair-tie."

Without questioning him further, I tugged it from my hair, my heat frazzled blonde locks tumbling to my shoulders in a mess.

"Ta." Bending on one knee, he wound the hair elastic around the mirror and the stick, creating a makeshift inspection mirror so he could look at our camper van's undercarriage without touching it.

"Clever," I said, and he winked.

"Keep an eye out for our explosive friend."

With a quick nod, I donned my work persona, shifting from the carefree girl I'd been over breakfast and back into the hard-headed woman who was constantly on guard. It felt like putting on dirty clothes after a refreshing shower, wrong and uncomfortable because it negated the point of getting clean.

In less than a minute, Toby returned throwing the stick on the ground and returning the mirror and elastic.

"And?" I asked anxiously.

"We need to get out of here."

"Noooo." My eyes went wide.

"Yes. That thing will blow sky high the moment the key turns. The guy doesn't deviate much from his MO." He pulled out the Blackberry and punched in a few numbers, holding it to his ear.

"What are you doing?"

"Calling it in."

"To the cops?" It connected, and he immediately explained where we were and that he'd seen someone attach a suspicious looking package to a van before disconnecting. I slapped him on the chest with the back of my hand. "Are you nuts? Cops are gonna swarm this place."

He tucked the phone away. "You want tourist jam on your conscience? We can't leave a live bomb in the parking lot. Too many innocent people."

"You're right. I just wish I knew how the hell Irish got here so fast?"

He knelt on the ground again, digging through his duffle. "I don't know, maybe they sped, maybe your friend's timeline was wrong and they left earlier. Maybe they got here in a bloody helicopter." He shrugged as he found a Swiss Army knife and a push button contraption. "Point is, they're here. And we need to go."

"If you need weapons, I have a taser, a tranq gun, and a handgun in my grab bag."

He lifted his brow and handed me his contraption. "We don't need weapons."

With a shrug, I turned the plastic box in my hand, indistinguishable as anything besides a remote of some sort. All that was on it was a switch and a button. "What am I supposed to do with this?"

"Find a car that isn't over ten years old. Flick the switch and hit the button while you hold the box next to the door. It'll unlock." He grabbed a weird-looking screw-driver from his bag then zipped the whole thing up. "Take your bag. I'll take mine."

"We're splitting up?"

"No. I'm getting some number plates. We've got a lot of road to cover and we can't be driving an easily identifi-able stolen car."

"Oh." I took the bag he handed me.

"Have a problem stealing?"

I opened my mouth. Besides some shoplifting as a teen, I hadn't done a hell of a lot. Ever since I'd started working, I'd been pretty flush with cash.

"It's a means to an end, Blair."

"I know. It's cool. I'm cool."

He smiled and stood up, grabbing my chin between two fingers before he leaned in and sucked gently on my lower lip. "Now hurry before the cops get here and people start gathering around."

After about five minutes, we were on the road in a Holden Ute that was so covered in red dirt I wasn't even sure what colour it was. It seemed like it was a rusty colour, but it also could have been white. It was that filthy.

"This cab stinks," Toby said, adjusting the seat until he found a comfortable position. He grimaced and came up with an old sock. "Animals." He threw it out the window and it tumbled along the highway.

"Looks like some guy's work Ute. Maybe he was out roo hunting in his free time?"

"It reeks. One of my brothers owns a Ute just like this. The twins use it for their lawn mowing business."

"Why do they have a lawn mowing business?" That sounded like a lot of hard labour when they were raised as thieves and could get their hands on easy money.

"It's complicated. They do some jobs to appear legit then we launder extra money through it. We have a bunch of different businesses that all feed into each other."

"You're right. That does sound complicated."

He shrugged a shoulder and hit the buttons to wind down the back windows. "Anyway, they spend long days in that thing sweating up a storm, stinking of grass, smoking, and whatever else. Even that Ute doesn't stink like this. I can't deal. Why did you choose this?"

Grimacing a little, I shrugged. "It was the one most hidden from view."

He scrunched his face up like he might puke and held his hand to his face. "I can't." Turning the wheel, he pulled into the first rest stop we came across and jumped out of the car, coughing and gasping like he'd just had his nose pressed up against Satan's bowels.

"You're a baby." I laughed, pulling open the back doors before taking bits of rubbish out. The car stank, that was true. But not that terribly. I guess Toby just had a sensitive nose. "Whoever owned this is an animal," I said, removing package after package of old food containers. Partially eaten burgers, chicken bones, and all manners of junk and packaging. There were also a couple of coke bottles with dubiously yellow contents that I held away from me as though they might explode. "This is gross."

Pulling his deodorant out of his bag, Toby sprayed it throughout the cabin then left the doors open while it settled. "I can still smell it. It's like rancid meat."

"Well, they did have chicken bones in there."

"Yeah." He sniffed the air. "I don't know. I think—" Stopping mid-sentence, he walked to the back of the Ute and popped the cover on the tray. Flies swarmed into the surrounding air, looking like static on a TV screen, followed by the stench of a thousand rancid farts.

"I'm gonna puke." I immediately jumped back, covering my mouth at the sight of a bloated carcass of a kangaroo, rotting in the back. "What is wrong with people?"

"Who the fuck knows," he muttered, covering his face with the neck of his shirt as he dragged the carcass onto the ground with a thud. The moment it hit, maggots came spilling out.

I screamed.

As far as the human experience goes, I've been through hell and back again. Not once, during all the crap that had happened to my person did I scream. But seeing those wriggling white things spill out of that roo was where my ability to cope ended.

"Get it away. Get it away. *Get it away!"* I bounced on the spot and shook my hands as he dragged the poor animal off to the side of the rest area. We'd seen a lot of kangaroo carcasses on our trek across the Nullarbor, they jumped in front of cars and trucks at night and ended up as roadkill, but this was our first one up close and personal.

"You're such a baby." Toby laughed, leaning down and washing his hands under a tap.

"I am not a baby. That was disgusting, and you know it." We'd switched roles so quickly. One minute I was laughing at him and cleaning out the car, while the next he was laughing at me and cleaning out the tray. At least we balanced each other out.

"Looks like our friend was a bit of a hunter." Toby pointed to the ute's tray where a long and narrow zip case sat.

"Rifle," I said, knowing the type of case by sight. "It might come in handy."

Nodding, Toby pulled the cover back over the tray to hide the gun from view. "We'll take it with us when we switch cars at the next stop. I reckon we drive straight through now. We can't afford to pause anymore."

"I know," I said, fighting tears as I helped secure the elastic rope to hook the ute's cover in place. This new development really sucked. I'd literally *just* opened up to Toby. In doing that, I'd woken up feeling unburdened, fresh to face a new day filled with these new emotions I'd developed towards Toby. I'd wanted to laugh with him and hold his hand. I'd wanted to kiss him in the open and lick him behind closed doors. I'd wanted to cram so much *freaking joy into seven small days,* and now… Now, I'd been robbed. The joy was gone. Just when I'd found it. Fucking typical. I hated my life. Hated this world even more.

All I needed was another seven tiny days.

"Hey," Toby said, reaching for me once the cover was secure.

I shook my head and shied away. "Let's just go, OK?" I knew he understood what was going on in my head. He had this uncanny ability to read me. But I couldn't handle that right now. I didn't want him to hold me, to kiss me, to tell me it would be OK. I didn't want any of that, because I knew it was a lie. We'd been found too soon and now this was over. *We* were over.

And it fucking sucked.

CHAPTER TWENTY

YOURS

A LITTLE LESS THAN sixteen hours later, we pulled into the underground car park of an apartment building in Anglesea; about twenty minutes out of Torquay. We'd switched cars *five* times, this last being an emerald green Nissan Patrol with two hundred and eighty thousand on the clock. We paid eight grand in cash for it and drove away without having to worry about being pulled over anymore. I actually slept for that final six hours.

Toby, however, drove the entire time, a grim determination on his face as he gripped the wheel. All the happiness and spark I'd come to expect from him was dimming the closer we got to his home. He still had his intensity, but it felt like that's all there was left of the man I'd grown to care for. All I wanted to do was turn around and go back to Madura, the last place we'd been happy. I'd give anything to feel that way again, to press pause on everything around us.

"I thought you lived in Torquay?" I said as we got out of the car and collected our things.

His jaw tightened and he shook his head slightly. "My family lives in Torquay. This place is mine."

"You aren't worried it's being watched?"

"No one knows I own it. The whole complex is run by a dummy corporation."

I looked at the concrete above us. "The *whole* complex?"

He nodded. "I rent most of them out and keep one empty for myself. I divided my time between here, the boat and my mother's house."

"And they seriously have no idea that this is yours?"

Keying a code into the pad next to the basement door, he shook his head. "I needed something that was just mine. Somewhere I could find a little peace without any of them dropping in on me." He pushed the door open and waited for me to walk through.

"Where did they think you were when they couldn't find you?"

He shrugged. "I told them it was none of their business."

"So many secrets between you all."

"Too many," he said, a tinge of sadness in his otherwise gruff voice. He was changing. I could see that. His proximity to his family having a profound effect on the way he held himself, the way he spoke, even the way he looked at me. Dread rolled off his body as he donned his old skin, the one we'd shed together. I could see my Toby slipping further and further away.

My Toby...

"Top floor," he said, leaning across me to touch the penthouse button on the elevator.

"Fancy."

"Hmm."

The lift moved and I tightened my grip around the leather handle of my bag, breathing slow while I did my best to accept our return to reality. I needed to put my old skin back on too. Problem was, I didn't want to. The idea repulsed me. But what choice did I have? We were there. At that place where shit got real.

"I fell over and bit my tongue," he announced, cutting through the stagnant silence.

"What?" I turned my head to look up at him.

"The most embarrassing thing I ever did in front of a girl I liked." He met my gaze, a small grin curving his mouth, his eyes glittering just a touch amid the storminess. "I was showing off on the beach and I tripped, my tooth went straight through my tongue and I spoke with a horrible lisp for a week."

My heart swelled. *He remembers.* Maybe he wanted to go back to that moment too. Before we were robbed of time. "Did you end up getting the girl?"

He shook his head. "She went out with Nate instead."

"Ouch."

The elevator stopped, doors sliding open. "After you," he said, gesturing with his hand.

There was one apartment door on this level, as well as a glass door heading out to what looked like a rooftop entertaining area. Toby entered a key code in the pad next to the main door then held his thumb against the tiny screen. The door clicked open.

"Very fancy."

"I don't like unwanted visitors," he said, ushering me inside what was probably the most beautiful apartment I'd ever been in. It looked like something out of a movie. The kind of apartment a high level executive would have, with sleek modern furniture, marble countertops, automatic tinted windows, and climate control. Black, white, grey and chrome dominated the colour palette with a little blue and yellow splashed here and there. I was…dazzled. But it didn't feel like Toby. Well, not the Toby I knew anyway.

"This is…" I ran my hand along kitchen counter, looking around the open living area as I searched for the right word. "Sleek."

"Hungry?" he asked as he moved to stand in front of me, taking my handbag from my shoulder and setting it on a barstool.

"Not particularly," I said, looking into his eyes and searching for the man I was missing. I saw hunger and I saw loss with just a shimmer of light. Just a shimmer. *Don't leave me.*

He ran his hand through the side of my hair, brushing it behind my right ear. "Thirsty?"

I shook my head. "No."

Then his fingers curled around the back of my neck before his mouth covered mine, taking me hard, his tongue colliding with mine possessively. Moaning, I practically collapsed against him, hands grabbing fistfuls of his shirt as his other hand reached between us and unbuttoned my jeans.

With his fingers poised at the waist of my panties, he tore his mouth from mine and stared down at me, his eyes filled with a mix of anger and desire. I couldn't help wonder if they were both directed at me, or if they were a reflection of what we needed to do.

"I don't think I have ever wanted a woman more than I want you," he said, slipping his fingers beneath the lace of my panties, dragging the middle digit across my clit before sinking two of them inside me. I moaned and pulled harder on his shirt. I didn't think I'd ever wanted a man as much as I wanted him either.

Holding me tight against him, he stroked me until my legs quivered and I whimpered, desperate for relief.

"Do you think this makes us weak?" he asked, quickening his movement as I rocked my hips against him, spiralling towards my release. He dropped his lips to my neck and spoke with his teeth against my skin. "Needing another person so desperately?" Then he ran his tongue along my pulse point before he closed his mouth and sucked hard, pressing his teeth into the delicate flesh to mark me with his madness. *He needs me too.*

As a sharp pain pierced my skin, my body gave in to his. I cried out and shook against him, wrapping my arms around his neck and grabbing handfuls of his hair, pulling him closer as I gasped. "We aren't weak, Toby."

He lifted his head as he withdrew his hand from my insides, catching the hem of my black singlet and pulling it over my head. "I feel weak," he said, palming my breasts through the lace cups of my bra, his head bowing to worship my cleavage. He moaned as his fingers found my nipples and twisted them into stiff peaks. "I don't want to give this up."

I arched into him as he unclasped my bra and slid it from my body. "Then don't," I whispered, just as he pulled his shirt from his torso and gathered me against him, his mouth devouring mine as he walked me to the bedroom and held me tight, lowering me to the bed.

He kissed me until I was gasping for air, lips bruised,

skin alive with desire. "You are mine, Blair Page. Do you understand that?"

I nodded, touching him everywhere I could as he sat back and pulled my remaining clothes down my legs and shucked the rest of his.

Climbing back on top of me, he leaned down and sucked my left nipple into his mouth, releasing it with a pop then settling the tip of his big cock at my entrance without pushing in. I almost cried from the aching need. "I need to hear you say it," he said, his eyes holding mine, desperate.

"Yes, Toby," I gasped, moving my hips towards him. "I'm yours."

He still didn't push in. "That means you do as I say."

"Yes."

"It means you let me protect you."

Now *I* was getting desperate. "Yes."

"OK," he said, leaving me whimpering for one more beat before he pushed inside, giving me exactly what I wanted. No, what I *needed.*

I was his.

That's what I just agreed to. To be honest, I wasn't exactly sure what being his meant, but as long as it meant we would find a way to keep doing exactly this, I was pretty much willing to do whatever he wanted.

"Oh yes," I moaned as he thrust inside me, in and out, slow and fast. I exploded more times than I could count, taking everything I could from his body with blissful greed as we altered our positions and lost ourselves in carnal worship. I never wanted to stop fucking him.

When we were both finally spent, we lay in a tangled heap on the bed, the sheets and blankets twisted on the floor. I was so tired I could barely move, barely think. We'd had sex with feelings and I hadn't even freaked out. I'd simply enjoyed him, wanted him, revelled in the fact that a man such as him wanted a woman such as me. He *wanted* me. I was his. He was mine. And somehow—*somehow*—we were going to find a way to make this work. To have more than seven days, more than a moment of being unapologetically ourselves, unapologetically together. In my entire life I'd never felt that I belonged to anyone. Now that I did, I was going to protect that connection with everything I had. I couldn't let him go.

CHAPTER TWENTY-ONE
I'LL HOLD YOUR HAND

DARKNESS ENVELOPED me from all sides as the cold whispered across my skin. My confused mind tried to count the visits and the sporadic meals, trying to figure out how long I'd been there. I had no clue.

My breath caught as I heard a shuffle, the creaking of a door handle then finally a sliver of light that spilled into the room, causing me to hold my hand up to protect my eyes from the harshness. "I hear you're not fighting anymore," the monster said...

No. Don't.

Forcing my eyes open, I swallowed hard, looking around the bright and airy room inside Toby's apartment. It was too much to hope that my nightmares would be over the moment I talked about them, but at least it had ended before anyone touched me. That was progress.

Letting out my breath, I snuggled under the thick doona and rolled to my side, expecting to find a warm body still sleeping beside me. Instead, I found a note lying in the depression in Toby's pillow with the words, *Had*

*some errands to run (no food in the house) won't be long.
T.* Pushing up on my elbows, I ran a fingertip over Toby's
neat handwriting. I loved that each letter looked carefully
formed, not one messy loop or hurried line. He'd been
precise and sure, exactly the way he was in almost all of
his actions.

Folding the note in half, I rolled onto my back and held
it against my chest, watching the thin curtains billow softly
in the morning breeze. My mind drifted back to last night
and the pained look in Toby's eyes before he'd kissed me,
the words he'd spoken, the emotion I'd taken from him.
He was just as frightened of what was happening between
us as I was, he'd even called it a weakness. And I suppose
it was, there had been more than a few moments where I'd
wanted us to turn around and run the other way, continue
being together instead of facing our problems head on.
Unfortunately, being an adversary of my father didn't work
that way. If he wanted you gone, he moved heaven and
earth to make sure it happened. There would be nowhere
we were safe, not until Grey and his entire operation where
taken down once and for all.

We didn't have a choice.

With a heart that felt full and heavy, I hefted myself out
of bed. I was pretty much out of clean clothes, so I grabbed
an undershirt from Toby's neat drawers and dragged my
feet into the bathroom. The rainwater shower pure bliss
against my weather effected skin, my aching muscles
sighing happily after our long hours on the road, working
in the harsh Aussie sun. I had a tan about ten times darker
than any I'd paid for in a salon, and my hair desperately
needed a treatment, my nails in dire need of a manicure,
but I didn't care. I felt more like me than I ever had before,

and I was relishing in this newfound peace, thankful for the man who'd led me there.

"Toby?" I called out when I shut off the water and thought I heard a voice. It was a little far away, so I wasn't sure if it was in the apartment or possibly from outside. Drying off, I slipped the clean shirt over my head and followed the sound, spotting bags of groceries and clothes on the counter. *Clothes?*

I peeked inside a stiff paper bag that had black ribbons for handles and pushed the tissue aside, finding a dress that was flirty and feminine and just my size. In another bag, I found sandals to match.

He bought me clothes? I held the dress up, swirls of coral and blue covering the soft fabric. It was beautiful, empire cut, down to my knees. Toby had great taste.

"I'm really happy for you, brother." I put the dress down and turned towards the sound.

"What the?" If I hadn't known the sound of Toby's voice like I knew my own, I might have startled and pulled the revolver from my duffle bag, training it on the man I found standing on the balcony with a phone pressed to his ear. With his back to me, he was almost unrecognisable. All business: tailored navy pants, a mauve button up shirt with the sleeves rolled to the elbows, shiny black shoes. And the clothes weren't all, he'd had a haircut. The too long hair I'd grown used to running my fingers through was now neatly trimmed and styled: a little longer on top, shaved close at the sides. There was no way it would fall into his face now. *His face*. When he turned a little, it was clean shaven, smooth as a baby's bottom. When he heard me open the sliding door, he faced me fully.

For a moment, I didn't move. Startled by the clean-cut look, a little untrusting of this new man before me. Then he smiled. The same heart-stopping grin that reached his always hungry eyes as they took in my oversized T-shirt look. *My Toby.* He held out his hand and gestured for me to come closer. My heart flitted in my chest, and I rushed to him.

"Tonight is fine," he said into the phone as he pulled me close. I'd landed against his hard chest, a woodsy cologne filling my nostrils and delighting my senses. "I think it's best that the whole family is there. Brothers only looks like a meeting." With his eyes locked on mine, he ran his free hand down the fabric of the T-shirt until he reached the hem and slid his hand underneath, fingers connecting with my bare backside. His eyebrows lifted in approval. "If that's necessary. I need you all to bring me up to speed…"

Gesturing to the small glass outdoor table, he indicated that he wanted me to sit there. "Perhaps. Not for good." After I did as he wanted, he took a seat in front of me then guided my legs so my feet rested on his thighs, knees apart so he could see right between my legs. He met my eyes then licked his lips. I reached out and touched his stubble-free jaw. He kissed my palm. "I'll fill you in when I see you. But it can't be left any longer. We need to finish what we started."

Lifting his free hand, he trailed the tips of his fingers through the centre of my folds, closing his eyes for a split second as he connected with my wetness then pushed inside. I gasped and widened my thighs, allowing him better access to push deeper.

"She shouldn't have interfered. I'd have come back on my own when I was ready."

Using his thumb against my clit, he pumped his fingers in and out, the zipper of his pants straining against his growing cock. I opened my mouth as my climax drew nearer, swallowing my moan into silence as he continued his conversation.

"That's bullshit. She always interferes. She can't help herself."

He picked up speed, curling his fingers up into my G-spot and stroking me in his expert way. My orgasm hit all at once, and I had to press my lips hard, biting into them to stop the sound from coming out. He stood and unbuckled his belt, quickly working the button and zip on his pants.

"We'll finish this tonight," he said, seeming to cut into whatever the brother on the other end of the line was saying before he disconnected and tossed the phone on the table beside me. "I have something far more important to do." With a grin, he freed his cock and plunged into me, one hand gripping my hip as the other slid into my damp hair before he completely engulfed me with his hungry mouth.

Hips thrusting in time with his tongue, he fucked me out in the open, his new look doing nothing to change the way he felt during our connection. *Thank god that hasn't changed.*

"Good morning," he said with a pant and a smile when we finished, slowly pulling out of me and tucking himself away, moving back to sit while he watched the semen spill out of me.

I smiled and placed the balls of my feet on his knees, letting him enjoy the view. "I thought you didn't like theatrics."

"I have no desire to shoot cum in your face or on your

chest. But watching me pour from inside you?" He released a grunt, an animal sound telling me it turned him on to no end.

"What's with the new look?" I reached out and touched his smooth face before sliding my fingers through his neat hair.

"It's an old look."

"The old mask." I remembered this look from the file photos Big Jim had sent me to find him. It made sense now. This was the man he needed to be to get the job done. A uniform of sorts.

"An uncomfortable mask," he admitted, taking my hand and kissing the palm. "One I hope I won't be wearing long."

"I don't know if I can put mine back on," I whispered. I liked the woman I had become with him. I wasn't ready to switch off my emotions and become that badarse I always was. This woman felt more right than any of the guises I'd donned in my years as a PI. I felt sick over the idea of locking her up to return to that ruthless version of myself.

"Then don't. Let me take care of you. Wait there. I'll get something to clean you up," he said, standing before disappearing into the apartment, returning with a warm cloth which he used to carefully wipe himself away. So soft. So gentle. I couldn't help but smile while my heart swelled. *I like him taking care of me.*

"If I was ever to love someone, Toby. I think that someone would be you," I blurted, surprising even myself with the admission.

Lifting his eyes from his cleaning, he studied mine for a moment, possibly searching for the truth in my statement. Upon seeing it, he stood and took my head in his hands, his thumbs moving against my cheekbones. "Love yourself first," he said, then he kissed me softly while my mind whirled. Love myself first? Isn't that what I'd been doing for most of my life? Being selfish and keeping everyone else at bay? I didn't understand.

Actually, I did understand. He wanted me to get my head straight, to quit drinking, to quit using sex as a bandaid to my mental anguish. *Love myself first? I don't know if I can do that....*

"Was that your brother on the phone?" I asked, changing the subject when he pulled away and I pressed my knees back together.

"Nate. Yes. There's a family dinner on tonight. We can find out what's been going on in my absence and why the hell Jasmine hired a private investigator to find me."

"A family dinner. That's why you bought me a dress?" I shifted uncomfortably where I sat, the idea of meeting his family setting off butterflies.

"Yes," he said. "I saw it and thought of you. I hope that's OK?"

"It's perfect," I said. "But a family dinner? I don't know…"

"You'll be perfect. It's just siting down, eating food and discussing things. All things you're amazing at. You'll get to meet my sister-in-laws. They all have kids now, Nate says his is almost walking."

"What?" I was getting confused. "I thought we were going there to talk about what we're going to do about Grey. Not have a family reunion with a bunch of screaming babies."

"You don't like kids?"

"I think they're fine. From far away. I'm not maternal by any stretch of the word."

Toby smiled.

"Why is that funny?"

"It's not funny. I just think you're gorgeous. And you'll be fine. Ignore everything that comes out of my mother's mouth, but feel free to talk all you want with everyone else. They're great, actually."

"Even Nate?"

He sighed and placed his hands on my thighs, moving them up and down. "Nate and I have a complicated relationship. We clash, but he's still my brother. That means more than all the other shit that's gone down."

"OK. I'll reserve my judgement then."

"Pissed on my behalf?" He grinned, amused.

"A little. I feel like they use you to run their businesses and do their dirty work while they run off having relationships and babies, reaping the rewards of the work *my man* put in."

"My man? She's protective."

"Of course I am. Just like you said that I'm yours, I consider you mine too. I will fight for you. I will stand by you. And I don't care who it's against. My loyalty is to you and you only. Everyone else will need to earn it, whether they're your family or not." Loyalty was one quality I'd always placed a huge emphasis on. It's why I'd worked the same job for Big Jim all those years. I did right by him. He did right by me. That was how it worked. It normally took years to build that kind of trust, my early loyalty to Toby was an exception where my heart overruled my head. No one else would slide by so easy, especially not after causing my beautiful man such pain. No.

The rest of the Cartwrights needed to earn a place at *my* table.

"She may be small, but she is fierce."

"Stop teasing." I tapped him on his chest. "And I'm not even a little bit small."

He gathered me in his arms until I was standing in front of him on my tip-toes. "To me you are."

"Everyone is small compared to you."

"Believe it or not, I'm the smallest in my family."

"Bullshit."

"I kid you not. I'm the runt. The tallest is Sam at six-four. Then Nate, Kris and Abbot are all around six-three, and I'm six-two."

"That's crazy to me. You're giants. How tall is your mum?"

"Six-one, I think."

"And your dad?"

He shrugged. "When I was a kid, I thought he was the biggest man in the world. But I haven't seen him since he went to prison. He was taller than Jasmine though."

"Jasmine. You don't call her mum?"

He shook his head. "Never."

"Because she was never like a mum or for professional reasons?"

"Professional reasons."

"What am I walking into tonight? I mean, I get that there will be four brothers, their wives and their kids—are there four babies too?"

"There are."

"That's really weird. Did they all get pregnant together?"

"Practically."

"That's super weird. Did they plan it that way?"

"No." He laughed. "It was a happy accident."

"That's so fucking weird."

"If you think that's weird, wait until dinner. It gets weirder."

Placing my hands on either side of his face, I stared deeply into his eyes. "You seem way too calm. Are you quietly freaking out about going back there?" His eyes flashed, and I knew that he was. "I'll hold your hand the whole time," I whispered.

Resting his forehead against mine, he let out a sigh. "That makes me feel better already."

CHAPTER TWENTY-TWO
THAT BIKER COULD REALLY BAKE

"TOBY! OH MY GOD!" A tall dark-haired woman came tearing out of a large white-brick house and jumped at him, causing him to drop my hand to catch her. I didn't know who she was, but I already had a problem with her. The rest of the family came filing out behind her, brothers, wives and babies. They all stood in an overwhelmingly massive group.

I was glad that the house was on a secluded block of land. The only way to see us all would be to enter the actual property or use a drone. Even though we were in the open, I felt quite safe here.

"Hey Leesh," Toby said, patting her a few times on the back as he set her down on the gravel driveway. "It's nice to see you too."

With wide saucer eyes, she turned to me. "Who is this?"

Toby reached for my hand again. "This is Blair," he said, prompting a few raised eyebrows and weighted looks. I took it that it was unusual for Toby to bring a woman to the family home, but the fact I was here seemed to delight his mother who was grinning broadly as she made her way to the front of the group.

"I *knew* you'd come back eventually," she said, tears in her eyes as she reached both hands up to cup either side of his face. She was tall as I'd expected, almost waif-like in her build and ballerina-like in her movements. She had dark blonde hair with streaks of grey, sharp blue eyes, and a complexion so clear I was sure she looked younger than me. She was stunning in a pair of dark pants and a white blouse, jewels about her wrist, but nothing anywhere else. *Classy.* Something I—even though I'd stepped out of a BMW sedan in a fancy new dress—was not.

"Blair," Toby said, his voice careful. "I'd like you to meet Jasmine, my mother."

With bright and happy eyes, she turned my way and clasped one of my hands in both of hers. "Blair," she said, testing my name as though she'd never heard it before. "It's wonderful to meet you."

"Likewise?" I said, the word sounding like a question. *Why was she acting like she didn't know who I was? Didn't she hire me?*

She placed a gentle hand on my shoulder and turned so she was standing beside me, *between* Toby and me. "Let me introduce you to the rest of the family, Blair. This is Nathanial, his wife, Holland and their son, Daniel." She indicated a man who was a harsh-looking version of Toby, taller with the same dark hair, darker blue eyes, and a slightly bigger build. He stood next to a short stocky woman with long bleached hair and interesting honey-coloured eyes. She held a wriggly boy who pulled fistfuls of her hair and giggled while he said, "Mum, Mum!"

"Hi," I said, shaking their hands for a short moment before they embraced Toby and welcomed him home. Our greetings were a stark contrast to each other but expected. It seemed the prodigal son had returned to the fold. I wondered if Nate was truly happy for that.

"This is Samuel and you've already met Alesha. This is their baby boy, Jake." Jasmine touched the baby's head cradled in his father's arm. "He is the youngest grandbaby. Only four months." She smiled again as I shook Sam's hand. He was by far the biggest of the bunch, his hair slightly lighter and longer than the older two. It was uncanny how similar looking they all were. Sam's face was familiar to look at yet different at the same time, almost boyish compared to his older brother's. Once he'd greeted me, he reached a long arm out to hug his big brother. He said a few quiet words, to which Toby nodded, then he stepped and back nuzzled his wife in her dark hair, Alesha still had tears in her eyes. She obviously cared a great deal for my man. By the way she'd greeted him, I had to wonder how much. Jumping on him in front of me like that felt like staking a claim.

Jasmine continued along. "This is Abbott and Sloane. They have our only little girl, Willow, who's a whole week older than Jake. We expect they'll be great friends," she said, introducing me to a red-headed woman who was rake thin and over six-foot tall. She was standing next to yet another Toby clone with messy surfer hair and a cheeky grin that told me he had mischief in his heart.

"Big bro," Abbot said, clapping hands with Toby before bringing him in for a hug. "You haven't changed."

"Good to see you upright and breathing."

Abbot shrugged. "Took a bit, but I'm fighting fit. Just

another scar to add to the collection. I've missed you, man. Real bad."

"Thanks," Toby said, clapping him gently on the arm. "How's my favourite smithy?" He directed that to Sloane who was cradling a dark-haired baby girl who looked like a sleeping doll.

"Busy on mum duties these days. Things are pretty different around here now. We missed you, buddy." She leaned in and whispered something near his ear I couldn't catch.

Toby responded with, "I know."

"And this"—Jasmine pulled on my arm as she gestured to the final son, obviously Abbott's twin with a cropped haircut—"is Kristian, my baby, and Veronica with *their* baby, Oscar. They all got the Cartwright good looks don't you think?"

"They sure did," I responded, feeling fairly sure she was talking about the grandbabies, but also agreeing in case she was talking about her sons. They were all so ridiculously identical that it surprised me they lived a life of crime for so long without being noticed. I mean, they were huge, they were gorgeous. How were people not staring?

"It's great to meet you, Blair," Kristian said, taking my hand. "You can call me Kris, and my Mrs prefers Ronnie." His smile was easy, carefree, the kind of smile Toby had exhibited when I first met him. It only served to show me how much of the burden Toby had been taking from the family compared to his younger brothers. That needed to change. Toby needed to have an easy smile too.

"Nice to meet you both," I said, looking to Ronnie and taking in her small frame, sun-kissed skin and naturally blonde-curly hair. I remembered her as the girl who had ties with Grey's operation. "Congratulations to you all on your children. They're lovely."

"You think?" Holland grimaced as her boy squealed and leaned back, using her hair like a set of reigns. Nate laughed and rescued his wife, taking Daniel from Holland and blowing a raspberry in his neck. Daniel squealed in delight. "I suppose they're OK," she added, love in her eyes as she tousled the hair of her little man now that he wasn't hanging off hers.

"Shall we go inside?" Jasmine asked. "Breaker is in there cooking up a storm. Just wait until you taste the dessert he made, Blair. Baked Alaska with homemade ice cream in the centre. If you have a sweet tooth, you will just die for it."

"You have a cook called Breaker?" I turned to Toby, my mind reeling from the mass of introductions. He was giving Kris's arm a squeeze and telling him they'd talk more inside.

Slipping his arm around my waist, Toby pulled me to his side then touched his nose to the top of my head, inhaling deeply. "That's better," he said before pulling back and walking me to the front door, following the rest of the family. "Breaker belongs to the Grim Order. Jasmine is his ole lady. I think I told you a little about him."

"Oh yes. I think the whole baked Alaska thing really threw me."

Toby grinned. "He's rough as guts, but get an apron on that man and he'll bake the best damn cake you've ever tasted."

"How weird."

"So you keep saying."

Dinner was a mix of chaos and conversation with babies getting passed around while they bombarded Toby and me with questions. I didn't get to say much more than who I was and where I was from because the focus was primarily on where Toby had been all this time and whether he was back for good or just a visit. Jasmine made it clear she thought he should be back for good now that he was 'obviously settled' and I sat there trying to take it all in without going too crazy trying to keep track of things.

"I'm back for as long as it takes," Toby stated with a tense jaw. "I've had a long time to think, and I have to be honest, I'm not comfortable coming back to pick up where I left off, and there's nothing any of you can do to change my mind about that." His eyes landed on his mother, and I noticed the biker boyfriend straighten up a little and slide his arm around the back of her chair defensively. I had done little more than say 'hello' to the man when I'd first entered the house. He was a quintessential biker—tattoos, long hair, and beard. He didn't say much. That may have been because he wasn't sure of me, or it could have been that he was the strong silent type. I hadn't worked that out yet.

"But you're here with a woman," Jasmine replied, her expression even. "You know what that means in this family. Why would you bring her if it wasn't to stay?" *Wait. What?*

"Truth be told, mother," Toby said, adjusting slightly in his seat. "She's the one who brought me. You hired a private investigator to find me and bring me back. You owe her money."

"I did what now?" Jasmine pulled her head back in surprise.

"Hired Blair to find me. Good choice by the way, you haven't lost your touch."

I'm lost.

Jasmine laughed as she leaned back in her chair and toyed with her cutlery. "You're mistaken, son. This"—her eyes swung to me—"wasn't my doing."

"Stop," I said, holding up my hand because I needed some sort of clarification here. The entire table had gone quiet to listen in as Jasmine and Toby lobbied their cryptic words back and forth. I hoped they understood all this because I had no fucking idea what it meant to bring a woman to the Cartwright table, or what kind of 'touch' Jasmine was supposed to have. Those questions would have to wait until later when Toby and I were alone. For now, the important question was, "Are you saying you *didn't* hire me?"

Jasmine nodded once. "That's precisely what I'm saying. As with all of my boys, I want them close, but I won't force them to be here. Toby could choose when he came home. Are *you* telling me coming back wasn't his choice?"

"I was hired by someone—I was told it was you—to find him and bring him back."

Everyone around the table exchanged looks, including Toby and myself. *Oh shit.*

"Come on, Jasmine," Toby said. "This has you written all over it. A beautiful woman, who just happens to be perfectly compatible with me, tracks me down to one of the farthest corners of the country. That's exactly the kind of thing you would do."

"I swear on the lives of everyone at this table, it wasn't me," Jasmine insisted. *No, no, no.*

"Must've been Grey," Breaker spoke up, his voice like gravel as he pushed his fork into the last potato on his plate. "Explains why they were so quick to blow up ya boat. They were followin' this one." He pointed at me with his fork. *I need to be sick. I've been played.*

"Makes sense," Nate said. "We were all in agreement to leave you be."

Abbot nodded. "Word was, Grey wanted your head for the Nagambie killings and that couple you executed before you hit the road."

Breaker narrowed his eyes at me as he chewed his food, speaking as soon as he swallowed. "What I don't get is if this here's the Black Widow, why the fuck is Grey usin' a fake mother story to hire you? You go after crooks in hiding all the time, no questions asked—am I right?"

"Yeah, you're right," I confirmed, my mouth twisted downwards as I pieced my role in this together. "But Grey wouldn't hire me directly. He and I have…history. He knows I'd never take a job from him. So, yeah. The fake mother story makes sense." *Fuck.* I met eyes with Nate and he nodded once before I turned my attention to Toby. "We probably should have figured that out. It was all too coincidental. I should have fucking *known*…" I shook my head, feeling even worse for messing up his happy life while regretting my 'no questions asked' policy. Had I looked close enough, I would have seen a discrepancy. Did Big Jim know about this? Or was he played too?

"Hey. It's OK," Toby said in a whisper, his hand squeezing my leg. "You didn't know."

"He played me. Us," I gasped, my blood pounding in my ears as reality hit. Grey had orchestrated this whole thing. He'd een watching me all this time. He'd used me to get to Toby. Did he want me dead too? Kill two birds with one stone? My god. We were targets, and I'd brought him here, to his family, around babies. "Holy fuck, Toby. This could all be some massive trap."

Murmurs went around the table.

"Hey," Toby said, touching my face so I looked his way. "We're gonna get the bastard."

I nodded, my chest tight as my head swam. How could I be so fucking blind?

"This place is Fort Knox," Breaker put in, reassuring everyone.

"What I wanna know," Kristian said, stretching his arm around Ronnie's shoulders while she rocked their baby to sleep in his pram. "Is are you gonna go all John Wick on Grey's arse for killing your dog. Cause not only does he deserve it, but I kinda wanna see that."

"That's the plan," Toby said with a nod. "I came back here to finish what I started before I left. I'd hoped that with the backing of Breaker's guys you could get rid of Grey without me, but with the cops watching too, I get that you've needed to lie low. However, this needs to stop. You guys have kids now, we can't risk sitting on our arses and doing nothing. Who knows when Grey will send his psycho bomber after one of you? This has to end. You know it does. Just like we all know that I have to be the man to do it."

"The man *is* majestic," Abbot said, his eyebrows raised, impressed. "After I got hit, he walked straight through the middle of a sea of men. Took them all out one by one like he was in the middle of an action movie. It was epic-level shit."

"You were delirious," Toby countered. "Loss of blood and oxygen can do that."

"I know what I saw, brother. Just like we all know we'd be dead if it wasn't for you."

"Well," Toby said with an intake of breath. "That's exactly what we will be if we don't sort this out. But, unlike in Abbot's story, I can't do this on my own. I'll need everyone's help if we're going to plan this out and stand a chance of walking back out of there. It has to be perfect."

Breaker nodded. "You have the MC's full support."

"I appreciate that, man. Thanks."

"You have all of ours too," Sam said while Alesha nodded. "We've got a hell of a lot to lose, and I'll be fucked if I'm letting that cunt anywhere near my family."

Murmurs went around the table as the rest of the family offered their services, anything we needed they all said. They wanted the threat of Grey over and done with too.

"Can I just say," Holland piped up. "That I think it's so very brave what you're all doing. But, I think my personal strength will be best used staying behind and taking care of the babies. While I've always liked to think of myself as the Belle in this story, I don't mind playing the part of the woman with all the children shrieking about five eggs for a day or two. It's for a worthy cause." She gave a small smile to the rest of the table, most of them nodded in understanding and told her they thought that was a good idea. I, on the other hand, had no fucking clue what she was talking about. Who the hell was Belle and what did five eggs have to do with any of it? By the time dessert rolled around, I was completely lost and sick from the idea that my father had been plotting my death all along.

Dessert was, however, absolutely delicious. Even in my frazzled mind, I couldn't help but moan with pleasure from the taste. That biker could *really* bake.

"BABABA." Sticky hands grabbed at the hem of my dress as I sat on a white leather coach in the grand house's living area, trying not to scream.

"I really think he'll be walking soon," Holland said to the others, who nodded and watched the little boy pulling on my dress without doing anything to stop him.

"Ma da ba."

He looked up at me with the same honey eyes as his mother and drool running down his chin. *Oh god. Get him off me.*

"I reckon he'll start talking soon too," Ronnie said from the floor where she sat with Oscar between her legs. He was chewing on plastic blocks and drooling up a storm like his older cousin. The other two babies were sleeping.

Did I die and enter the kind of hell women who never wanted babies were sent to?

"Why are we here?" I blurted suddenly, earning myself some curious glances.

"Like, on this planet?" Holland asked. "Or here in this specific room?"

Sloane chuckled. "I don't think she's after the meaning of life, Holl. She's looking a bit shell-shocked. And for what it's worth, we were all the same coming into this family. The way they do things... it's a little archaic and off-putting, but they'll fill us in on the details when they come out of the war room."

"The war room?" I asked.

"That's my name for it," Ronnie said with a smirk. "They go in there and beat their chests while we women folk stay out here with the children. It used to piss me off because I like to be part of planning our jobs. Then I realised it was actually beneficial. They argue with their egos in there, and by the time they present a job to us, they've reached a compromise."

"They just decide everything?" I was *not* OK with that.

"Not really," Alesha put in. "We get as much input as we want on the actual job. But they decide what the job is and who has a role in it." That was bullshit.

"Since we've had children," Sloane said. "We've all taken a big back step. We don't work outside the cover businesses unless our specific skills are necessary in the field."

"And what are your skills?" I asked, looking at each of them.

"I jack cars and drive," Ronnie said, pride in her eyes.

"I'm a locksmith by trade," Sloane put in. "So I pick locks and open safes."

Alesha went next. "I don't really have any particular skills. But I do have access to a crematorium, so I suppose my specialty is cleaning up when things go wrong."

"Is that a threat?" I asked, light teasing in my tone because she was the one I was most concerned with.

She laughed and shook her head. "Not at all. I just didn't have much of a crooked history before I married Sam. I'm still learning."

"And what about you?" I asked Holland, who had thankfully collected her toddler and was now bouncing him on her knee.

"I can sing?" she said, scrunching up her nose which caused the others to laugh.

"Holland is our token non-criminal," Ronnie explained.

"I just don't have the stomach for it," Holland added. "I mean, I accept that's how things are, but I prefer not to know the details. I'm too afraid of losing my beast and would worry incessantly."

"Your beast?" This woman spoke in riddles.

Alesha grinned and filled me in. "Nate is her beast. Holl likes to merge her own life with the Disney version of Beauty and the Beast. She and Nate have this massive library in their house and dream of retiring to run a bookshop."

Holland's eyes glittered as she nodded. "He even built me a ladder that runs along the shelves."

"I'll have to take your word on it. I've never seen any Disney films," I said, shrugging.

Holland looked horrified. "No fucking way!" She gasped and covered her mouth. "What kind of life have you led without Disney in it?"

"A realistic one?" I replied. I wasn't getting defensive

at all, and I wasn't even trying to have a dig at her. I was simply being honest because dreaming and hoping for a prince to save me wasn't constructive during my upbringing. That would just lead to a world of disappointment.

"Oh ignore her," Ronnie said, waving a hand in the air. "She can't imagine living a life without pop culture. I was the same when I came into the family. I'd never watched any of the nineties classics and she lost her ever-loving mind. Made me watch marathons for months until she was satisfied I'd get all of her references."

"*Pretty Woman* is life," Holland added.

"I'm sure it is," I said, deciding to skip telling her I hadn't seen that either.

"Why don't you tell us how you went from tracking Toby down to being the woman he brought to Sunday dinner?" Alesha asked, leaning forwards a little.

"Why don't you tell me why you threw yourself at him in the driveway?" I asked in return, eying her with suspicion. Something told me she considered herself above the others in her position within the family. Like she was the next female behind Jasmine. I'd picked up on it in the way she acted during the cleanup after dinner. With Jasmine in the office with her sons and Breaker, Alesha had taken control.

"I can answer that one," Holland said, smiling at her friend. "Leesh has been socially awkward all of her life."

Alesha went bright red and placed a hand on her face. "Please shut up."

Holland smiled. "She used to be incapable of stringing a sentence together around good-looking men."

"I'm fine now," she argued, her cheeks still pink.

"It's crazy, actually. All our lives she'd been this stammering mess. Then she walks into this house and suddenly, she's cured."

"I was scared out of my mind."

"Anyway, the Cartwrights are the first men she's ever been close to. She's like their little sister because she lived here with them for the first few months of her marriage to Sam."

"They made me feel more welcome than my own family ever did," Alesha added. "Jasmine taught me to cook, Kris taught me to surf, Abbot taught me to see the humour in pretty much everything. I don't think I need to detail what Sam taught me"—she pressed her lips together as her blush returned—"And Toby, well, he was like this guiding light. Whenever I felt lost, he was there." She looked around the group of women. "I think he was that guy for all of us. He's special in that big brother, favourite uncle kind of way. Does that make sense?"

Sloane and Ronnie both nodded while Holland kind of shrugged. I was pretty sure her relationship with Toby had differed somewhat from the others since he'd actively pursued her and all. Seemed funny to me that it wasn't her I felt wary of. Only Alesha. I suppose that was because of her over-the-top greeting. *You don't wrap your legs around another woman's man.* You just didn't. But, I'd let it go this time—primarily because of how quick Toby was to set her back down.

"He's a special person," I said, pressing my hands together in my lap.

"He is," Ronnie agreed. "Seems you're lucky to have found each other in the chaos."

"We were," I said, keeping it short and sweet, my cards close to my chest.

"Aw, come on, Blair," Holland said. "We need some details here. Well, I do. My soul thrives on romance."

"Abbot says Toby always lived like a monk. He was really quiet about his free time, and they never saw him with a woman," Sloane put in. "So we're all super interested in you, and how you two got together."

"I'm just happy he's found someone," Alesha said. "He deserves to be happy."

"More than any of us," Ronnie added, nodding.

"There really isn't much to tell. He was a job. I hunted him down, and after we escaped the boat explosion, we travelled together. And well, he's gorgeous. One thing led to another, and here we are." They all looked a little disappointed at my summary of events, but I still felt protective of Toby's and my relationship. We'd been behaving as though two weeks was all we had, circumstances had turned that into one, and now we weren't ready to let each other go. I didn't really know what our future held, or if we'd even have one after we confronted Grey, but I was willing to try because Toby was worth it. He was the best man I'd ever met.

"Well, he looks happy," Sloane said before correcting herself. "Happier, anyway. Coming back here can't have been easy for him. He really earned his freedom, you know."

I nodded because I did know. And I felt seriously stupid for playing right into Grey's hands by bringing him back here. Grey was a smart man, he couldn't be in his position if he wasn't. He'd sent me after Toby, knowing that if the boat bomb failed, I'd herd him back to his mother the way I was trained to. We'd returned to what was probably a trap, and now I was afraid of what came next, and when….

"Maybe you'll all feel better once you have your freedom," I said, rising from my seat and moving over to the window. I pulled back a blind and searched the darkness, unease bubbling through my chest.

"No one can see in," Alesha said. "There are gates and sensors all around the property. We'd be alerted if anyone was out there."

I swung my gaze upward. "That's why, if I was Grey, I'd use a drone."

"What's a drone gonna see?" Ronnie asked. "We're all inside."

Releasing the blind, I let out a sigh. "Until we aren't."

"There are infrared ones," Sloane put in, not really helping anyone.

"Why don't you sit down, hon?" Holland suggested. "There's a fully stocked bar in the rumpus. Relax a little, grab a drink. The guys will fix this, but we'll be here a while." Now she was rocking her little boy in her arms and he was nodding off, his little fingers twisted in her hair. Between me and myself, I felt a little pang of 'awww' go off somewhere in the dark recesses of my heart. But I wasn't going to admit that out loud.

"Anyone else want a drink?" I asked with a sigh, thumbing over my shoulder.

"There are vodka mixes in the fridge if you want to bring some back," Alesha suggested.

"Any particular flavour?"

"Whatever you grab is fine."

The way the first level of the house was laid out, there was a formal lounge and dining towards the front, a kitchen and office in the centre, then a rumpus room towards the back that opened out onto the backyard and an in ground pool. The rumpus held a long grey couch, a pool table, and a marble-topped bar on the farthest wall.

Placing my hand on the cool marble, I walked around to the working side of the bar and kneeled down to open one of the glass-front fridges, pulling out four bottles of vodka mixed with guava—the kind of drink I always referred to as 'lolly water' because it was so sweet. As I set them on top of the bar and looked around for something stronger for myself, my eyes landed on the door that lead into the office, the place Ronnie had referred to as the 'war room'.

Grabbing a scotch glass from the shelf, I selected a vanilla-flavoured vodka and unscrewed the lid, my eyes straying again to that closed door as I sniffed the sweet notes.

I wanted to be in that room, listening to them plan, taking part in the decision-making process. The man they were after was *my* father after all. He was the monster under my bed more than anyone else in this house. I would be the ticket that allowed them to get close to him. Didn't I have a right to be a part of this?

"Fuck it," I muttered to myself, abandoning my drink preparation and marching across the slate flooring. I didn't even take a moment to reconsider, just reached out and placed my hand on the knob and turned.

I was met with silence as seven sets of eyes swung my way.

"Is there something you need?" Jasmine asked, placing the tips of her fingers on the desk where she was standing. The others were all around her, some in chairs, others leaning on filing cabinets or bookcases. Toby was on his feet, closest to the side of the desk, looking like he was literally Jasmine's righthand man.

"I need to be a part of the meeting."

"Family only," Jasmine replied, her words sharp.

"Jasmine," Toby warned, an edge to his voice.

"Family? Considering you're plotting to murder *my* father, I think I qualify. Don't you?"

Toby hissed under his breath as the shock registered on his siblings' faces.

"Your father?" Jasmine repeated, suddenly interested. "Why haven't we been told this?" She directed that at Toby.

Instead of answering her question, Toby took a few strides towards me and placed his hand on my elbow. "Can I speak with you outside?" He waited until we were on the other side of the kidney-shaped pool before he released me and turned my way, letting out his breath. "You agreed to let me protect you." He put his hand on his hip and the other against his temple, like I caused all his stress.

"Ah, yeah. But that doesn't mean you get to cut me out."

"Maybe I was doing it because I don't need them using you as fucking bait, or worse, deciding you're somehow the enemy."

"I don't know if you remember or not, but I happily volunteered as bait. No matter what he decides to do with me, he'll see me. If you stay close, you'll get your shot."

"That is the stupidest fucking idea I've ever heard," he blustered, eyes flashing as he took hold of my arm. "After what he did to you? I am not serving you up to him so he can do it all again, or worse—kill you the moment you walk in. It's insane, Blair. You've given this zero thought."

"I've given it a hell of a lot of thought, actually."

"But it's suicide," he yelled. "You're planning with anger and revenge, and I won't let you be reckless with your own safety."

"Let me?"

He jostled my arm. "Yes, Blair, *let* you. You are mine. Mine to take care of. Mine to protect. And you do as I fucking say, or I can't do what I'm good at."

That means you do as I say.

It means you let me protect you

Those were the terms I agreed to. He'd used that big cock of his as a weapon of persuasion and now he was holding me to my word. *Fucker.*

"Are you saying I can't be involved?"

He released his grip and smoothed his hand down the length of my arm. "You're too emotional to be involved."

My mouth fell open as I stepped back. "Emotional? That man is *my father*. He put me to work in one of his whorehouses when I was too young to know what was right and what was wrong. Then he ordered my torture, raped and beat me as an adult before trying to blow me up. *Twice*. He represents everything evil in this world, and I need to watch him die, Toby. Don't you dare take this away from me."

"I'm not taking it away, sunshine."

"Don't call me a pet name when I'm pissed off at you." He reached for me and I stepped back.

"Fine. I'm not taking it away, *Blair*. I'm doing this *for* you. I can't go in there and do what needs to be done if I'm worried about you as well. We'll both end up dead and then this will have been for absolutely nothing."

"And if I don't go in there and do this, then I will be tortured for the rest of my life." I pointed at my head. "I need to watch him bleed."

"I'll take a fucking video and show you so you can watch over and over. Just please, I can't concentrate with you in a room, and if anything happens to you, I'll die, Blair. Please. It will be so much easier for me if I know that no matter what happens to me, you will be OK."

"No. We both knew the risks coming here. Just because we've let our feelings get out of control doesn't mean the job is any different."

"*Goddamn it, Blair.* I love you too much to risk your life."

His words hit me in the chest, stealing my breath and causing me to stumble back slightly. "You *love* me?"

He held his hand out, gaze softening. "With everything I have."

Looking from his outstretched hand to the sincerity that shone from his eyes, my chest tightened, constricting my throat. I shook my head. "Not yet, Toby. You weren't supposed to. Not until after. It was only supposed to be a maybe until then."

"I love you now, Blair. I can't help it. And if you love me, even if you just think it's possible that you could love me, please stop fighting me on this. Killing that man will be my greatest gift to you."

"I want to kill him myself."

Stepping closer, he caught my hand then tugged me until I collided against his chest and stared up at him. "How many men have you killed, Blair?" he whispered, his fingers slipping into the sides of my hair so my face was still and I couldn't look away.

"None," I whispered back.

"You think it will make you feel better, but I promise you it won't. Watching a man drain of life is the least cathartic thing you will ever do. All it does is leave you feeling hollow. Take it from someone who knows. Keep your soul clear. Let me take on this stain for you. I'm begging you."

Blinking rapidly, I struggled to come up with anything to counter him with that didn't sound childish.

"Toby," I whispered, hoping the inflection in my voice would be enough for him to understand. I was fairly sure he knew exactly where I was coming from, but his insistence he knew better was far stronger than my pursuit for revenge.

"Let me protect you, sunshine."

When I opened my mouth, I wasn't sure what I was going to say. I wanted to say something like, "I'm going Toby. I'm going and there's nothing you can do to stop me," or even something really deep like, "You can't protect me from myself." But I didn't get to say anything, because a whirring sound buzzed above our heads and grabbed my attention.

"Get the rifle," I gasped, pushing against his chest.

"What?" Releasing me, he immediately looked up to the sky where I was pointing.

"There's a fucking drone watching us." I ran after it, following it around to the front of the house with Toby hot on my heels.

"What the fuck are you doing chasing it?"

"To see where it goes. They're obviously here

watching us. We played right into his hands and now we're all in one place. Get the rifle from the car." I skidded to a halt and turned to him with wide eyes as he pulled the hunting rifle we'd carted across the country out of his car. We'd transferred that thing from boot to boot because I insisted we might need it. And now we did. "What if they're planning on blowing up the house, Toby?"

"We'll stop it." He pulled the rifle from its case and pulled back on the bolt, aiming it into the sky where the drone hovered. Then he pulled the trigger. *Click*. "What the fuck?" He took aim again. *Click*.

"Is it loaded?"

"Of course it's bloody loaded. That filthy bastard who never cleaned his ute just didn't look after his fucking gun either." With a growl, he tossed it on the ground then kicked it to the side. "Useless."

"It's going. Hurry." With a gasp, I spun on my heels and ran even faster, grabbing onto the entry gate and tugging at it to no avail. "How the hell do you get this open?" Wedging my foot in the bottom, I climbed before there was a sudden click and the whole thing moved with me still attached.

"It's electronic," Toby said as I looked his way.

"Oh," I said, jumping off it and dusting off my hands. "Quick. It's over there."

I went to run out of the gate but Toby's hand wrapped around my upper arm and stalled my movement. "Running out there is nuts. You just said we were playing right into their hands. Don't you think they *want* you to chase the drone?"

"Not if the drone was just planting explosives, and…

Oh my god, Toby. The babies. There are babies in that house! We have to stop them."

Slipping his hold, I took off at a sprint, not having any sort of a plan as I raced off the property and into the street. All I could think was what if there was a bomb, what if I was the only one who could stop it going off? I couldn't say any of it made a hell of a lot of sense, but since I'd survived three of Irish's explosive attempts at the detriment of a house full of girls and one poor little dog, I wouldn't be responsible for standing by while Irish added babies to his kill count. I had to act.

"Blair," Toby yelled from behind me, obviously not as quick on his feet as I was. "Stop!"

As I rounded the corner and came up on a dark-coloured van that would look suspicious even in the daylight, I realised the stupidity in my actions. Toby had been right, I was coming at this all wrong, using my emotions and anger to guide me when there was a better, more logical way to get what I wanted. But all of that was too late now. The driver's side of the van opened, and a man got out in front of me.

"Nice to see you made it in one piece, toots. You were supposed to call me."

Planting my feet, I slipped slightly on the gravel under my feet, gasping and confused. "Nick? What the hell are you doing here?"

"Blair, get back," Toby said from behind me. I turned to look over my shoulder and found him standing with his chest puffed out like he was an animal ready to pounce.

"What the fuck is going on?" I demanded, looking between them. Nick was supposed to be on another job. It made no sense that he was here. Unless…

Nick twisted his mouth down a touch as he shook his head. "I'm just here collectin' for a job."

"What job? You want the money for finding Toby?" *Please tell me that's all it is.* My guts twisted, knowing there was more but not wanting to believe it.

"Blair," Toby said again, holding his hand out, trying to encourage me to move back with him.

"No, Toots. I want the money for findin' *you.*"

"What?" And that's when I saw why Toby hadn't moved closer, coming around the back of the van was none other than Irish, brandishing a big silver handgun. "You're working for *Grey?*" I directed to Nick, disbelieving. How could he? He was supposed to be my friend. He was supposed to be on *my side.* What the fuck possessed him to go to work for the most vile man on the planet? *This isn't happening.* My world tilted and bile rose in my throat. *This is* not *happening.*

"I go where the money is. It's nothin' personal."

"It's fucking personal to me," I hissed. "What the fuck is wrong with you? Does Big Jim know?"

"Jim?" Nick laughed. "He hasn't got a fuckin' clue. Thinks me and you are off somewhere rekindlin' the old flame." He sniffed, his eyes landing on Toby. "Yeah. I fucked her too."

Toby lurched forwards, fist flying into the side of Nick's face, sending him colliding with the side of the van before dropping to the ground, clutching his face as he spat blood on the ground.

"We all fucked her, buddy," Irish sneered, cocking his gun right next to Toby's head. "You ain't anythin' special."

A growl rumbled out of Toby's chest and I felt sure he

was about to turn on Irish, bringing his fists to a gunfight. Knowing that couldn't possibly end well, I flung myself into his arms, getting in between him and the barrel of the gun. "Toby."

He caught me, stumbling back just enough to create a little distance between us and them.

"Funny," Irish started, squinting at me in the dim light as I turned in Toby's arms. "I didn't recognise ya back on the docks. But now, the ole memory's clearin' up." He tapped his index finger against his head "You were such a fighter. I can't believe I passed up a chance to reminisce." He lifted his eyebrows, leering at me, that gold tooth flashing in the moonlight. "But then, I can't really be expected to remember all the girls I break in. You kind of blend into one long dirty fuck." I wanted to tear his fucking face off and shove that tooth up his arse.

"You motherfucker." Pushing me to the side, Toby lurched forwards, growling like an animal, ready to carry out my thoughts in actions. And I reckon he would have too. If I hadn't called his name.

"Toby. *Stop*!"

He froze at the sound of my voice, turning to find me teetering back, a barrel pressed against my temple as Nick held me in a headlock.

"Wouldn't do that if I was you, my friend. We're just here to pick up Blair and deliver a message to you," Nick said.

"You can't have Blair," Toby growled through gritted teeth, his shoulders so tense I thought a vein might pop in his neck. "I'll rip you to fucking pieces with my bare hands."

"It's funny," Irish said again, keeping his gun trained

on Toby as he reached for the handle on the side of the van. "The boss has these big thick files on the lot of you Cartwright bastards. But nowhere inside any of them was a mention you had a daughter."

Holy fuck. No.

The world seemed to drop into slow motion as Irish pulled on the handle of that van. Toby's eyes went wide, I wrestled against Nick's hold, and the door slid open, revealing a frightened woman, shaking, bound and gagged. *Lucy.*

Oh god.

"You bastards," I shrieked as Toby surged forwards, grabbing Irish by the front of his shirt and lifting him off the ground, slamming him into the side of the van with his fist cocked back. I expected a gunshot, or at least some yelling about killing. But all I got was maniacal laughter before Toby growled and dropped Irish, placing his hand flat on his chest so he stayed pinned to the side of the van.

"If you harm a single hair on her head—"

"You'll what?" Irish leered, holding up a fist. "Kill me? We both know how that will work out. I die, she explodes."

"What the hell?" I gasped.

Toby stepped back, turned around and roared, his fingers scraping through his hair, pulling in impotent rage.

"The girl's sitting on a bomb," Nick explained, his hot breath on my ear. "It's hooked to a deadman switch. Anything happens to Irish or me and she dies."

"You sick bastards. What is wrong with you people?"

"What's wrong with us?" Irish countered, pointing his gun sideways at me. "His family came to us for help then reneged on the deal. When we went to collect what was rightly ours, *this* man killed more than a dozen of my brothers. Wanna find a bad guy in this story, Miss Page? He's standing right here." He shifted his aim towards Toby.

"You're fucking delusional," I spat, hating that there was absolutely nothing either of us could do right now to get Lucy out of that van and out of harms way. We were trapped in whatever sick game Grey was playing with us, mere puppets because of my own blind stupidity. How was it possible I shared DNA with that guy?

Looking bored, Irish gestured for Toby to back up, which he did, because all he could do was comply. Each step, each twitch of his muscles was a fight against his mind, desperate to maintain control instead of giving into the rage that bubbled visibly under the surface.

"The ladies are coming with us," Irish said, his head tilting like a bird as he studied Toby's restrained reaction. "But you're allowed to go. Mr Grey has a task for you."

"What task?" Toby forced out, his words bloody and raw.

"Get your family and the Grim Order to stop interfering with our business, and we'll quit trying to blow you up. We'll even let your girl here live." He inclined his head backwards to the sobbing Lucy.

"I don't control the Grim Order."

Irish shrugged. "But you have sway. You're a resourceful man, Mr Cartwright, with a lot of incentive. I'm sure you'll come through. Your daughter's life depends on it."

Lucy whimpered, and I heard the crack of Toby's knuckles as he clenched his fists by his sides. I'd experienced his protection and love for only a short time. But his daughter? He'd given up so much to protect her from this. How was he even standing right now? He loved with everything he had. So fierce. So powerful. *This must be killing him. And it's all my fucking fault.*

"What about Blair?"

"What about her? Mr Grey has requested that his daughter be returned to him. She's not yours to bargain for."

"No deal," Toby yelled.

"Too bad for you, sweetheart," Irish teased, indicating to Nick that he wanted me in the van with Lucy. "It's the only deal you're getting. So hop to it. Mr Grey will be in touch shortly."

"Blair, don't," Toby started as I moved towards the van without a fight and allowed Nick to bind my hands behind my back.

"It's OK," I said, smiling at him as best I could under the circumstances. "I can look after Lucy while you do whatever you need to do. I'm OK."

"This is fucking bullshit," he argued, running his hand through his hair in agitation, the emotion and frustration straining his voice. But there wasn't a single thing he could do to stop this without killing us all in the process. I knew that, saw the anguish etched on his face as he stood there coiled tight but unable to explode. The *only* option available to us at this point was compliance.

So I climbed back into that skin I'd shed while I'd opened my heart to Toby, donned my old mask of indifference and re-erected the walls of my mind, becoming the woman I was before, the fighter, the survivor. It was the only way I'd get through this.

"I'll be OK," I told him again, fighting the pain in my heart as I watched the fear pool in the corners of his eyes.

"Blair," he gasped, the sound of defeat coating each letter of my name.

I'm OK. Turning away from the beautiful man who owned my heart and had somehow put together my broken soul, I sat in the seat next to Lucy and checked her over as best I could, trying to focus on what I could do as opposed to what I was losing. *Just when I found it...*

"You'll be all right," I whispered as she looked at me with wide eyes and whimpered, a scared animal sound fighting through her gag. "I'm so sorry I got you involved in this." Her eyes shone with confusion as a tear slid down her dirt covered cheek, quickly absorbed by the fabric across her face. In her eyes, all I could see was her father mirrored right back. *Oh god.*

"Belt up, princess," Irish grunted, securing the seatbelt around my waist. "Gotta make sure we take you back to daddy all pretty like." I closed my eyes as he moved away and pulled the handle on the door.

Good bye.

"Fuck. *Blair*," Toby yelled as the van slammed shut, his voice muffled as he hit against the side. "Lucy!"

The van started.

No.

I felt a surge of panic rise and press behind my eyes as we lurched forwards, our next destination a place where dreams died and souls were crushed.

Jagged nails clawed up my throat. *I can't go back there.*

Memories flashed as fire and screams flooded my

senses, grabbing hands, darkened rooms, the unbuckling of a belt… *Don't!*

Please.

No.

Sucking in my breath, I swallowed hard, forcing it all back down, down as deep as I could, locking it back up as tight as I could, telling myself to harden the fuck up. I survived once. I'd survive again. I had to. I couldn't let Toby's daughter experience the nightmare. I had to protect her. Even if it was my last act on this earth. I would save Toby's daughter.

It was the least I could do for the man I loved, the man I'd destroyed. *I'm so sorry, Toby. This is all my fault.*

CHAPTER TWENTY-FOUR
A TERRIBLE MAN.
REALLY BAD

"WHAT THE HELL IS GOING ON?" Lucy shrieked, tears streaming from her red-swollen eyes when I pulled the gag from her mouth and untied her restraints. They had put us in a room much like the one they'd put me in after my last interaction with Grey. A locked bedroom where they kept the girls they classed as 'broken in'. It had a window with bars on it and not much inside but a bed and a few items of clothing. But at least you could tell what time of the day it was and wash in the attached bathroom that held nothing more than a sink and a toilet.

"Have they done anything to hurt you?" I asked, my voice soft as I took a damp cloth and ran it over the dirt on her face, my memories coming hard and fast now. It didn't matter how hard I tried to lock them away. I was flailing.

"Not r-really," she stammered, her body shaking. "They g-grabbed me from my h-house and brought me s-straight here. I d-don't understand why. W-what is *happening*?"

Swallowing hard, I finished cleaning her face and

moved on to her hands, treating her like a child while she cried and shook from fear. I couldn't get my thoughts straight. I'd spent years avoiding what had happened to me. Facing it by talking to Toby had only been the tip of the iceberg. Being here was bringing everything rocketing to the surface. I wanted to curl into a ball and sob. But I needed to be strong for Lucy. I would do everything I could to keep her from going through even a sliver of what I endured. I wanted to protect Toby's daughter with my life.

I love you too.

In my relationship with Toby, not saying that back to him was my only regret. The rest of it had been perfect, and I'd miss him during every moment I had left in this world.

If I can get Lucy back to him safely, I'll be able to face anything.

"I'm so sorry you got dragged into this."

Lucy pushed my hand away to stop me cleaning, her eyes flashing as her fear slipped into anger. "Dragged into what, Nikki? Tell me what the fuck is going on. Why was my dad calling you 'Blair' and why did you call him 'Toby'? Who the hell were those men? And why in god's name *am I here*?"

Oh god. Here goes.

"Your dad and I, we aren't in the navy, Lucy," I said, lifting my eyes to meet hers as she watched me intently.

It's so hard to look at her when all I see is him.

"Are you… are you *spies*?" Her eyes went wide.

I shook my head, almost laughing at the suggestion. She was so innocent. "It's worse than that. We… we're criminals. Your father is a thief and I'm a private investigator. But not the good kind. I'm the kind who hunts people down who are hiding from the bad guys. You know, so they don't testify in court."

She pulled her hands from mine as if she'd been burnt. "What the fuck? No. No. That's not true. Dad would never...."

"I'm sorry, Lucy. It's the truth. He was trying to protect you by keeping you away. He never wanted you involved in this life."

"I don't believe you," she whispered, a lifetime of believing her father was a hero so ingrained that she couldn't see him any other way.

"Whether or not you believe me isn't really the issue. The fact that you're here should be evidence enough."

"Why am I here?"

"Because a very bad man wants to hurt your father, he figured taking you was the best way to do that."

"What bad man? I'm an adult Nikki, Blair—whatever the fuck your name is. Explain this to me."

"I'm trying." I swallowed. It really wasn't easy spilling the details of what Toby and I did to a regular person. The details made us sound like the bad guys, and while we weren't exactly good, we weren't evil either. To me, my job was pretty normal, as was Toby's. "Your father did something that pissed off a smuggler. That smuggler wants revenge. So, we came here planning to kill him before he could get us."

Her eyes grew bigger. "My dad was going to kill someone?"

Now's probably not the time to tell her he's killed quite a lot of people.

"Well, yes. But he's a terrible man. Really bad."

"My dad or the smuggler?"

"The smuggler." I was really fucking this up.

"Why couldn't he just call the cops?"

"Because that would mean your father would have to explain how he knows the smuggler which would put him in jail. I don't think any of us want that."

"He could bargain for immunity. They do that all the time on TV."

I ran my hand over my head, frustrated. "This isn't TV, Lucy. I don't think you're understanding the gravity of our situation. It isn't something the cops can fix. You're being held to ransom by a very powerful man with powerful friends and powerful enemies. Your father is somewhere in the middle of all that, and I'm, well, I'm just fucked either way you look at it." I laughed a little, even though nothing about this was funny. "But, since you're OK and they've put us in a room with a bathroom and a window, I think we should be all right." I reached out and patted her on the knee.

"What does a window have to do with any of it?"

I turned and met her eyes, so filled with confusion, anger and sadness. Powerlessness.

"It's just safer in these rooms," I told her, trying not to even think about what happened in the rooms that didn't have windows and bathrooms.

"Have you been here before?"

"Once." I nodded. "I was here once."

"And you got away?"

"They let me go."

"Well that's good." She perked up a little at that. Hopefulness widening her eyes. "We might be let go too."

"Yes," I said, giving her a smile I didn't feel. "I'm

going to make sure they let you go, Lucy. I promise you that."

"OK. OK. So we're not going to die here?"

"No, Lucy," I whispered. "I won't let you die. I'm not sure how long we'll be here for. But I promise you'll get to go home."

"OK." She breathed, nodding slightly as she looked about the almost naked room. "W-who is this bad guy we're being held by, anyway?"

"Did you ever read about a smuggler who was arrested over a big drug robbery about a year ago?"

"Uh…yeah. Grey something?"

"Grey. Yes. That's who this belongs to." I gestured around the room, my nervous heart skittering about in my chest as I hoped to god all of my promises could be made true.

"And my father is a thief?"

"His whole family is, actually."

"His whole family?"

"Yes. He has four brothers."

"I never knew I had uncles." Confusion knitted her brow. This was a lot for a frightened girl to take in. I was sure hardly any of it made sense, and she probably felt trapped inside a shitty dream. But the distraction helped, so I kept going.

"You have aunties too. They're all married and have kids."

"I have cousins?"

I nodded. "Babies right now."

"What are their names?"

I told her, detailing everything I could remember about them and all the other members of her extended family.

She sat there wide-eyed, listening and asking questions; more questions than I had answers to. But I made them up just the same, because if we were talking she didn't have time to be afraid. And if I was honest, neither did I. Talking to Lucy kept the walls from pressing in.

CHAPTER TWENTY-FIVE
FAILSAFES

IF DAREDEVIL WAS AN AUSTRALIAN-BASED SERIES, Brendan Grey could play Kingpin. He'd have a salt and pepper goatee and a navy suit, but the rest of him would look pretty much the same: formidable stature, shiny bald head and beady eyes that showed little to no feeling. When he smiled, it came off as unimpressed and his laughter sounded empty. His voice was commanding and his movements arrogant. The man knew the world quivered at his feet. Just the sight of him caused my hands to sweat and shake.

"You seem different from the last time we met," he said as a waiter with a straight back poured red wine into oversized glasses.

Grey had sent for me a little over an hour ago. A staunch looking woman escorted me into a dressing room and ordered me about as I changed into provided formal wear and had two other women do my hair and makeup, dressing me up like some glorified doll.

"I suppose I am," I said quietly, coaching myself to

keep my cool as I nodded to the waiter and eyed the silver cutlery in front of me. *Could I get across the table fast enough to stab him with that knife?*

"Yes. You're calmer. More refined, perhaps."

"And you don't have blood on your knuckles. So I guess this is different for both of us."

He smiled, his black-beady eyes creasing. "Perhaps I'll take the refined comment back."

"You do whatever you like."

"A toast then." He lifted his glass, and I did the same, mindful that my behaviour could cause Toby's daughter undue pain. I was eager to get back to her, nervous that I couldn't keep her with me. "To new beginnings."

"To new beginnings," I parroted before taking a sip of the rich burgundy liquid, tart on my tongue.

They served a first course of potato and bacon soup in gold rimmed bowls with wide lips. I wasn't at all hungry, but I forced myself to eat, struggling to keep the food in my belly. *He makes me sick.*

"I must apologise for my man, Irish. Had I known you'd taken up with Toby Cartwright, I would have called him off sooner."

"And if he'd blown me up, what would you have done then?"

He spooned a mouthful of soup past his thin lips, swallowing before moving on without answering my question.

"The fact you've taken up with a Cartwright works to everyone's benefit in the long run. I've been watching them for a long time. A rather industrious family. Interesting mother. I believe she handpicked each of her son's wives as a way to strengthen their business holdings. Fascinating, don't you think?"

"Manipulative might be a better word."

He chuckled. "Yes, I suppose so. However, it got me thinking. If *you* were to marry the oldest Cartwright we could strengthen *our* business."

"Ours? Nothing in your life has to do with mine."

"You're my daughter. It may surprise you, but you're the only heir I have. One day all of this will go to you." He moved his gaze around the large dining room, giving me a moment of panic as I realised what I was doing here. I didn't want to be groomed to take over the helm.

"I don't want to be your heir. Give it all to someone else."

"I don't recall saying you had a choice, Blair. I sent for you because my time on this earth is running short. I need to get my affairs in order, see my vision come to pass so I can leave this world knowing my legacy will carry on. Your marriage could create the biggest crime cooperative this world has ever seen. Thieves, smugglers, drug lords and bikers, all working in harmony towards a common goal: anarchy."

"That's insane," I responded. "None of them will ever go for that."

He grinned and picked up his wine, taking a sip. "I think they will. And I think Toby Cartwright is the man to sell them on it."

"Why would he ever do that?"

"Because I have his daughter, and I have you. That man mowed down an entire troop of my best single-handedly because of brotherly love. Imagine what he could accomplish for his daughter, for his woman. Men have moved mountains for less."

"You really think he'll join forces instead of gunning you down?"

"I do," he said, nodding his head.

"What makes you so sure?"

"The same reason you're sitting here speaking to me instead of plunging that knife you keep looking at inside my neck—you're afraid of what I can do."

"I already know what a monster you are. I've experienced it firsthand."

"That pretty little thing you were brought in with doesn't know that, and something tells me you're both willing to do whatever it takes to keep it that way. And let's not get into the safety of all those tiny babes Jasmine is so fond of showing off. I feel certain we can all come to an agreement that benefits us all and stops this silly little war we have going on. Don't you think?" *He's psychotic.*

"When you said your time is running out, did you mean you're dying?"

He nodded once.

"What of?" I had to fight the urge to smile.

"I have an inoperable blood clot in my brain. It could cause an aneurysm at any time."

"So you're walking around with a time bomb in your head?" How fitting.

"Quite literally, yes."

A pang of something that felt like a mixture of regret and satisfaction radiated through my belly. Nature could possibly rob me of the chance to murder my own monster. I didn't know how I felt about that.

Moving my spoon about the bowl of creamy-coloured soup, I ran over the details of our conversation in my mind, worrying my lips as I wondered if this was the way the world always worked for men like Grey. Were they so powerful and far-reaching they could force almost anything to their advantage?

"If I agree to marry Toby and he unites the different entities, what will our life look like?"

"You learn the ropes and together, when I'm gone, you'll rule over everybody."

The waiter returned, whisking away my barely touched soup and replacing it with scallops on top of caviar and some orange-coloured purée.

I poked at it with my fork as I tried to imagine my life like that. Toby had slipped into this other kind of man since we'd returned to Torquay. He was still the man I loved, but he had pulled on a mask of detachment that would only fuse to his skin if we were to immerse ourselves in this world. I knew in my heart we could never be happy this way. The contrast to the Toby around his family and the Toby I'd met on that wharf was so stark I could barely marry the two personalities together. He was happy before, harsher now. I couldn't imagine a future forcing him to make soul-eating decisions as the head of a criminal empire. I loved him far too much to do that to him.

"What if I told you I didn't want to marry Toby Cartwright," I said.

"That's not what I'm offering."

"In that case, I have no interest in learning anything from you."

"No problem. I'll just rid the world of the Cartwright family and send the daughter to work in my whorehouses."

"Then I'll kill myself and you'll die with nothing and no one." I picked up my knife and held the tip against my throat, showing him how serious I really was. "Take it all away and I have nothing to lose."

He narrowed his eyes. "You wouldn't."

"I would." I pushed the knife point into my skin and felt the heat of blood trickle down my chest, disappearing into my cleavage. It was tempting; pushing the knife in all the way. A moment of pain and it would all be over. My light would extinguish and I wouldn't have to fight, I wouldn't have to worry, I wouldn't have to *concede*.

"Do it, and I swear to you, I'll kill them all. Are you really that selfish, Blair? You'd allow those *babies* to burn alive?" His volume rose with every word, chilling my bones as my hand shook.

Fuck!

"Blair!" Grey boomed, causing me to release my grip, dropping the knife with a clatter as our waiter rushed over and pressed a cloth against my wound. I sat there. Numb. I couldn't do it. I couldn't end my life and condemn them all. Grey had me between a rock and a hard place and he knew it.

I hate him, I hate him, I hate him.

"It's not deep, sir," he said, checking the tiny slice in my skin. I wished it was deep. I wished I wasn't sitting here listening to my monster and his distasteful plans. I wished I had the power to stop him. I wished I knew what to do. But I was lost. I was broken. I didn't know how to fight anymore when no matter which path I chose, people I cared about suffered. *I don't know what to do, Toby. I'm sorry.*

We sat glaring at each other as the waiter took care of my cut, retreating from the room and quickly returning with antiseptic and a bandage.

"He'll still have to broker a truce," Grey said as the waiter withdrew from my side, the knife removed from my possession.

"What?" Was I hearing right?

"Even if you didn't marry him, he'd still need to broker the truce."

"Will you release his daughter when he does?"

"Yes."

"Untouched. No one defiles or even torments her."

"She'll be treated as a guest."

I stared at him, not sure if I could trust the words his lips were forming.

"What happens after Lucy leaves?"

"As long as the truce is upheld, nothing. The Cartwrights, the Grim Order and the Cartel can go about their business as I will mine. You will sever all ties, work for me, *learn* from me and become the heir I should have made you in the beginning."

Did he really mean that? If I joined him, he'd let everyone else go?

I'd have to give up my future, so they could have theirs. But that was something I was more than willing to do. I didn't give a fuck what happened with the bikers or the cartel, but to Toby, well, I loved him. That meant I would protect everything important to him, and I'd protect it with my life.

How could I say no?

"OK," I agreed in a whisper, my chest feeling so tight I could barely breathe.

"Good." Grey smiled, satisfied that he had what he wanted.

I forced a tight smile, reminding myself that those

babies deserved a life without a smuggler breathing down their necks, and Toby deserved the chance to be a permanent fixture in his daughter's life. That would be my gift to him, given in love. I could endure anything if it meant he would be free.

And if I was lucky, nature would soon take care of Grey and I'd be free too.

Free to be with Toby...

Grey clicked at the waiter who quickly scurried from the room. "I'll have the paperwork drawn up immediately with the appropriate failsafes in place."

"Failsafes?"

"So you can't kill me in my sleep, or kill yourself the moment that girl goes home. You will be bound to me, to my organisation, running things exactly as instructed or my reach will extend from the grave, killing them all while you're forced to watch." A shudder ran down my spine. "Is that understood?"

"Yes," I whispered, my last shred of hope shrivelling.

Toby. I'm sorry.

CHAPTER TWENTY-SIX
FOREVER YES

THREE DAYS LATER, I was sitting in Grey's 'conference room' which was just a concrete basement with no windows, a steel door, and no other entry or exit point. It smelled of dirt and damp and echoed every time you moved.

Beside me, my father was dressed for the occasion in his signature three-piece suit. I wore pinstripe pants and a white silk blouse because that's what was set out for me when I woke this morning. My treatment in Grey's home had been far different than it was during our first meeting all those years ago. Back then, I'd been just another inconvenience before I became a surprise. This time, I was the prodigal daughter coming into the fold. I felt sure that Grey was revelling in the fact he'd found a way to control me. The moment I showed any sign of a fight, he reminded me of the stakes. Dangled Toby's life from the tips of his fat fingers.

Perhaps love was a weakness.

During the past days, I'd been immersed in the business side of Grey's world, an intense training regime that saw me shadowing him through almost every step of his day. I had my own living quarters—locked from the outside—but was allowed to visit with Lucy for one hour each evening. She seemed okay. I'd taken her books and magazines to keep her from going stir crazy. While it didn't really make up for the fact someone had kidnapped her, at least it was something. At least she was safe. Despite not growing up with Toby's constant presence, she exhibited a similar amount of strength and fortitude that most women in her position wouldn't have. Toby would have been proud that she was handling her confinement like a trooper.

The one bonus was that she didn't have much to fear besides captivity. Grey had given his word she would remain untouched, and that's how she stayed. One thing I had learned about my father was that he was nothing if not a man of his word and never reneged on a deal.

"They're here," Grey said, checking the message that lit up his phone, those two simple words sending my heart into rampaging rhythm in my chest.

They're here.

Toby is here.

I was going to see him.

I also had to say goodbye....

If you'd asked me a week ago if I could ever imagine joining my father's organisation, I would've sneered and insulted you, calling you insane. But stranger things could happen. When a person was backed into a corner with compliance the only foreseeable option, anything was possible, unlikely alliances were drawn.

"Agree with everything I say," he reminded me, hard eyes on mine. "Understood."

Pressing my fingertips into the top of the table, I nodded. "I do."

Working this close to the man, I'd had many opportunities to commit patricide as planned. And every time I didn't take that chance it cut me a little deeper. The satisfaction of ridding the world of his stain was an intoxicating thought. But I couldn't risk the reality. If Grey died by *my* hand, the cost would come in blood. No matter how much I wanted the satisfaction of revenge, I couldn't seal another person's fate that way. And so I stood by, played the dutiful daughter and learnt how to be a crime boss. My unwanted apprenticeship had begun.

"Welcome," Grey said as the door opened and Breaker entered, followed by Jasmine, and then Toby. He looked exhausted. Dark circles under red-rimmed eyes, sallow skin. He'd styled his hair, shaved his face and put on his suit, looking the part of the man in charge, but I knew him too well not to see the signs. He'd been beside himself. He was hurting just as much as me, if not more.

My heart jumped into my throat the moment we locked eyes. His seemed to ask me if I was okay, so I tried to use mine to tell him I was, to tell him I was sorry. I knew this was all on me.

Taking the seats they were shown to, Toby sat directly across from me and reached one hand out just a touch farther than his other. The tiny connection felt like everything, and it took all of my energy to stop myself from jumping across the table and into his arms.

Run away with me.

We can't.

"Well," Breaker said, leaning back in his chair like he didn't have a care in the world. He was wearing typical biker attire: jeans and a T-shirt with a leather cut proclaiming him a founding member of the Grim Order MC and listing the positions he'd held, right up to VP. "You got us here. How 'bout you talk?"

"Where's Lucy first?" Toby demanded, looking from Grey to me, the strain of worry etched into the lines in his face.

"Safe," Grey said. "If you've achieved what I asked, I'll have her brought up at the conclusion of our meeting."

"If you've touched a hair on her—"

"They haven't," I blurted, reaching a hand towards him. "She's fine. I promise."

His eyes closed for a moment as he slowly released his breath. *Thank god*, it said.

Thank god.

If only there really was some benevolent deity watching over us right now. We could use the help.

"Are you OK?" Toby asked, soft voice, gentle gaze.

I nodded. *God, I want to rewind time so badly.* I wanted to go back to the night we spent in Toby's apartment and never let it end. I wanted to go back so I never chased after that drone. Back even further so I never trusted Nick. Back further still so I could have killed Grey before he even knew who I was. Then none of this would be happening. Toby would be safe.

If only I could turn back time....

I sounded like a Cher song.

Breaker lifted a hand and shrugged. "Are we fuckin' doin' this or what? I got better shit to do."

Toby sat back and frowned. I hated seeing him stressed

like this. Being out of control in a situation severely pushed him outside his comfort zone, much like it did me. I learned in our short time together that he and I were two sides of the same coin. It's why we'd fit so well together, why we worked.

And why I know he'll understand why I have to push him away...

Grey checked his watch. "There's still one more party left to arrive."

Before anyone else could even fire off a question, the door opened and in walked Robert Conway, the country's biggest producer of opiates and Grey's sworn enemy. It was for Conway that the Grim Order had struck a deal on behalf of the Cartwrights. The deal that begun the war that saw everyone in this room reach the current stalemate: watched by police, unable to operate fully due to attacks from other parties. They were all bleeding money. Well, all except the Cartwrights. They were the smallest party in the room but the catalysts for the current trouble. They were making serious cash before Toby up and left. They'd gone practically dormant in the time since. Grey attributed it to the fact that Toby was the brains, and they couldn't operate successfully without him. I had to agree, but quietly thought it had a lot to do with the fact they'd all just had babies and were shifting their focus, but I didn't say that out loud.

"Afternoon," Conway said, taking the seat his security thug pulled out for him like he was a king or something. He looked more like a pimp with his dark receding hairline and 70s porn moustache, accompanied by chunky gold jewellery that disappeared into the thick chest hair that poked out of his business shirt, unbuttoned a couple of buttons too far. The deep V look didn't suit him at all. In fact, he made my skin crawl.

Leaning back in his seat, Grey folded his hands together and looked at each person in the room individually. "It's time we discussed peace," he started.

Breaker scoffed. "We wouldn't need peace if you hadn't tried to take somethin' never meant to be yours," he said, sniffing as he nodded in acknowledgement towards Conway and his man. "Now you're cryin' cause we got you backed into a corner and you know it."

Grey shrugged. "Backed into a corner? I don't think so. Those drugs you stole and framed *me* for were always mine. It was *my* shipment they confiscated."

"Finders keepers, old man. We did the work. And it was fuckin' perfect too. All this trouble came from your own greed. You smuggle anythin' and everythin', sell sex and kink without battin' a fuckin' eye. You're a rich man with a massive racket goin' and you just had to interfere with ours. So yeah, you caused this. Thinkin' you were so big and untouchable we couldn't get to you. But we did. So we *know* you really are in a fuckin' corner or we wouldn't be here. Your goods ain't travellin' nowhere, and we're the fallen tree in the middle of your road."

"Great analogy, baby," Jasmine noted, patting Breaker on the knee. She looked perfect and unflappable in a soft mauve pantsuit, her hair pulled back in a French roll, eyes sharp.

Grey just smiled as he eyed Breaker. "It's true I'm experiencing some roadblocks, and from what I understand everything isn't smooth sailing on your end either, Travis." *Travis?* It took me a moment to remember that Travis was Breaker's real name. I'd read it on Toby's file when I'd first gone looking for him. I was pretty sure it was incredibly disrespectful to call a biker by their first name instead of their road name.

"The name's Breaker, old man," he said, narrowing his hard eyes and confirming my reaction. *What is Grey doing?* Pissing Breaker off wasn't going to get this deal sorted. And Breaker looked fucking *mean* as he glowered across the table. A huge juxtaposition to the man I'd met a few days before.

"What are your terms?" Conway asked, cutting the altercation off before it could go any further. "You wanted to talk peace and swinging dicks about won't accomplish anything. Spit it out."

"I propose a merger," Grey stated as I nodded along as he told me, expecting the words "A compromise" to come out of his mouth.

"Wait." I stopped nodding toot suite. "What?" I was breaking my word, but he had said nothing about a merger when we discussed this meeting earlier. A merger how?

"A merger how?" Jasmine asked, echoing my thoughts as she craned her neck forwards, tilting her head a little.

"We all have something the other wants. To you"—he turned to Conway—"I can provide access to raw product: a new poppy crop, Australian grown and ready to harvest within the month. In the meantime, I can help lift supply levels via my international contacts and private trade routes."

"That's quite an offer," Conway said, eyes narrowed as his fingers ran across his bushy moustache. "What do you expect from me?"

"Distribution. It's my understanding the MC is your

partner in the East, and various other entities are working the smaller major cities in the other half of the country."

"Correct."

"I want my amphetamines distributed along with your opiates: an easily accessible smorgasbord for junkies everywhere. If we work together, we can double our current drug revenue and push out those pesky smaller vendors; dominate supply."

Conway lifted his brows and exchanged glances with Breaker.

"You know where the MC stands on this." Breaker left the rest unsaid. I took the comment to mean that the MC had agreed to distribute for Conway, and if Conway changed that deal, they may quit distributing all together. Breaker didn't have the power to make that decision on his own. He'd need to take it back to the MC for a vote—at least that's what they did in *Sons of Anarchy*, anyway. I was still new at this whole crime boss thing.

"What does any of this have to do with us?" Jasmine asked, her arms folded across her chest now as her lips pursed, giving her a restless and annoyed look about her. "My boys want nothing to do with the drug trade."

"You, madam," Grey started. "Are here because your family started this war." There was no kindness in his eyes as he looked at her. "Broken promises. Running between factions and pitting us against each other. Killing messengers, collectors, conspirators. This meeting wouldn't even be necessary if you'd just kept to your own thieving path. But you strayed onto ours and now you're somewhat of a problem."

Breaker growled. "You don't speak to my woman that way."

Grey held up a hand and kept talking to Jasmine. "A problem with powerful protectors. Your only true loyalty exists with those you consider family, which is *specifically* why you're here. I want your son." He nodded towards Toby.

"You can't have him," Jasmine stated, maintaining her cool. "What kind of stupid truce is that?"

"I don't want to kill him, Jasmine. I want him to marry my daughter and unite our families—merge our interests."

"This is not what we discussed!" I hissed, leaning in to keep my voice low. Everyone heard, the echo in the room amplified each word, but I couldn't just sit there and nod. This wasn't a part of our deal.

"I made no promises," Grey hissed, glaring at me, my mind warring with confusion as I fought my anger and tried to recall his words at dinner, realising that he was right. He didn't make a single fucking promise. "You shut up and you do as I say."

I gulped as a growl emanated from across the table, originating out of Toby's chest.

"I'm OK," I said quickly, reaching across the table to place my hand on his. He flinched slightly, his anger making him jumpy. Then he visibly calm and linked his thumb with my fingers.

Grey took a breath and continued untroubled. "Merging our families merges our business, protects our interests"—he slapped the table with a flat hand—"*maintains* power. Our children will be the gods of the underground, generations from now we'll be more powerful than ever."

"You want my son to inherit your organisation?"

Jasmine asked, her brows high on her forehead as she seemed to ingest the meaning behind Grey's speech.

"That's exactly what I want. Your son. My daughter. A powerful entity that joins us all."

Looks were exchanged around the table while Toby met my eyes, a deep longing coupled with untold sadness inside them. "I'll do it," he said, his voice so soft I almost didn't hear him.

While I knew I was expected to say yes and go along with everything, I simply couldn't stop my mouth from blurting the words, "What? No. No, Toby. This is crazy. You can't want this."

"I'll do it," he said again.

Grey gripped my thigh under the table and squeezed. Hard. I struggled not to wince.

"Let her go or I swear I'll kill you right here and this whole thing is off," Toby growled, his massive frame leaning over the table, ready to attack Grey who smiled and slowly released my thigh.

I looked to Jasmine and Breaker as if they'd be some kind of allies against this deal. But neither of them seemed incensed by the idea at all. If anything, Jasmine looked delighted, like this was the greatest plan she'd ever heard. *What the hell is wrong with her? She can't want this.*

"Can I at least speak to him? I'll do it. But just let me speak to him, please," I whispered. Grey narrowed his eyes at me, but he kept his hands to himself.

Conway slapped his hands on the table with a loud drumming tap, stealing attention back his way. "Personally, I like the idea. We're stronger united. I kind of wish I had a son or daughter old enough to add to the mix, but they're all married with kids already." He turned to

Jasmine and tapped her on the shoulder. "But hey, I hear you have grandkids now. Maybe in eighteen years' time, we tighten *our* bond, take over the fucking world." With a chuckle, he winked and pushed to stand, scraping his chair back. "A marriage merger. It'll unite the Greys and the Cartwrights which will unite the MC, and in turn, the Conways. I like it. I really do. As for the distribution/supply deal, Brendan, I like that too. Let me run some numbers, chat to some of my people, and I'll be in touch. But I feel pretty fucking positive about this. All of us joined…" He clapped his hands together and held them in front of him. "We could make magic." He headed for the door, pausing to place his hand on Jasmine's shoulder and giving it a squeeze like they were friends or something. "We have a lot to discuss. Set it up with my people when you have more details." And then he was gone, and I was sitting there wondering if I'd missed something. I thought Conway and Jasmine were on opposite sides?

"Can I talk to you outside?" I said to Toby, taking the opportunity to stand so Grey couldn't grab my thigh again. I would probably get a beatdown for this, but at this point, I didn't give a fuck. This marriage was between Toby and me, and I didn't want him sacrificing his happiness for it. He'd already given up so much.

"What's to discuss?" Toby said, with a slight bounce of his shoulder. "I'd marry you under any circumstances, Blair."

In the middle of a crime lord gathering, I swooned. Trying not to cry out and profess my undying love, I moved around the table. "We still need to talk."

When I touched his arm, my nerve endings sung a poorly written tune about being home. It made my heart happy. I belonged to this man, that much was true. But I needed to be sure that this was what he wanted. I couldn't stand it if he woke up married with nothing but regret in his heart. There'd be no room for love then.

With a nod, Toby stood and followed me out of the room, his hand on the small of my back as he acted the gentleman even when he had every right to be a total cunt.

"We won't be long," I said to the room, catching the daggers directed my way from Grey's eyes. My stomach flipped. I would definitely pay for speaking out.

Jasmine waited until we stepped through the door before speaking again. "I'll need more details," she started. "Exactly what interests are we aligning, and under what capacity will the rest of my family be involved?" *Details? What the fuck?* She was seriously considering this? I saw how she loved her family just a few nights ago. *How the fuck can she be siding with these animals now?*

Had I read her all wrong?

EXITING the room didn't exactly give us a lot of privacy. We weren't allowed past the cramped foyer to the meeting room where one of my father's goons stood in the corner, keeping a watchful eye and listening in.

"You don't want this life," I said in a hushed tone that still sounded harsh in the echo.

"You're right. I don't. But I want you." He placed his hands on either side of my face and I wrapped my hands around his wrists. *His touch feels so good.*

"That's not good enough. I saw how happy you were when we first met and you're different here. You don't have that light in your eyes anymore and I can't be responsible for removing it. I have to be here. But you don't. You can say no to this, take Lucy, go back to Wannanup and have that life you've always wanted."

His thumbs moved against my skin. "I can't do that, Blair. My life isn't anywhere unless it's with you."

Tears pricked my eyes. "Toby," I whispered, struggling with my emotions. "Please. Let me do this for you."

"Blair." Leaning in, he kissed me tenderly, not caring that a security goon was watching our every move. "Just say yes," he said, pressing his forehead to mine, before kissing my cheek and whispering into my ear. "None of this matters." He moved and kissed my forehead, moving to my right ear. "Just be ready. Tonight."

He's coming for me?

Pulling back, he lowered his hands to my shoulders, fingers brushing the skin on my neck. I had so many questions as I looked into his eyes, but I couldn't ask any. I couldn't even show my joy, or my concern. I just had to keep an impassive expression and hope Toby knew what he was doing. *I trust him.*

"You're mine, right?" he said, trying to convey more than just those words I was sure.

Clearly remembering the moment I promised myself to him, I nodded.

That means you do as I say.

It means you let me protect you.

"I'm yours," I whispered, swallowing hard.

"Then say yes, sunshine."

"OK." I nodded. "Yes."

Forever yes.

CHAPTER TWENTY-SEVEN
NOT WEAKNESS

AFTER TOBY and I agreed to the marriage offer Grey had pushed for, the meeting concluded with an assurance they'd all meet within the week to 'hash out the details'. Jasmine was so convincing in her role, accepting Grey's offer with greed in her eyes, a sense of power and everything. I had to wonder if it was an act or if it was a reality. Did she know Toby planned to come for me? Or was he keeping her in the dark and her reaction today was real? And if that was the case, could she happily marry her son off for the sake of her own personal gain? The idea boggled my mind as I tried to align the Jasmine I'd first met with the woman in that meeting today. They looked the same, but her concern for her family was gravely different. Surely it was a farce?

Blowing out my breath, I dragged my fingers through my hair as I paced back and forth inside my room. Grey had been so pissed at my mouthiness he'd had his goon escort me straight up to my room like a misbehaving teen so he 'didn't have to look at me anymore'. I was tossed through the door unceremoniously, landing on all fours before the goon slammed the door and slid the bolt locked in place. *My ivory tower.* I'd need heavy artillery to blast my way out of here. I wasn't exactly sure how Toby thought he would get in.

He's the brains of the operation, I reminded myself as I stripped out of the uncomfortable business attire and opened my cupboard, full of clothes that weren't even mine. *He can do anything.*

His entire family had the utmost confidence in him, spoke about him in reverent tones. If anyone could get through Grey's security, it would be him. *My Toby.*

As I stood in front of the mirror, my fingers touching the bruises forming on my arm while my eyes noted the bruising on my thigh, I couldn't help feel an abundance of loss. Toby's passion had caused a similar kind of bruising. Where he'd held me so tight in the throes of our love-making I was marked afterward. There was a beauty in that, evidence of his desire, hunger and need like love tattoos on my flesh. But this—I ran my hand over the marks on my thigh—was an abuse of power. Marks that echoed forced compliance. They marred the happy memories of my time alone with Toby, mocked it with their violence and reminded me that in this place, I was a prisoner, that I didn't have choices.

None of this matters. Be ready. Tonight.

Pulling on a pair of black harem pants and a blue t-shirt, I walked over to the window, wrapping my arms around my torso as I surveyed the extensive grounds, marvelling at how something that looked so beautiful in the fading daylight could be the façade to a dungeon of terror, the physical mouth of hell. *I hate my father.*

I hated myself even more for taking him at his word and believing he'd keep it. It was one thing he'd repeated ad nauseam during his 'Quick and Dirty Guide to Running a Smuggling Ring' speeches—he never backed out of a bargain. I'd swallowed his bullshit and thought he'd taken my offer. Turned out, he didn't balk at the thought of me taking my life, he balked at me taking away his bargaining chip: the bride in his marriage bargain. The man was a narcissistic psychopath.

Looking up to the sky, I watched darkening clouds move across an apricot-coloured backdrop while I prayed silently for a sign that showed me I was about to be saved from this place. Lucy had been released to Toby as the meeting ended, a scene that brought relieved tears to my eyes while they cried tears of joy and embraced each other. After that moment, even while I was being dragged up to my room, all I could focus on were Toby's words and the fact he mouthed the word, 'soon' at me as they departed.

Soon.

We would be together soon.

How soon?

Give me a sign....

Those failsafes Grey had mentioned tormented me in every moment that passed while I waited. What was going to happen if I left? He'd said I couldn't kill him. I couldn't kill myself. I couldn't do anything but what I was told, or he'd blow up my world. What kind of father did that? What kind of human did that?

He'd dragged me back here, blackmailed me into

behaving and was now forcing me to marry. I loved Toby. But, being a part of this world wasn't what either of us wanted. We had to get out of this somehow. I was conflicted over a desire to flee or to stay put.

Although, after today's blindside in the meeting, I couldn't trust that staying would keep us safe either. I honestly didn't know what move was the right one, what Toby, or even the Cartwrights, could do to protect us all from Grey's wrath. Stay or go. Either way, we were sitting on a powder keg, waiting for it to explode. How were we supposed to win this?

Stepping back from the window, I paused, spotting something small and dark moving across the sky. *Is that?* I moved closer again, watching the tiny speck glide past the clouds. If I wasn't looking directly at it, I'd think it was a bird, or maybe even a distant plane. But it wasn't either of those things.

It was a drone.

"Toby," I gasped, knowing this was the first sign. *He's coming.*

Suddenly, there was no question in my mind. I wanted to get out of here, to escape this soulless place and take my chances living in the metaphorical Fire Swamp. We knew to beware, surely we could figure out a way to survive without whatever evil Grey had planned getting to us... *God. I'm going crazy.* I touched my fingers to my forehead, letting out a sigh because if I was honest with myself, I was petrified right now. Scared that Toby wouldn't make it. Afraid that if he did, Grey would find him and kill him before he got to me. Terror-stricken that Grey would get to me first, punish me for the way I behaved in the meeting, leaving only a broken version of me for Toby to find.

"I hope you know what you're doing," I whispered to the drone, because clearly, I had no clue. Stepping back, I blew a kiss at the sky, wishing them luck while quaking with fear.

What do I do if Grey gets to me before Toby?

Bouncing my knee as I sat on the edge of my bed, I wrung my hands, my mind whirling.

I had to kill him.

There were no two ways about it. Chopping the head off the snake would give us time to regroup, figure out what his failsafes were and combat them. It was the only way we'd have a fighting chance. It was the only way I'd get out of this without losing my mind. It had to happen.

Lying back on my bed, I tried to think of a way to get out of my room and take the bastard by surprise. Looking up at the high ceilings didn't give me any ideas at all. They were all painted with replicas of nineteenth century art depicting orgies between gods and humans. It was... unsettling that Grey chose this room for me, all those men and women with their open mouths and rolling eyes. I didn't know if he was taunting me after the last time they'd brought me to this property, or if he just didn't give a fuck that those images might mess with my head. I didn't know my father well, but I had a strong feeling it was a little bit of both.

Actually, those open mouths and wide eyes did give me an idea. In my MMA training, I'd learned plenty of choke holds, ways to cut the oxygen supply from my opponent to force them to tap out. I'd never used them outside the cage before, but with no weapons available, all

I had was my strength. And if there was one thing I definitely knew about my father, it was that he couldn't let anything go. His need to make me pay for embarrassing him at the meeting would be eating him alive. There was no way he could pass my door without coming inside to 'teach me a lesson'.

I shuddered and sat up, my hands clenching. *I'll be ready for you, you evil son of a bitch.*

If this went down anything like the way my 'punishments' did the last time I was here, Grey would come into the room alone with a guard stationed outside. He'd beat into me, call me names, do whatever else he pleased, then walk straight back out. The guard wouldn't interfere. But at what point would he?

Pacing about the room, I ran my hands through my hair, blowing out a nervous breath as I shook the jitteriness out of my hands. I couldn't lie; I was freaking the fuck out. Part of the reason I learned MMA was as a confidence booster after the torture I endured here. I'd fought my best then, but I'd had shitty skills, making my efforts futile. Training had helped me feel badarse again. But when I fought at the gym, I fought against women in my weight class, I never went against men who were bigger and meaner than me. This would be my first hand-to-hand combat in a real world setting. No referees. No trainers. Just me and the other half of my genetic code in the battle to the death. *Oh, my god.* The idea caused a flash of tightness to take hold in my chest as I fought for enough air. *I can do this. I can do this.*

In the field, I'd had a few close calls and tussles with my marks, but I'd never had to full-blown fight. I was way out of my comfort zone and wished there was something in this fucking room to use as a weapon. I didn't even have a lamp.

Where the hell is he? Looking at the dark window, I blew all the air out of my lungs, trying to calm that skittish feeling that vibrated about in the centre of my chest. The sun had set long ago, meaning I'd had at least two hours to get myself all worked up. At this time of year with daylight savings in effect, it'd be about eleven at night by now. I'd skipped dinner, my empty stomach adding to my sickening nerves. I just needed this—whatever was going to happen—to be over. I couldn't handle this limbo state, caught between the need to be rescued and the need to fight. Something had to happen.

The bolt slid against the other side of the door before the lock tumbled and the handle turned. I turned towards it and stopped breathing. *Here we go.*

As the dark brown door swung on its arc inside the room, light spilled in from the hall, silhouetting Grey before he stepped inside and waited for his man to close him in.

"I feel as though our lessons aren't quite sinking in," he said, taking a step closer as he unbuckled his belt and started pulling it free from his belt loops.

No.

Not wanting to give him the chance to wield a weapon, I sprang to action, sprinting towards him. He froze for a moment, mouth open to speak but no words coming out. My movement too fast for him to react before I launched myself off the ground, both feet landing against his chest with an echoing thud.

"*Oof.*"

He fell back, coughing as the air left his lungs and his

eyes went wide, shock and surprise settling in only a moment before he switched to anger.

"You," he garbled, forcing the word on an empty breath as I landed on his chest, my knees pinning his shoulders as I pressed my forearm against this throat and pushed down.

"This is where you die," I grated out through clenched teeth. I took triumph in the way his eyes bulged as he fought for breath and writhed for control beneath me. "Fucking *die*."

He was strong, bucking like a wild bull, lurching me side to side, up and back, forcing me to switch my hold to the traditional choke, two hands around his thick neck.

I'm slipping.

With a growl, he flipped me on my back, my hands flying back to try to catch myself before my head hit against the wooden floor. *Fuck.*

"Ungrateful *bitch*," he grunted as he slapped my hands away then placed a big palm over my face and shoved my head against the hard floor. *Ow.* "I gave you a gift. A *fucking gift.* And you repay me with insolence and violence? Which of your little friends am I going to pick off first?" His spittle landed on my face as he leered in so close I couldn't focus on him. "Or do I teach you a lesson the old-fashioned way?"

"*No.*" With my legs over his shoulders, I was bent up like a pretzel and struggling to turn this to my advantage.

"It's hard for a man to look at a grown woman and view her as his daughter when he didn't raise her from a child. My cock doesn't know the difference between your cunt and the whores' downstairs." Panic flashed behind my eyes as he shifted his weight, pulling his belt free before wrapping it around my wrists and binding them over my head.

"Stop!"

"I am king." He leered at me, perspiration and saliva dripping, like a wolf hungry for its kill. "Learn." Transferring his weight to his knees, he kept a hold of the belt while using his other hand to unbutton his pants.

"You're a sick fuck," I yelled, spitting in his face a split second before I lifted my hips and wrapped my legs around this neck, twisting my ankles and clamping my thighs together as hard as I could.

He released the belt as he stumbled some of his weight to his palms, trying to return me to the compromised position I'd been in. I fought with everything I had as his fingers dug into skin, his teeth sinking into my upper thigh.

Mother fucker!

Teeth bit through fabric, and I howled with pain while I squeezed tighter, clenching my eyes shut as he slapped, hit, and scratched, his fight weakening as small choking sounds gurgled from his throat.

Tighter, tighter. Hold on.

With an almighty grunt, I put all of my strength into closing my thighs, focusing on cutting off his air. *Hold, please hold.* His movements slowed, tapping instead of hitting, scraping instead of grabbing. Then he fell, limp. *Oh god.*

I burst into tears, pushing away as my stomach heaved and I dry wretched on the floor.

Is he dead?

Freeing my hands from the belt at my wrists, I shuffled across the floor on my knees, reaching out shaky fingers and pressing them against the pulse point in his neck.

Thump...thump...

Shit.

Releasing a burst of emotion, I covered my face with my hands. *Why? After all that effort, he's still alive.*

Leaning over him, I held my hands at his throat, tears streaming from my eyes as I shook and willed myself to take what was left of his miserable life. But no matter what I did, I couldn't make myself do it.

I couldn't kill him.

"Fuck!" I cried, hating myself all over again for giving up too soon, for not having the fucking intestinal fortitude to go back in there and finish the job.

Grey needed to die, and I needed to be the one to make sure that happened. Why couldn't I take the chance when it was right in front of me?

"Fuck, fuck, *fuck*," I cried, dropping back on the floor and pushing myself away from his body, sliding across the floor until I hit against the wall. Overwhelmed, I sobbed into my hands, knowing I was only moments away from getting found by his guard. "*Argh!*"

My stomach lurched, and I lifted my head, grabbing for the belt when a scraping sound came from the other side of my door.

Oh god. I'm dead. I'm dead. I'm dead. I'm dead.

Forcing myself up on weakened legs, my thighs screamed and shook, adrenaline the only thing keeping me upright.

With my eyes on the door, I wrapped the ends of the belt around my hands, creating a garrotte that I held taut, ready for another fight. I was pretty sure I was bringing a belt to a gunfight, but I didn't really have a choice, I had to do something. I couldn't die now. Toby was coming.

The door creaked.

It cracked open.

I held my breath.

And steeled my heart.

I will survive.

"Sunshine?"

I'm alive!

Now, I sounded like a Gloria Gaynor song.

"Toby!"

Releasing a gasp, I dropped the belt.

Thank god. I'm saved.

When Toby stepped in, my first response was to sprint towards him, flinging myself into his arms and hugging him so hard that I think I nearly choked *him*.

"You came."

Toby squished me right back. "Of course I did."

"How?" I pulled back enough that I could look into his face, his smiling, happy face and watering ocean-clear eyes. *I love him so much.* "How did you get past security?"

"With a lot of help." He nodded towards to the door where Sloane stood keeping watch. She lifted her hand in a small wave.

"We need to move," she said, her large eyes as serious as the tight braid in her red hair.

Toby nodded then looked to where Grey lay on the floor, barely breathing. "He dead?" he asked, looking into my eyes with deep concern in his.

I shook my head. "I couldn't finish the job." It was a pitiful admission.

In an instant, he gathered me in his arms and pressed a kiss in my hair. "It's OK," he whispered, making me feel a thousand things at once, mostly grateful.

"I tried. I just… I couldn't."

Taking my face in his hands, he pulled back and looked into my eyes. "Let me do it for you. He needs to go."

Pressing my lips together, I nodded, knowing the man had to die but also hating that it was Toby doing it. He'd left his family because he'd had enough of dealing death. Now, here he was killing in *my* name. I felt like I was robbing him of that last piece of his soul.

"Wait." I placed my hand on his arm as he pulled a gun from the back of his pants.

"He needs to die, sunshine."

"I know. But—"

"Ah! Just the man I was looking for," Jasmine declared as she burst into the room with Breaker right behind her. She had a pistol held at her side, pointing to the ground as she sauntered over to Grey's body. "Is he already dead?" She bent over slightly, peering into his face for the briefest of moments before she lifted her gun then shot him between the eyes without waiting for an answer or even checking. *Whoa!* She stood up and brushed a loose strand of hair back like she'd just completed a little light house cleaning. "Who killed him first?" She looked at us.

"He was just unconscious," I blurted, a little shocked at her flippancy, my mind spinning as I stared at the meat sack that was once a man, my father.

The monster under my bed was just a man. And now that man was dead. Gone. But my hatred and anger was still right there. An aching ball in my chest, exactly where

I left it. *This was supposed to make me feel better. Why don't I feel relief?*

She lifted her gun and shot him again, this time in the heart. "Well, he's good and dead now. Wanna shoot his balls off? It's the least he deserves after all he put you through." She held her weapon out and I shook my head, my eyes lifting to Toby's.

"She knows?" *He told her?*

His eyes said, "I'm sorry," while his mouth said, "A little. I filled her in on what we knew while we were planning."

"Most of it I guessed," Jasmine informed me. "Brendan Grey was the worst of them all. He had to have lost his mind if he thought I'd ever allow my family to align with him." She shook her head as Breaker leaned over and spat on the corpse.

"He was dying," I told her. "Blot clot in his brain."

"Explains the haste," she said. "Not the stupidity."

"We should go," Breaker said, touching a comms device that wound down from his ear. "Everyone is gathered."

"Well," Jasmine said, smiling as she looked towards me. "Ready to watch the fall of an empire?"

"Honestly," I said, my entire body feeling heavy and numb. "I just want to go home." Wherever that was.

Toby took my hand and gave it a squeeze. "Let's get out of here."

"This place won't be safe in about ten minutes, guys," Sloane called out, hurrying everybody up.

Toby lead the way downstairs where several of Grey's men kneeled, tied up and gagged on the floor of the massive foyer. Around them stood the remaining

Cartwright Brothers along with Alesha, all dressed in black and brandishing weapons while looking badarse as fuck.

"Welcome to the family," Jasmine said, smiling as we reached the ground floor. "Didn't think we'd ever leave you to the wolves did you?"

"Honestly, I didn't know what to think." I'd simply felt trapped.

"Well, this is what family does. We protect each other. All of Grey's men on the property are here. Any off-site are being hunted as we speak. This ends tonight. His reach won't be capable of extending to you anymore."

Holy fuck. A chill ran down my spine coupled with a great sense of relief. *There it was.* It was wrong to be happy about a mass killing. But when the men were all evil minions, I struggled to see the wrong in that. I was just glad that Toby and I didn't have to do it. I didn't think we'd be walking out of here if it had been just us. For the first time in my life, the idea of having a family felt pretty great. *We protect each other.*

"They're ready to go," Nate said, touching the comm in his ear.

Jasmine nodded then used her gun hand to gesture towards the men on their knees. "Bullet or burn?" she asked me, giving me a little control over the situation.

Distant screams from the house fire in Adelaide echoed in my mind. As I took a moment to survey the group of men, my lip curled as that ball of pain in my chest throbbed uncomfortably. *They caused this.* When my gaze landed on Irish, his evil eyes glared at me as if he still thought he could win this. Suddenly, my decision was not a difficult one at all.

"Shoot them in the legs so they can't run. Then burn them."

One side of Jasmine's mouth pulled up, almost looking proud. "I *really* like her Toby. Couldn't have chosen better myself." Then she turned to the rest. "You heard her, boys. Bullet to the knees. The fire will do the rest."

Bang, bang, bang, bang.

I couldn't express the level of satisfaction I got from those sounds and the accompanying groans. I thought I'd feel a little guilt. But there wasn't a single shred.

"We'll make you pay somehow, bitch," Irish grunted, writhing in pain as he clutched at the wounds on his legs.

"No," I said, numb to his plight. He had no idea that anyone connected to Grey was being taken out as we spoke. "Tonight is when it ends. This is *my* revenge. Everything you ever were is about to burn to the ground." Whatever failsafes in place would never eventuate without men to carry them out. After tonight, Grey's rule would be nothing but a memory.

"You weren't even worth the fuck," he spat, the moment I turned my back and headed for the front door.

I turned around, but Toby was faster, brandishing his gun and pressing it against Irish's temple. "Say one more shitty thing about her. I dare you."

Irish laughed. "She's a dead root, mate."

Toby cocked the hammer, and I had no doubt in my mind he was about to shoot Irish in the head. As much as I wanted that stain of a man to die, I wanted him to suffer even more.

"Stop," I commanded, placing my hand on Toby's outstretched arm. "This is what he wants. And he doesn't deserve an easy death."

With a low growl, Toby lowered his weapon to his side.

"Whipped pussy," Irish snarled.

Not even a beat passed before Toby lifted his weapon and fired, shooting off Irish's lower jaw in a spectacular spray of blood and gore.

"Shut the fuck up," he said before taking my hand and getting us the hell out of there, each step forward, a weight lifted from my shoulders.

Once outside, I turned and looked up at the formidable building, beautiful on the outside with so much darkness within.

It's over.

I was almost afraid to believe it.

The moment we were all clear of the blast zone, a voice rang out with the words, 'Light her up!'. It was then that a series of charges went off, imploding the house and setting the whole damn thing ablaze. Toby slipped his arm around me and pulled me close into his side as we watched the fire take hold. The orange glow lit our skin in the dark night, illuminating the grounds surrounding the house and showing me how huge the operation to get me out of there had been.

Bikers were positioned all around the property. In amongst them, men in plain clothes who I guessed were friends of the Cartwright family or part of Conway's organisation. And best of all, about a hundred metres down the property's long driveway, was a bus driven by Ronnie that was being boarded by a group of girls in various states of dress.

"You saved them," I said, emotion welling up inside me as the exact thing I'd tried to do in Adelaide was actually happening before my eyes. The innocents were being taken to safety and the bad guys were paying the ultimate price. It might have made me a horribly sick person, but it was the best gift anyone could ever get me. The core of Grey's operation was burning to the ground and the rest of us were free.

I was finally free.

"We had to save them. It was one thing everyone in the family was in complete agreement on."

"You all risked your lives coming here to save me. To free all those women."

"You're worth it. I'm just sorry this took so long to organise."

I almost laughed. "Toby, you did this in *three days*."

"And even that was too long without you," he said, pressing his forehead to mine.

A few tears escaped my eyes just as a yell rang out among the surrounding men, interrupting our tender moment.

A burning figure ran from the house moments before gun fire sounded and he dropped onto the grass in a fiery motionless heap. No one would escape.

"It's really over," I sighed, the knowledge that all the evil in those walls would never break free making me weep with relief. "It's finally over."

Wrapping his arms around my torso, Toby held me close. "For us, it's just the beginning, sunshine. We survived this. We thought we wouldn't, but we survived."

"Perhaps love isn't a weakness after all."

Looking into my eyes, he smiled before tucking my hair behind my ear. "No. I think it might be the most powerful thing I've ever known."

"I love you, Toby," I whispered.

"And I love you too, Blair," he replied, leaning in to kiss me as the walls of the house crumbled and everyone in attendance cheered.

We're free.

CHAPTER TWENTY-EIGHT
MY PARADISE

THE FOLLOWING months became filled with meetings followed by hours of police questioning as we dealt with Grey's demise and the destruction of his organisation. News outlets had been abuzz with stories and theories regarding the mass takedown, but no one could put it all together. Too many smaller factions had worked as one to create a superpower that no one ever saw coming. Not even Grey himself. It was ironic that his dream had been to unite everyone under his own rule, but they'd joined against him instead. It was poetic, really.

With every criminal involved unwilling to talk, the police couldn't really make a case against any of us, meaning Grey's Will (that, surprisingly, had me written in a few months after he'd learned I was his daughter years ago) was deemed legal and I inherited everything that remained of his estate, as well as the insurance payout for the levelled house.

It had been one of the bonuses of being engaged to my very own criminal mastermind with some pretty epic contacts. Everything had been planned so meticulously that the cops had nothing but supposition to work with and zero evidence to pin on any the three entities involved. We really were free.

And I was ridiculously rich.

On top of what Grey's liquid assets netted me, I was also well compensated by Conway and the Grim Order for the unrestricted rights to Grey's remaining business holdings. I willingly handed it all over and would have happily done it for free, except that wasn't the way things worked in our world. Paying a fair price was the only way to ensure a clean break with no favours owed. I walked away with heavy pockets, and the Cartwrights were released from all of their debts over Nate's poppy field fuck up. All was right with the world again. We were on the other side of an incredibly dark tunnel and the new sky was so bright.

"I've gotta say, kid. It's good to hear ya voice. I thought you'd gone crazy gettin' back with Nick, and then he turned up dead and I had a fuckin' panic. Thought you were gone too when I hadn't heard from you. Almost had another heart attack," Big Jim said. I contacted him now that the world felt safe enough to live in again, needing to let him know I was alive and well. I also just wanted to hear his voice.

I couldn't help but smile at the sound of relief in his tone. "I don't know why Nick told you we were together. But I was always fine. Just had some personal stuff to take care of." I thought it best to keep him in the dark over the true events behind Nick's demise and my disappearance. I didn't want to give him an actual heart attack.

"Personal, huh? Wish you'd called sooner, kid."

"I know, and I'm sorry you worried. But I have some good news: I quit drinking."

"You did?"

"Yeah. I haven't touched the stuff for weeks," I told him, a grin fixed on my face. "Turns out I'm responsible for another life now." I touched the slight swell of my stomach with my free hand. "I'm told drinking while pregnant is a big no-no."

About three weeks after being rescued, I was sitting in my psychologist's office—yes, I was getting help for the mess in my brain. While love had set me on the road towards healing, it couldn't magically fix me, I needed a professional for that—and the topic of children came up. She wanted to know if I saw motherhood in my future, and it dawned on me that I hadn't had a period since before Toby and I had gotten together. He'd been ecstatic. I'd been... shocked. Motherhood was never something I'd contemplated for myself before that moment. But the idea had grown on me, and now I was excited to have this future presented ahead of me, one I never thought possible for someone like me. *A family.*

One of my own making.

"Whoa, kid. That's amazin'. I was gonna ask if you was ready to come back to work. But you've got yourself a more important job now, huh? Who'da thought, the kid, a mum."

"Crazy, right? I didn't think I ever wanted kids. But it turns out I just hadn't met the right guy yet. I'm gonna be great at this, Big Jim. And I won't fuck this kid up the way I was. I'm gonna give it a great life."

"Of course you will. I've no doubt about that. And this man of yours, he good to you?"

"He is." I smiled as I looked over to Toby who was working up a sweat on the treadmill that lived out on the master bedroom's balcony. One of my favourite things to do was lie on our bed and watch him be all manly with the gym equipment he had out there. He was positively stunning, and that pregnancy libido boost was a real thing. I couldn't get enough of him, lately. "You know, I never thought I wanted any of this, but now it's here, I think it's actually all I ever wanted. Does that make sense?"

"Yeah, kid," Big Jim said, voice gentle on the other end of the phone as I heard him puffing on his cigar. "I know exactly what ya mean. Couldn't happen to a better person either. I wish you all the happiness in the world."

"Thank you. You know you're the only person who gave a shit about me for a long time."

"Well, you were my best earner," he teased.

I laughed. "I was. But I wanted to ask you something."

"Anything, kid. You know that."

"Give me away at my wedding?"

"Wow. Married. This guy must be real special if he's gettin' you down the aisle."

Hopping off the treadmill, Toby wiped a towel over his face and chest, giving me a wink through the glass wall. It made me all warm and gooey inside. "He really is, Big Jim. He's my entire world."

"With such a glowin' review, I'd be fuckin' honoured to give you away. Lookin' forward to meetin' him."

After a few more words, I disconnected, placing my phone on the side table about a second before Toby walked into the bedroom, his now overgrown hair sticking up at odd angles from the sweat.

My Toby was back. With the light dancing in his eyes,

and the relaxed attitude to life, he'd found his happiness again. I loved seeing him smile.

"Well?" he asked, slinging his towel over his shoulder as he stood at the foot of the bed.

"Come over here and kiss me, and I might spill."

With a grin, he did exactly that, tasting of salt and hard work. "Spill."

"Well," I said, placing my hands on his corded arms to cop a feel of the solid muscle. "Big Jim said congratulations on the baby and the wedding."

"And?" He lifted his brow.

"And he'll give me away."

He beamed. "Excellent."

I grinned. "It is. And I also spoke to Lucy. She's agreed to be in the bridal party as my matron of honour. So that's really awesome too."

He sat down and took a hold of my hands with a relieved breath. It had taken a few weeks for Lucy to come to terms with the fact that her father wasn't the man she thought he was—well, that he didn't have the career, she'd thought he had. He was still the same kind, loving and patient man, it was just that he was a crook instead of a hero in common circles. But, he was a hero in our world.

Getting the chance to spend time with the family in Torquay, listening to their stories, and seeing the love they all had for each other, helped Lucy realise that they really were good people at heart and that her dad had only kept her away so she could have a normal life. A life she was more than happy to get back to.

In the following weeks, we'd chatted on the phone, emailing back and forth and FaceTiming, giving us the chance to normalise our relationship and allow her and

Toby to get back to where they were before the day his boat exploded. Things were looking up, and up, and up.

"Did Big Jim mention Nick to you at all?"

"He did. Said he turned up dead which was what we expected, I guess. Kind of a shame. At the end of the day, Nick was only doing what he was trained to do. I doubt I'd have done the same to him, but then, there's a good reason he and I didn't work out as a couple. I don't hate him though. I just feel sorry he got mixed up with the wrong people and died because of it."

"You're a good woman, sunshine."

"And you're a good man, my heart."

He smiled before he leaned in and kissed me again. "I cannot wait to make you my wife," he whispered.

"Four weeks and counting," I whispered back, just as a text message alert sounded on both of our phones.

Toby groaned as we leaned over the bed in opposite directions and checked our screens. "Jasmine reminding us about dinner," he said. "Guess I should hit the shower before she strokes out over us being late."

I stood with him and trailed my finger down the center of his chest, stopping at the waistband of his workout shorts. "I think she can handle it if we're a little late," I said, pulling at my bottom lip with my teeth.

Toby's eyes darkened as he pulled me close and took two handfuls of the fleshy part of my arse. "A little? Sunshine, once I get started with you, you know we'll be a lot late."

"Do we care?"

He grinned. "No. We don't care at all."

"Better late than never. Right, brother," Kristian laughed, clapping Toby's shoulder in welcome the moment we walked through the sliding doors that led to the pool. The entire family was gathered, the outdoor table laden with food.

"Nice of you to join us," Jasmine said, eyebrows raised as we took our seats and the dinner began.

"We had something important to discuss," Toby replied, trying not to smile as his eyes landed on me, that glow I'd watched fade away back in full force. It was amazing what a second chance at happiness could do for a person.

"I'm sure," Breaker replied, handing over the basket of bread while food circulated around the table. It all looked so good, and I was starving.

"How are you feeling, Blair?" Holland asked while Nate filled both her plate and his with schnitzel and salad —exactly what Toby was doing for me. Funny that the two brothers who'd been most at odds in their lives were actually quite similar men. Each loved taking care of their women.

"Hungry," I said with a smile. "Like, all the time."

Toby added an extra schnitzel to my plate. "One for you, and one for the baby," he said, dropping a kiss on my shoulder.

"Oh god," Ronnie said, placing salad on Kristian's plate while he buttered her bread rolls. "I was the same. I swear I gained a whole new arse while I was pregnant with Oscar."

"Which was sexy as fuck," Kristian added, nodding while he focused on the bread and butter. When he slid the finished roll onto his wife's plate, he found her glaring at him. "What? Big arse. Big tits. It was hot."

Ronnie rolled her eyes and laughed.

"I was just happy I *got* tits," Sloane added, her blunt nature shining right through. "Pregnancy does some weird and wonderful shit to your body."

"Things we probably don't want to talk about while eating," Alesha said, laughing as she and Sam exchanged a knowing look.

"Totally worth it for these little tykes though," Sam added, sparing a doting look for their sleeping son who was lying peacefully in his pram.

"Definitely," Nate agreed, chuckling a little because Daniel had just stuck his finger inside a cherry tomato and was showing everybody as he squealed and kicked at the tray on his highchair. He thought he was hilarious, and I had to admit he kind of was. In the months since I'd arrived in Torquay, the little rascal had grown on me. As much as I thought I'd struggle to even like Toby's family, I found myself coming to care for them all greatly and see them as mine. Things had changed a lot in the year Toby had spent away, and even he was feeling more content around them.

Ronnie told me once that they were an odd assortment of life's misfits who somehow fit together despite their irregular shapes. I had to agree. The Cartwright family was chaos in the best way.

"Looks like you ended up getting everything you ever wanted, Jazz," Abbot said, taking a swig out of his bottle of beer while his eyes focused on his mother.

Jasmine shrugged. "I don't know about *everything*. There've been a bunch of jobs that have passed us by of late. We're going to lose our clout if we keep letting it all go."

"Maybe letting it all go is a good thing," Sloane said, her eyes large and serious. "We have so much now. Don't you think it's time to step back from all that risky business and enjoy life?" There had been a lot of talk about what direction to take the family business in of late. Criminal activity was out of the question because of police heat, and on top of that, the entire Cartwright clan seemed ready for an extended sabbatical. Except Jasmine.

"Of course I want to retire," she said. "But I can't do that until you're all running things on your own."

"I think we're doing just fine," Toby said, using a napkin to wipe his mouth as he sat back and slid an arm around the back of my chair.

"Really? Because from where I'm sitting, everything I built, everything I worked hard for is slipping right through our fingers."

"You know," I started, holding my finger in front of my mouth as I finished chewing. "I've heard both sides of this. But if you change your thinking a little, Jasmine, you could alter your disappointment into pride." Her brow lifted and Breaker looked down to hide his smile. I'd grown to like him too during all of this. Turned out I didn't hate bikers as much as I thought I did. I simply hated evil motherfuckers.

"Pride?"

"Of course," I said. "Look at all this. Look at everyone sitting here. From what I've been told, you masterminded the lot of this. You fought your way from nothing to practically owning this entire town. You taught your sons to be *good* men in a cruel world, and you found them equally wonderful women who have given them love and children."

"Mostly," she said, tipping her head to the side a little. "I didn't choose Holland or you, but the rest is true."

I grinned. She was so stubborn and couldn't see her own accomplishments. "Point is, your sons are healthy and happy. Your empire is vast and profitable, and your real estate holdings are growing. By the time we finish laundering the cash you've all collected, you could actually run all of this completely legit. No risk. No worry. There are plenty of big corporations and wealthy people out there who started off as criminals then straightened out with success. That's the ultimate goal here, right? Enough wealth that you can sit back and watch future generations flourish?"

"I suppose." She shrugged.

"So instead of thinking exiting the game is a failing, pat yourself on the back and be proud that in a single generation *you* built this family up enough that they *could* go straight. That's an amazing gift, Jasmine."

"Here, here!" Abbot yelled, clapping his hands together and starting a Mexican wave of cheers and applause around the table. By the time it finished, the babies were all awake but Jasmine was smiling. There might have even been a tear or two in her eyes.

"OK," she said, nodding slightly as she touched a finger to the corners of her eyes. "I hear you. You want to stop."

Toby reached across the table and took her hand. "We really do, mum," he said, voice soft, eyes genuine. "We want to *live*."

Real tears spilled from Jasmine's eyes as she pressed

her lips together. "God, what are you doing to me? You haven't called me mum since you were a boy. And now I'm crying. Lord." She wiped away her tears, accepting the napkin Breaker handed to her before he kissed the side of her head. "Well, I suppose if that's what you all want..." She looked around the table to find everyone nodding and Holland saying, "Oh lord, yes, please."

"OK. Then I officially hand Cartwright Enterprises over to you all for safe keeping and ethical growing. You're right. At the end of the day, I have all of my sons safe and happy and I have a whole bunch of grand babies —one grown up I will never forgive you for hiding by the way"—she directed that at Toby who just shrugged because he had no regrets over hiding Lucy—"and I suppose that's all that really matters. Right?" She looked to Breaker who gave her the nod.

"You are a queen," he told her, giving her a look filled with nothing but love.

"OK." She kept saying that. "Well, I suppose we should break out the champagne. Turn this into a celebration. My retirement party."

Nate and Sam obliged her request, pouring a glass for everyone—sparkling apple juice for me and the same for Holland, who'd tried to keep the different drink discreet since Nate poured it for her without a word. But we all noticed, causing her to go a little red in the cheeks and shrug. "Seems pregnancy is contagious. So watch out, guys," she said, pointing at the other women at the table.

We all congratulated her whole-heartedly before turning our attention to Jasmine who stood from her seat with a raised glass. "I want to thank you all," she started, her voice sounding a little strained with emotion. "Blair is right. Building an empire strong enough to sustain future generations was always my goal. As you know, I come from very humble beginnings: absent parents and drug addiction just a couple of the challenges I faced from a young age, challenges many of my beautiful daughter-in-laws also faced, in a life where we were all brought up as much as we were *thrown* up." A light chuckle rippled around the table. "It took a lot of fight, and a lot of guts to get to where we are today. Not just from me, but from every single one of you here. My fight became your fight, and you took it all on board and conducted yourselves beautifully. I couldn't be prouder of the people you all are and the strength you share as a unit." Her eyes landed on me. "Something we all saw firsthand when we pulled together to make sure Blair wasn't lost to us and to our Toby." With a short pause, she looked around the table, meeting each and every person's eyes. "Family above everything else. Forever and always. That is our creed. It's our strength, our power. I know that over the years, I've come across as ruthless and unwavering, but it was something I had to become to ensure our survival, to keep you all safe. And now…" She reached out with her free hand and entwined her fingers with Breaker's. "I think I'm done. It's time for me to step back and enjoy all of this love we have. That's our real power, don't you think? Love."

I nodded as I wiped at my eyes, now leaking a little. I wasn't the only one, Ronnie and Holland had a few tears running too. Toby ran his fingers up and down my arm as he pulled me a little closer.

"I love you," he whispered, brushing his lips along the shell of my ear.

"I love you too," I said back, kissing him quickly while I'm guessing everyone watched, or perhaps engaged in their own loving moment. I didn't really know anything except the fact that the table was silent in that moment, and when I looked back up, Jasmine was grinning and openly crying happy tears, her glass held high.

"To family, love and strength," she said. "May it be ours for generations to come."

"To family, love and strength," we chorused, lifting our glasses before taking a sip. It was a fitting toast to the future of this family. Finally free of the criminal life that had challenged, built, and plagued them for much of their lives. Now they were at a point where they could all breathe easy and watch their children grow up in a world that wasn't dripping in secrets and danger. Everything they'd ever longed for growing up could be provided for the next generation—freedom and safety. It was the most important goal of each and every brother. Whether they'd agreed with the thieving life they'd always led, or rallied against it, each of them wanted something different for their offspring. It was why they'd been so understanding when they discovered Toby had hidden Lucy from them. It stung, but they got it, a couple even admitted they'd probably have done the same.

But now, it was over. We were free, and from the smiles and laughter about the table, we were all happy. In the months after the Adelaide job, and even the years that had followed, I'd stopped placing value on myself and in my life. I'd thought happiness was something that would never happen for me. Then a chance job, a manipulation from my biological father, connected me to the man I considered my soulmate, and my life changed. Suddenly I had a future, something to look forward to each day when I woke up, a reason to live. While I had been the one to save Toby from that explosion on his boat, he'd been the one to save me from myself.

He'd once said I needed to love myself before I could truly love him. And while I fell madly in love with him first, I was definitely learning to love myself. Therapy and a more positive outlook was helping me with that and putting my nightmares to rest. Not that I didn't have them, but they were certainly few and far between, and even when they happened, I had the arms of the man I loved to curl into to help them fade away.

Toby was the best man I'd ever met and the only man I'd ever loved. In four weeks, I would be his wife, and I already knew that day would go down as one of the happiest days of my life. I had to say 'one', because the real happiest day was the day I met him. Nothing could top the moment we locked eyes standing on that pier, it was the moment everything changed for me. The day I found my paradise.

TOBY

five years later…

———

"DADDY!"

"Granpop!"

Three heads with shiny dark hair, blue eyes and button noses came running at me, the expectation that I catch them clear on their faces.

Not one to disappoint, I kneeled down and opened my arms, gathering them all up and lifting them into a spin while they giggled and squealed.

This was what life was all about, what I'd always wanted. Marriage, children, happiness. I had it all, and this time, I didn't have to run away, and I didn't have to hide it.

"When are the fireworks, daddy?" Amy asked, her big

eyes and heavy lashes blinking up at me as I set them all back on their feet. She was four now and already acted like she ruled the roost with a stubborn streak like her mum and a big heart too. She loved to sing and dance and she brought out the best in us.

"Yah," Clara, my one and only granddaughter said as she swiped at her nose. "When are da firewerps?" Clara was three and was almost like a sister to Amy and my two-and-a-half-year-old son, Asher. They spent most days together now that Lucy and her husband had moved to Torquay with the rest of us. It had taken a while to get used to our relationship and it's new dynamic. I'd never planned to tell her about my real life, but I was glad it had all come out in the open. Fighting Grey was a horrific time in all of our lives, but it was something that brought us closer together and cemented our decision to go straight as a family unit. A decision I will never regret for a moment.

"The kids fireworks are happening at nine. You still have two whole hours."

"Two ows!" Asher slapped his face dramatically, even though he had zero concept of time.

"I'll play with them, uncle Toby," Daniel said, a little out of breath from running over here. He was six now and a little bookworm like both of his parents. He was sweet and gentle, and every time I looked at him, I was so glad we didn't have to harden that soft heart of his with violence and crime. The future felt brighter for the Cartwrights with every passing day.

"Planning on making any New Year's resolutions?" my beautiful wife asked, settling in beside me and sliding her arms around my waist as we watched the kids run towards the jumping castle my mother had hired for the evening.

Jasmine was so much more fun now that she was focused on being 'grandma' and not constantly searching for a new score. Retirement suited her.

"What could I possibly improve on?" I asked, looking into her bright green eyes. They were what drew me to her in the first place. Most guys would have gone for her tits or her arse because her curves were as perfect as curves could get. But I was all about the eyes. I loved their colour, I loved their depth of emotion, and I loved that I could know exactly what she was thinking with one look. It had been like that from the beginning and hadn't changed over the years we'd been together. We'd always had that simpatico with each other. It was how I knew she was the one. It was also why I thought my mother had been up to her old tricks by sending her to find me. Although, I'm glad I was wrong on that. It made what Blair and I had even more special.

Many would call Jasmine Cartwright controlling and manipulative over the way she ensured most of her sons found a wife. But in her own way, it was the ultimate act of love. Sure, she wanted grandchildren to carry on the name and business. But if that was all she wanted, she could have chosen any random girl off the street. Instead, she found women compatible with the man as well as our lifestyle.

The first attempt at partnering her sons had been quite random. Holland was never supposed to be a part of it, but Alesha had caught her interest. She'd mused aloud during our private meetings that she thought she was the kind of girl Sam would like. At first it had been dismissed as nothing more than an offhanded thought, but when Alesha and Holland had shown up at our home, the opportunity presented itself and the first match up was born. As was the idea to instigate a match for all of her sons.

It was no accident that Alesha and Sam's wedding reception was at the function centre Ronnie worked at. Just like it wasn't random that Jasmine took Abbot out to Rochester to hire Sloane to open that safe. Each meeting was researched and planned, with myself being the willing accomplice who manufactured circumstances and guided them along their joined paths.

Why did I help her get my brothers to the altar?

Because I had a goal too. And the realisation of that goal—a happy family with no criminal ties—was all around me as children played and my brothers held their wives, laughing and smiling as we gathered to ring in yet another new year, another successful year, another year of freedom.

Everything we went through. Every roadblock we encountered. Every painful moment we endured, led us here. I for one was the happiest man alive. And I was pretty sure my brothers would all tell you the same thing.

"Get over here, you two," Nate called out, beckoning us to where the rest of my brothers had gathered around my mother. "Breaker has something he wants us to see."

I nodded in acknowledgment. As the oldest of five boys, I'd always had to fill the role of 'man of the house', looking out for them and being the person Jasmine leaned on when she needed support. At the time it had come fairly naturally as it was just something I had to do, but once Breaker entered the picture and she began to lean on him, I realised what a burden it had been. I had always wanted to break away from the family business, but being so intrinsically tied to it had kept my feet firmly in camp

Cartwright. Having another 'man of the house' around gave me enough of a pause that I felt the ties that bound me loosen and slip free. I realised how messed up my relationships with my brothers had become. The animosity and resentment I'd developed towards them because, while they were all out partying and living their lives, I was at home planning for the next job. There were times when I hated them for that. My year away had given me the time to let go of that anger and find my centre, the man I could be without a mountain of responsibility. Since I'd returned, our business focus had changed. We divided roles between brothers and wives, taking each of our strengths into consideration. Now, instead of having one person responsible for overseeing it all, we congregated around a circular table and shared the burden. Our relationships were much better for it. I was friends with my brothers now, something I didn't think I'd get to be.

"Something he wants us to see?" Blair raised her eyebrows. "I wonder what that could be."

"A new tattoo?"

"A cake?"

With a shrug, I took her hand and together we joined the others, standing in a semicircle while the children all played off to the side. Ten in total: two belonging to Blair and me, one to Lucy, two to Holland and Nate, *three* kids to Kris and Ronnie, with Sam and Leesh keeping it at one, along with Abbot and Sloane. We were growing our own football team.

"As youse all know," Breaker started, standing next to Jasmine with his hands on his hips. "Jasmine has been my lady since that first day I walked into her office."

Abbot visibly shuddered. "I'm still scarred over that. Don't remind me."

Ronnie laughed and Kristian punched him playfully in the bicep.

"You're going in the deep-end over that," Abbot warned, flashing his twin a warning glare while Kris flipped him the bird behind his hand so the kids couldn't see. I didn't think those two would ever fully grow up. But they were good value, and they kept things fun.

"Enough," Jasmine said, laughing at her man-child sons. "Breaker is speaking."

Thanking her, Breaker cleared his throat. "Anyways, my point is, I want to make an honest woman out of her. Officialise it all and shit, you know?" He narrowed one of his eyes like we should all know exactly what he was talking about. I thought I knew where he was going, but I couldn't be sure since I didn't really speak biker. I'd always thought the fact he called her his 'ole lady' and she wore a cut that said as much was the official part of their union. Obviously I was wrong, because when Breaker slipped his fingers into his pocket and pulled out a diamond ring, my mother just about fainted.

"What are you doing?" she gasped.

Breaker lowered to his knee, a little stiff because like all of us, he was getting on in years. "I'm askin' you to marry me, baby. Be my queen." He held up the ring and through her tears, Jasmine nodded.

"Yes," she cried, holding out her hand for the ring. "Yes. I'll marry you, baby."

Helping Breaker back to his feet, they kissed in a way that was probably a little over the top for the audience, but we were used to them being over the top, so we cheered while the kids squealed even though they didn't really understand what was going on.

"Now I really do have everything I ever wanted," Jasmine said, looking around at her family with her hand on her heart. "Life is pretty fucking perfect right now. Who'd have thought."

"Grandma used a bad word!" Willow yelled, pointing at Jasmine as she gasped in horror. We all tried not to laugh as the kids gathered to find out exactly what was said, Willow proudly declaring that it was the F word. Sloane settled them all down with a game of cat and mouse and it was forgotten pretty quickly.

Before we knew it, the kids were all inside asleep and the adults were outside waiting for the midnight fireworks to light up the sky from where they were set off at the beach. With a drink in hand, we sat around the pool, cuddled up on loungers, talking about kids and the renovation on the surf shop we'd been working on lately. It was all so normal and so right; the dog curling up between Blair's and my legs the icing on the cake.

I reached down and scratched her head. "Ready to do this all again next year, Coco," I said with a smile. It had taken a couple of years for me to feel OK bringing another dog into my life after losing Rogue. But Coco, a chocolate-coloured Labrador, had been a welcome addition to the family with her zest for life and her love of chasing balls and licking sticky children. She made everything about my life just that bit more complete.

"Ready?" Sam said, looking at his watch before counting down from ten.

We all joined in, the stroke of midnight punctuated with the first boom of fireworks, a passion-filled kiss from my wife, and the crazy barking of my dog. Absolutely-fucking-perfect.

Life didn't get any better than this. My dreams had come true, and I was living in the middle of a real-life Hallmark movie. I was the luckiest bastard in the world.

"Happy new year, Sunshine."

Blair smiled and looked into my eyes as she placed her hand against the stubble on my cheek. "Happy new year, my heart. Here's to many more."

I grinned as I brushed her soft hair back from her face. "Forever should just about do it."

"Yes," she whispered, sucking lightly on my lower lip. "Forever sounds perfect."

The end.

Sign up to the Lilliverse Newsletter to discover more titles, limited offers, and upcoming releases by Lilliana Anderson
https://www.lillianaanderson.com/newsletter

Next for Lilliana fans, a brand-new laugh out loud comedy about second chances, wrangling kids, and crazy relatives.

THE DAY DARCY learned the news of her husband's remission she expected a celebration, or at least a nice piece of cake. Instead, she was served with divorce papers. Oh, and the knowledge they were bankrupt.

With her twenty year union over and two children to support on her own, she moved in with her eccentric grandmother, hoping to find peace and quiet in the seaside town of Hampton.

What she wasn't expecting to find was a set of saggy old man balls upon arrival.

Needing to bleach her eyes, calm her screaming teen daughter and stop her eight year old son from filming the chaos to upload, Darcy was already reconsidering the sanity in her decision. Turned out, Nana was quite the player in the retirement circle.

She also fancied herself a bit of a match maker.

Deciding local football legend, Leo Murphy would provide the ultimate distraction for Darcy, Nana enlisted the help of her trouble-loving great-grandson with somewhat disastrous results. Leo didn't even know what hit him. Literally.

With a great smile and a body to die for, it wasn't hard to convince Darcy to give Leo a chance. It also helped that he had a lot of patience for one particularly rambunctious young boy and couldn't run too fast on his busted knee—a captive audience was easily swayed, after all.

But with a teenager in the midst of a meltdown, a heart cracked and bruised, and a son who wouldn't stop acting up, even a chance could prove too much for Darcy and not enough for Leo, who wasn't the kind of man who gave up easily.

https://books2read.com/u/3L0zNX

All Preorders (2019)
Love is a Beach
A Beautiful Destination
Lying Game

ALSO BY LILLIANA ANDERSON

Confidante: The Madame

For more information on upcoming releases visit

www.lillianaanderson.com/preorders

Bestselling Author of the Beautiful Series, Drawn and 47 Things, Lilliana has always loved to read and write, considering it the best form of escapism that the world has to offer.

Australian born and bred, she writes New Adult Romance revolving around her authentically Aussie characters with all the quirks you'd expect from those born Down Under.

Lilliana feels that the world should see Australia for more than just it's outback and tries to show characters in a city and suburban setting.

When she isn't writing, she wears the hat of 'wife and mother' to her husband and five children.

Before Lilliana turned to writing, she worked in a variety of industries and studied humanities and communications before transferring to commerce/law at university.

Originally from Sydney's Western suburbs, she currently lives a fairly quiet life in suburban Melbourne.

For more information on Lilliana and her work:
www.lillianaanderson.com
info@lillianaanderson.com

To join her Facebook reader group and talk books
https://www.facebook.com/groups/438800699591852

facebook.com/LillianaAndersonAuthor

twitter.com/confidante_lili

instagram.com/lilliana_anderson

ACKNOWLEDGMENTS

AS ALWAYS, there are people to be thanked! Many sets of eyes go in to the creation of each of my books and I am very grateful to every person who takes time out of their lives to help me.

To, **Marion Archer**, I thank you all for your keen eyes and funny comments. **Margaret Neal**, thank you for helping to proof the final copy—hopefully we got them all!

To my team of author friends and sharers, you're all so wonderful. I don't ask you to do what you do, but you see something I post and share it far and wide. I'm eternally grateful. Thank you all so much. I love you!

To every blogger and reviewer who has an ARC or has signed up to post about my book – I thank you too. You are the first step to announcing my work to the world. No author can do this without you xoxox

Also, a big thank you to my husband for putting up with my bitching and moaning and his unending support and encouragement.

Thank you to my kids for being so patient while I stare at a computer screen and finish typing out a thought. I love that you all come and sit with me while I work just to spend a bit of extra time with mummy!

And of course – thank you to all of my readers. You are the most important of all. Without you, I would be writing to the crickets.

Mwah! xoxox

www.ingramcontent.com/pod-product-compliance
Lightning Source LLC
Chambersburg PA
CBHW031026120726
47905CB00007B/2064